Lifting the Sky

Lifting the Sky

Mackie d'Arge

I hope you enjoy Blue's story!

Mackie d'Arge

BLOOMSBURY

NEW YORK BERLIN LONDON

Published by Bloomsbury U.S.A. Children's Books
175 Fifth Avenue, New York, New York 10010

Library of Congress Cataloging-in-Publication Data
d'Arge, Mackie.
Lifting the sky / Mackie d'Arge. — 1st U.S. ed.
p.   cm.
Summary: Twelve-year-old Blue, always on the move with her ranch-hand mother,
yearns for a real home where her father can find them, and on a remote ranch
on a Wyoming reservation she finds that and more, including a mystical ability
to heal injuries.
ISBN-13: 978-1-59990-186-2 • ISBN-10: 1-59990-186-2
[1. Ranch life—Wyoming—Fiction.   2. Aura—Fiction.   3. Healers—Fiction.
4. Single-parent families—Fiction.   5. Animal rescue—Fiction.   6. Indians of
North America—Wyoming—Fiction.   7. Indian reservations—Fiction.
8. Moving, Household—Fiction.   9. Wyoming—Fiction.]   I. Title.
PZ7.D2434Lif 2009   [Fic]—dc22   2008030311

First U.S. Edition 2008
Book design by Nicole Gastonguay
Typeset by Westchester Book Composition
Printed in the U.S.A. by Quebecor World Fairfield
2 4 6 8 10 9 7 5 3 1

For Charlotte, and for Arielle and Alena

Lifting the Sky

Chapter One

The principal crooked his finger at me. "Come to my office," he said.

I almost choked. *Please let it be something horrendous I've done,* I prayed. *Just don't let it be . . .*

But deep inside me I already knew.

It was my mom.

She'd done it again.

My heart crumpled as I pushed myself out of my seat. I tried to ignore the snickers and stares as I trailed after him to his office. There stood my mom, arms crossed, silently waiting. Clearly she'd already said her piece and didn't feel the need for more words.

The principal scowled as he flipped through my records. It was all there, the number of schools I'd attended—I'd been plucked out of four schools already that year. "Well, Blue," he said gruffly. "Given the time left until school lets out for the summer, I'll make you a deal. Take the books you'll need to finish up, only promise you'll send them back, along with your last assignments." He frowned at my mom, but she didn't notice. She was staring out the window already anxious to be on her way.

My hands shook as I cleaned out my desk and locker. "I get to go on vacation early," I bluffed to the class as I stuffed my things into my pack. "It's been great knowing you all," I added, swallowing hard. Then I slung my pack over my shoulder and marched out the door. No sad good-byes for me. No promises to keep in touch. I'd learned it was easier that way.

I followed my mom out to the pickup, kicking at the gravel as I muttered under my breath, "Just four more weeks until summer vacation—couldn't you have managed four more measly weeks?"

Even if she'd heard me it wouldn't have made any difference. All our worldly belongings were piled into the back of Ol' Yeller.

I tossed my stuff onto the heap, climbed into the cab, and wrapped my arms around my dog. As we turned onto the highway the load in the back of the truck shifted, then settled into place again.

Frankly, I wasn't the least bit surprised that she'd quit another ranching job just like that. Two months in a place was our average. This time we'd barely made one.

That's the way it's always been. She leaves in the blink of an eye. It comes on suddenly, as though a heavy thought has fallen from the sky and hit her on the head. She'll put her hand up to her forehead and her eyes will get all faraway looking like they can see through walls and out beyond the hay fields and the hills to someplace no one else can see. "It's time to hit the road," she'll say, and she'll finish up whatever she's been doing, tidy up neat, and start loading our gear into the back of the truck. And if I get a certain look on my face when we've driven into some motel for the night, or into some ranch looking for work, she'll look at me and sigh and say, "Bloom where you're planted, Blue. Just bloom where you're planted."

As if we've ever stayed in one place long enough for roots to grow. Honestly, I've been potted and repotted so many times my roots have all but curled into a ball, like they're scared to death to fasten to the earth 'cause they'll just be jerked right up again.

My mom's worked at so many ranches back and forth across Wyoming that I've forgotten half of them, or tried to.

She's been hired on as a cowpuncher, fencer, hired-hand-of-all-trades, night calver, sheepherder, cook, irrigator, hay hand—you name it, she's done it, and as good as any cowboy only she's a cowgirl and proud of it. And everything will be going along all fine and dandy. We'll have settled in at some ranch. I'll have gotten over new-kid jitters at some school I won't bother to learn the name of. With luck I'll have made a few friends. But before you can say "whistlin' blackbirds," we'll be on our way once again.

Our worldly goodies don't add up to much. My clothes all fit into one battered suitcase, my mom's into another. There are two canvas bags full of boots, hers and mine—rubber irrigating boots, winter boots, cowboy boots, and some really scruffy sneakers. Our bedrolls and pillows. Her cowboy gear—chaps and spurs and lariat ropes. Her saddle. We had to sell mine. Her tools she carries around in the tool chest. She has her own fencing pliers and wire stretchers that she takes real good care of. And her special irrigating shovel with a pointed blade. She keeps the handle oiled and gets upset if someone uses it or leaves it caked with mud. It cost forty-three dollars plus tax. My mom has several pairs of leather gloves that she tries hard not to lose. I've got a pair too, but they're getting awful small. Then there's our aluminum tool box that's plumb full of books and stays in the back of the truck. We've carried it around forever and ever and keep adding to our supply, trading for books and giving some away. You could track where we've been by the books we've left behind. My mom says if you want to get high, books are better than whiskey or gin and you sure feel better the next day.

Not that she drinks anymore—or at least she tries not to. Back when I was little, after my dad took off like he did, there was a spell when she drank more than her fair share. But one night she didn't get back to the bunkhouse. Nor the next day, either. If it hadn't been for a sweet old rancher's wife who took me under her wing, who knows what might've happened. It scared my mom enough to almost make her stop drinking. Speaking of my dad, we used to carry around his treasured guitar, which he somehow forgot to take with him. Last year my mom hocked it. I got all snively because I knew how he loved that guitar. Besides, it gave him something to return for other than just little ol' me. My mom promised we'd buy it back someday, but I was sure she wouldn't. Then there's our just-in-case box and our radio. My mom's box of secrets. Mostly I think that's a few letters she got from my dad. She never would read all the parts out loud to me, no matter how much I begged. My Prismacolor pencils and my journals. My old journals I keep stored in my suitcase so they won't get left behind. The newest one I keep in the backpack I made all by myself, out of a pair of my dad's Wrangler jeans. I've drawn or written in journals since I was four-almost-five, and somehow I've managed to hang on to all of them. I used to have a teddy bear named Grub—I'd had him since the day I was born—but the last place we were at, a puppy chewed him up. All that was left now was one black button eye. It hurts to even think about that. And now to finish up—a good iron skillet we've had since forever, my mom's white china teapot, and her stash of medicinal teas, our blue enamel dishes, and two tin bowls for Stew Pot. He's a border collie, Australian shepherd, blue heeler dingo, and who-knows-what-else mix. He's eleven or so, and my best and usually my only buddy. The only piece of so-called furniture we own is Stew's monstrous fake-fur beanbag bed.

That's it, folks. All our worldly goodies.

The last time we packed up I had pleaded for a whole year in one place, or maybe six months. Even four would do. All I got was one of those looks that said, "Don't go getting your hopes up."

But I did have them up. I had *great* hopes. I wanted to unpack my suitcase. Call someplace "home." And maybe . . . maybe my dad would be able to find us.

"Wishes don't put fishes on dishes," my mom said after I'd whined and wished myself into a tizzy.

I puzzled over that for a long time—or at least until it made some sort of sense. Maybe I'd have to *do* something to help make this happen. But what?

I was sure he'd been looking. I could imagine him pulling out his wallet at coffee shops and gas stations all over Wyoming and passing around an old faded photo of us—of course I'd be little, but my mom would still look the same. Someone would say, "Oh yeah, didn't we see that pair at a branding at so-and-so's ranch?" or something like that. But up till now, if he'd tried to check out the tip, he'd have found that we'd left with no forwarding address.

Hardly a night went by that I didn't pour my heart out to Whatever's Up There. "Please let my mom's special place exist," I'd pray, "and please, please let us find it. And if you could, let her like it so much that she'll stay, and let my dad find out that we're there."

I even drew a picture in my journal of how I thought that place might look. I drew a secret place hidden way up in the mountains with canyons and cliffs and a long winding stream, and up in one corner I drew a house overlooking hay meadows. It wasn't a bunkhouse or a trailer or a sheep wagon. It was a high-tall two-story house. Over the house I wrote the word "home." Curving over the mountains I sketched in a rainbow and colored it all the colors of light.

At night I would lie in bed and march my fingers up the road I'd drawn on that paper, right up to the house, and then I'd take my finger and climb it up imagined pathways through the mountains. Sometimes I'd even put my drawing on the floor and I'd touch it with my bare toes. I'd concentrate so hard that sometimes it felt as if my toes actually touched solid ground.

So here we were, on the road once again. This time we'd left the high windy plains of southern Wyoming and were headed up north where my mom said things might be better.

"We're not going back to that ranch," she said, keeping her eyes on the road, "even if something got left behind."

I was still grumpy, so miles went by before I sniffed, "Okay, so what happened?"

"Never mind. I'd had it up to here," she said, slashing her hand across her forehead. "So I quit."

But I knew. This time it hadn't just been itchy feet. She'd had enough of the way that old ranch manager had acted like he was some big catch that she might want to fish for. There'd been something about him that had made me uneasy, and he'd insisted on calling me Runt or Pee Wee or Squirt, so good-bye and good riddance to him.

The next place just *had* to be better.

When we got off the interstate, we stopped in at a few ranches to see if they needed help. No one seemed anxious to hire us, though one place needed a cook.

"I've had enough ranch-cook jobs to last me a lifetime," my mom said, and we kept right on going.

It was dark when we got to Lander, on the edge of the Wind River Indian Reservation. We found a cheap motel, and the next morning we woke up to red cliffs and fresh snow on the mountains. In town, a light rain had fallen. As we drove down the street to have breakfast a rainbow popped out of the sky.

I knew it was rare and peculiar for one to show up in the morning. *We could sure use some luck,* I thought. I spit on my finger and crossed my heart seven times. It was Wednesday, May ninth, a few minutes till eight.

Not five minutes later my mom opened a newspaper and spotted the ad.

"When one door closes, another opens," she said, pointing to the ad section and pushing the paper across the table to me.

I gave her one of my looks. There were three "Ranch Help Wanted" ads in the paper—the first for a part-time night calver, the next for a nonsmoking cook. I shook my head and tried out the third. "Early-rising self-starting caretaker-irrigator needed on remote mountain ranch," I read. There was a local number and the name M. McCloud.

"This one sounds bearable," I mumbled as I took a bite of my eggs and slipped the rest into my napkin. I didn't want to sound too excited, and besides, I was still in a huff. But to myself I was thinking, *That's perfect—it fits her exactly,* and I crossed my fingers for luck.

My mom quickly finished her breakfast and slipped a five-dollar bill under her cup. The tip was almost as much as our breakfast had cost. I knew she'd tip her last dime without a thought as to how the next one might appear. She never seemed to worry about where her next paycheck might come from. She'd even joke that the reason she was always running from one job to the next was because she was fleeing her demons.

But believe me, it was no joke to *me*.

"Every exit's an entrance to someplace else," she said now. She got up and tore out the ad and tucked it into her pocket. I stuffed the last of my toast into my napkin along with my scrambled eggs and snitched eight packets of jam from the next table. Just in case. On the way out I crammed six peppermint candies into my pocket and smiled sweetly at the cashier as I followed my mom to the truck.

Chapter Two

We asked around and found out that the ranch was on the reservation way up in the foothills of the Wind River Mountains. We got directions and headed on up there, didn't even call or anything. My mom doesn't like phones any more than she likes unnecessary words. She says I talk more than enough for the two of us.

We'd hardly turned off the highway and onto a rutted dirt road when we came to a sign. We jolted to a stop and read it.

TRIBAL LANDS
ABSOLUTELY NO TRESPASSING
BEYOND THIS POINT

The small print said it was Eastern Shoshone and Northern Arapaho Tribal Land and that you had to be a member of one of the tribes to go on. No hunting, no fishing, and a big humongous fine for picking up artifacts.

I got the feeling the sign meant what it said.

"What now?" I moaned. "This *has* to be the right road. Unless we've been sent on a wild-goose chase."

From the looks of things it sure could've been possible. The two-track road crooked over the hills toward the mountains. One ranch peeked out of the hills on our right, but otherwise there was nothing but sage-covered hills stretching out till they butted into steep rosy cliffs and high snowcapped mountains. Junipers dotted the hillsides and still-leafless aspens and cottonwoods followed the curves of a creek.

My heart gave a lurch. It looked strangely familiar.

My mom shrugged and put the truck into four-wheel drive, passed the sign, and kept on going, dodging rocks and boulders, splashing through puddles and lurching over shaky bridges that crossed and recrossed a wide shallow creek until finally—after eight miles that felt like a hundred and eighty—we came to a pole gate with a sign that said "Far Canyon Ranch." We pried open the gate and headed for the shiny tin roof of a barn that stuck up behind some bare trees. We crossed another shaky bridge and there by the barn we came across a man.

"Are you the Mr. McCloud with the ad?" my mom asked.

The man had looked a bit startled to see us come rattling across his bridge, but he nodded and said, "Yes, ma'am." He was in the middle of doing something to his tractor, so he put his tools down and wiped his hands on a red cloth. "Do you have any references?" he asked politely.

My mom shook her head. "No," she said. "I quit my last job."

Mr. McCloud took off his gray sweat-stained cowboy hat and scratched his dark wavy hair and asked, "Well, do you know how to irrigate?"

She didn't answer, just held out her hands, palms up, for him to see.

My mom has big hands, with long, thin fingers. And calluses and scratches all over from shoveling and doing all kinds of ranch work. Mr. McCloud put his own big calloused hands under hers and lifted them almost to his face so he could see them real close-up. I thought maybe he was going to read her fortune, he studied them so hard. Finally he turned her hands over and looked just as carefully at the backs of them. No rings, no watch. Lots of scratches from barbed wire. By then I knew she was thinking she'd have been better off saying some words, but it was too late.

"Yeah," he said, giving her back her hands. "You do." And he looked into her eyes.

I don't know if my mom would be considered pretty, maybe not. She's kind of skinny but real strong and her arms have muscles that ripple almost like a man's— although because it was spring and still cold she had on her old navy-blue coat with feathers sticking out all this way and that where it'd been torn by barbed wire, so you couldn't really tell she had muscles. She doesn't do anything with her long, dark hair, so it's usually in her eyes, but she has eyes the color of a stormy sea, the kind of eyes that if you do look right into them you might find yourself drowning, they take you down so deep.

Mr. McCloud coughed and surfaced and said, "Sure looks like you can handle a shovel and do fence work. Can you caretake? Know a thing or two about calving?"

She gave him a look like, "What do you think?"

"Well, okay," he said. "I like girl-help. Females are usually gentler with the animals and a darn sight more careful with things in general and they don't say they know how to do something when they really don't. Last hired man I had around here didn't know the hind end of a cow from its front. Plus he got the tractor stuck for six weeks in a swamp. I thought it'd sink clear down to China." He glanced at Stew Pot, who'd jumped out of the cab and was now proudly perched on the tarp that covered the gypsy load in the back of our muddy truck. Then he turned and looked at me, sizing me up.

I was standing there trying hard not to think of the tractor plowing its way through the earth and popping up in China, and wearing such a silly grin he must've thought I was a happy camper. My dark reddish brown hair was all scrunched up under my blue baseball cap and sometimes I can almost pass for a boy till I open my mouth. I'm kind of substandard runt-sized for my age, so I stretched up real tall trying to look at least thirteen—which I was, almost. I puffed up my chest, not that it did any good. It'll probably be aeons before I'm not flat as Kansas.

Mr. McCloud nodded at me and I nodded back but kept quiet.

"You know," he said, turning to my mom, "it's a forty-five-minute trip back down that road you came up. You'd have to get your kid"—he glanced at me—"your young lady, down to catch the school bus. It's another hour to the school. No easy way around that. We haven't had a youngster on this place since I don't know when. Don't know how that'd work out."

My mom could've told him that by great good luck and fortune I was going to finish up the school year by mail, but she just stood there and said nothing, so I did.

"I'm homeschooled," I piped up, giving him the biggest smile ever. Behind my back I crossed all my fingers.

Mr. McCloud's eyebrows lifted. He looked from me to my mom and then to Stew Pot in back of the truck. He was silent for a long moment, as if weighing the situation. "This place has been left to the hired hands to handle for the past several years," he went on. "There are some heifers about to calve, and the fences and ditches are in pretty bad shape. But we're short of hands at the moment. I live on another place, mostly, on our main ranch off the reservation, about forty-five miles due east of here. I get out here only once in a while to check up on things. I'd like to be movin' along soon as these heifers have calved."

My mom finally spoke up. "I can handle it," she said.

Mr. McCloud gestured toward a small log cabin that was partly hidden by trees beside the creek. "That's where I bunk out when I'm here," he said. He jerked his thumb at a wooden building beside the barn and added, "And that's the bunkhouse for the hands."

He stopped as though his train of thought had taken another track. I could almost see the wheels churning as another thought hitched up.

"The old homestead's up there apiece on the hill. It's where I grew up. Where I used to live . . ." He gestured to a place up the road, though we couldn't see any house because the road bent around some aspen, cottonwood, and golden willow trees that glowed in the late-morning sunlight with the first yellow-green buds of spring. The ranch lay snuggled in a sheltered valley, and all around its fenced pastures rose hills and cliffs and canyons, and behind those, high mountains.

Mr. McCloud stared down at his hands. There was a long silence when all we could hear was the sound of the creek and some birds. "House hasn't been lived in for almost three years," he finally said. "It would need fixin' up, but it should be livable. You can bunk out up there."

"Okay," was all my mom said. She hadn't spoken more than a dozen words and she'd landed the job.

Chapter Three

Mr. McCloud tipped his hat. "Well, ma'am," he said. "Just follow me then, and I'll show you two up to the house." He climbed into the big diesel truck parked by the barn and we followed in Ol' Yeller.

My mom reached over and touched my knee and smiled. My fingers were now so stuck together from crossing and recrossing that I had to pry them apart.

As soon as we rounded the bend of trees, I felt like laughing and crying and shouting out loud—it was all just as I'd drawn it! A secret place up in the mountains with canyons and cliffs and a long winding stream—and there, up in one corner, on a hill overlooking hay meadows, stood a high-tall two-story house.

"Blue, you'll catch a fly if you don't close your mouth," my mom said as we drove into the driveway and stopped, but I'd already flown out of the truck. I ran to the house and touched it to be sure it was real. My legs started wobbling. I felt so dizzy I sank to my heels. Stew Pot trotted over, his worried ears cocked, and stuck his nose in my face.

"Oh, Stew Pot," I whispered. "I think we've just stepped into my drawing!"

The house I'd drawn had looked just like this one all right, but it had been a happy, sunshiny house. This one seemed lonely and sad, with its windows blank and dirty and dark. Sagebrush, rabbitbrush, and scraggly wild rosebushes had taken over the yard.

From somewhere that sounded far off I could hear a voice saying, "This whole place has been going downhill for the past several years. Maybe you'd be better off down in the bunkhouse."

No, no, it's perfect, I wanted to shout, but the words stuck in my throat as I looked over at Mr. McCloud. I squinted. I rubbed my eyes. No, they weren't playing tricks. He was standing in the wild, overgrown yard looking like he'd just stepped into a rainbow. Rosy pink floated out of his middle. Emerald green shot out of his chest. Out of his throat bubbled a lovely deep blue that floated up into bright yellow. Misty lavender circled his head like a cloud.

I'd seen them before. The lights. But never, ever like *this.* It was as if I'd never seen color before.

Truth is, I couldn't remember a time when I hadn't seen colored mists flashing around people and animals and sometimes even out of trees and rocks and plants. But almost as soon as I'd see them, *poof!*—they'd disappear. I used to wonder what I was seeing, but I just figured everyone saw the same exact way I did. The one time I did say something about flashing lights, my mom rushed me straight off to an eye doctor. He gave me some drops. But of course the drops hadn't changed anything. I still saw lights, but I learned to say nothing about them, and to pay no attention to them. As I got older the lights had grown dimmer and dimmer.

But *these* lights I couldn't ignore. Was it because we were so high up in the mountains? Or because of the pure mountain air?

I looked around. Even the sky seemed bluer than blue and alive with tiny balls of bright bouncing lights. The trees shimmered with a reddish gold glow. I stared at my mom, who was now looking intently at me. She glowed like a rainbow too.

My mind raced. And then suddenly I remembered the story my mom told me about how she'd come up with my name, Blue, when my eyes weren't even close to being blue—in fact they're greenish brown. The way my mom told the story, when I was born there was a deep blue hazy light around me that all those in the room could see. It was indigo blue, she said, as blue as the farthest mountains beneath an evening sky, and all the pretty names she'd thought of had flown right out the window and into the bluest of blues beyond. And that's why she named me Blue.

My mom said she never saw the blue light around me again. When I was little I'd look in the mirror, but those blue lights never showed up. Sometimes, though, I'd look at myself in the dark and think I could see a blue-white glow around my hands.

Just in case you think that with such an introduction into the world I might've turned into something special, you'd be wrong. In school I shine in art and I'm pretty good in English and history, but that's been the extent of my stardom. I'm a dud at basketball, for rather obvious reasons. And then there's track, which is my favorite sport even though I'm always stumbling over my feet. For some reason they've grown at a much faster rate than the rest of me.

I don't shine in the area of fashion, either, because when it comes to the subject of clothes, well, the less said the better. Or as my mom says, the less, the better. What fits into one suitcase is all I've got. I don't care, though. There are lots of things more important than clothes. My mom says it's not the clothes that make the man, and no woman should think they make her, either. And to be perfectly honest, I must've missed out on the gene that makes a girl give a hoot about clothes.

While I'm on the subject of me, my last name's Gaspard. It's French 'cause of my dad, who was born in Paris, France, oh my. He dropped off the earth the week before I turned five.

"He was a sweet-singing, dude-ranch-wrangling, ram-headed, hard-drinking, French-speaking, arrogant charmer," my mom once said, "and when he was sober he could be a delight, but when he was drunk he was horrid."

It was the longest string of words she'd ever strung together. I wrote them down in my journal under the title, "My Dad." Every time I remember or hear something about him I scribble it down.

After my dad took off we were on the go searching for him. The ranches my mom hired on at were dude ranches, mostly—the kind of places where sweet-singing French wranglers might be. Later I suspected the tables had turned and she kept moving on so my dad wouldn't know where to find *us*. The ranches she chose then were all rough-and-tumble hard-working places no dude would ever set foot on, especially someone like my dad.

Sometimes I wished I didn't look so much like him. Every once in a while I'd catch my mom staring at me, and then she'd sigh and slip into deep quiet, and I'd know she was thinking of him. I've got his same fiery dark auburn hair and his greenish brown eyes.

My mom's real name is Maggie, but everyone calls her Mam. From the time I was just a baby I heard the cowboys calling her ma'am, so that's what I learned to call her myself. As I grew I used to wonder why everyone we met already seemed to know her name, and why the cowboys tipped their hats politely when they said it. I thought maybe she'd been a movie star or a rodeo queen or someone really famous before I happened along.

But now my mom startled me out of my daze by touching my shoulder. "You okay, Blue?" she asked.

I nodded. I must've looked really dopey sitting there on my heels, blinking and shaking my head. I got up and took a deep breath to steady myself. I'd ignore the lights, do my best to just act normal—something I was feeling real far from.

I followed behind Stew Pot as he sniffed his way round

the house. Sticking out in the back was a big room made of logs that had obviously been added on but never finished because the logs had never been chinked. Stew Pot lifted his leg and put his mark on the side of it. Then we continued on, past a great big fenced area with a shed in it, past a spot where there'd once been a garden, and finally over to a ramshackle one-room log cabin that stood not far from the house. The door to this cabin lay flat on the dirt floor. Stew Pot's grand tracking nose was going about ten miles a minute. He trotted in and stared up at a pack-rat's twiggy nest in the rafters.

Mam had just pulled back the tarp that covered our load. She flashed me a look that warned not to go poking about, but when Mr. McCloud ambled over she joined us.

"This is the old homestead cabin," Mr. McCloud said quietly, reaching out to touch a log wall as if he were stroking his favorite horse. "It was built by my great-grandparents before they built the big house. It's been used for everything under the sun since then—as a schoolhouse, a blacksmith shop, a henhouse, and now just a storage shed. One winter, back when I was a kid, it even housed an elk. She'd turned up in the middle of a blizzard, starving, and with a hurt leg. My mother pitched some hay into the cabin so the elk would be out of the storm. Well, after treatment like that, you'd better believe the elk turned up her nose and flat refused to leave. She lived there happily until the spring."

He fiddled with the rusty hinges where the door had once hung. I stepped into the almost-empty cabin and the two of us lifted the old battered door. Years of dust slid off as we propped it sideways against the log wall.

"Thank you . . . ," he said, searching the air as he realized we hadn't yet been introduced.

"Blue," I said. "Blue Gaspard. And my mom's Maggie, but most everyone calls her Mam."

"Thank you, Miss Blue," he said. He stuck out his hand and I shook it. He and my mom looked at each other. Neither one stuck out a hand. Then my mom reached out and Mr. McCloud touched the tips of her fingers with his. I'd never seen a finger shake before. It was almost as if they didn't want to go through with that hand thing again.

"My friends," Mr. McCloud said gruffly, "just call me Mac."

"Mr. Mac," I said, quickly counting myself as a friend, "I'm confused. We saw that sign when we came off the highway. No trespassing, it said, unless you're a member of one of the tribes. But you aren't . . . ?" I didn't know how to put it.

"Good question, Miss Blue," he answered. "And you're right. I'm not Native American. It's mainly the Eastern Shoshones who live in this part of the reservation, here by the mountains. The Northern Arapaho came later, and ended up sharing the land. They settled to the east, in the flatlands. The two tribes were not exactly friends, you see, and even now there are still some hard feelings between them."

He pushed his hat low on his forehead as a gust of wind swirled by and looked at me from under the brim.

"As for the trespassing, I'd better warn you that the sign meant what it said. There's land back here that's considered sacred—burial grounds and places where the Indians go on spirit quests and where the medicine men gather sacred herbs for their medicines. There are petroglyphs etched into sandstone cliffs all along the base of these mountains that are said to hold powerful medicine. The old-timers say these places are dangerous to go near. The lakes and rivers are guarded by water ghosts, or so they say. The mountains are watched over by the feared *ninimbe*, or little people. And to tell the truth, I've lived here long enough to actually believe some of these tales."

He ducked his head as if he felt a little silly owning up to this nonsense.

Me, though, I shivered. I could almost feel eyes watching us, checking us out.

"You can go beyond our fence line to clean out our ditch," Mr. Mac continued, "and to get our appropriated water at the headgate up by the creek, but that's about it. Unless you're after one of our critters that has slipped through the fence, don't go ridin' out there on horseback. It might piss off the neighbors." He scratched his chin and smiled. "Not that we have many out here . . ."

Bummer, I thought. There went the horseback riding. If I did go exploring, I'd just have to sneak off on foot and be really careful not to get caught.

"But, Mr. Mac," I piped up, still confused. "If you're not Indian, how'd you get this place right in the middle of Indian lands?"

"Parcels of land here and there belong to non-Indians," Mr. Mac said, his voice all hoarse and gravelly. "That's what those of us who aren't indigenous to this land are called, here on the rez. As for this ranch, my great-grandfather bought it from a Shoshone. I'm sure he paid nowhere near what it was worth. The history of how white men got hold of native lands is a long, heartbreaking story. Maybe you'll learn more about this while you're here."

Mr. Mac looked down at the ground, as if he was embarrassed by his own ancestors' role in the history of these parts. He let out a sigh and looked up. Softly then, his words drifting skyward like a prayer, he said, "But I was born here, and to me this place is more precious than diamonds or gold."

Silently we walked back to the high-tall house. The clouds seemed near enough to reach up and touch. A herd of pronghorn antelopes stopped grazing on the hillsides to watch. An eagle circled above us. A moose jumped over a fence into a pasture where horses were grazing. A cow bellowed, and then another, and soon the valley echoed with calves answering back.

I crawled onto the load in the back of Ol' Yeller and started handing things down to my mom. She passed them on to Mr. Mac, who piled them onto the little front porch. Our canvas bags of boots and shoes. Our bedrolls. Two battered suitcases. Stew Pot's monstrous fake-fur beanbag. The porch was getting full. We slowed down, waiting for Mr. Mac to open the front door.

"I apologize for the mess you'll find," he said as he

went up the porch steps. "I was . . . well, we were doing some remodeling. Didn't quite get it done, as you'll see." He fumbled with a piece of baling wire that had been twisted around the doorknob and attached to a nail on the doorframe. "No need for locks around here," he said smiling. "This wire's just for keepin' the wind from blowing the door open."

And then, as if his words had stirred it up, a gust of wind swooped around the house and twirled his hat across the porch, past the cabin, and into the fields. We all scrambled after it and Stew Pot nearly nabbed it. I thought I'd captured the rascal, but it had other plans and took off spinning wildly again. It was my mom who finally caught it and held its brim down with the scuffed tip of her boot. Mr. Mac was hot on her heels, both of them breathless and laughing as they stooped to pick it up.

For a second time that day my eyes practically popped out of their sockets. Something was going on with their lights. They swelled out and fluffed up around them like rosy pink clouds. I watched as the two of them looked away from each other, watched as their lights seemed to reel back in close to their bodies, as if they were trying to keep them safely tucked in.

I'm such a snoop, but even I had to look away. Some things should really be private.

They walked silently back to the house. My mom plucked a feather out of her hair and looked anywhere but at Mr. Mac. He looked straight ahead, brushing back his dark hair and cramming his rascally hat on his head.

"Think I'd best leave you ladies to settle in," he said, coughing and clearing his throat. "I'll see you about the cattle and irrigating and the rest tomorrow. The pantry down in the cookhouse is full of canned goods, and the freezer's well stocked. Help yourselves." He opened the door to his truck, tipped his hat to us, and slid in.

My mom and I stood silently, watching as the truck rumbled down toward the barn and disappeared behind the reddish gold shimmering trees.

Chapter Four

"This house has surely been enchanted," I said as I stepped inside. "Like in a fairy tale where the spell's only broken when the maiden gets smooched by the prince." I smirked.

"Don't go getting smart," Mam said.

But my skin got all goose bumpy as I got my first look. I'd pictured much of the outside, but somehow I'd never imagined the inside. The mudroom was stuffy and cold and spiderwebs draped the small panes of the windows. I reached out to latch the open doors of a hutch that was crammed with cans of screws and nails and all sorts of tools and fencing supplies. An old pair of cowboy boots sagged in a corner beside a low table. It was a typical mudroom. I turned to Mam and gave her a big smile.

"Smells musty," Mam said, pinching her nose. "Mr. McCloud was right. We might be better off in the bunk-house."

It suddenly struck me—what if the picture I'd drawn had only been *my* special place? What if it wasn't my mom's?

Silently we moved our gear from the windy porch into the mudroom. We looked at each other, and then Mam creaked open a door that led into a little dark hallway. There we found three other doors. Mam opened one. It led down to a cellar. She opened another. It led up a steep, narrow stairway to what looked like a sunshiny attic.

"A house of doorways," Mam muttered as she opened the next door and stepped in.

"Entrances and exits and portals," I said from behind her in my deepest, most mysterious voice. "And when new doorways open, *leap!*" And I bounded into the kitchen and stopped.

The kitchen was like a piece of fallen sky—all the shades of noon and dusk and morning. The cabinets and an old threadbare sofa and braided rug and the lamp that hung over the table were all different hues of blue. Cobalt-blue bottles stood on the counters and lined the windowsills.

"It's a blue room made for me 'cause I'm blue too," I said, and I whirled around the table and crashed into a chair that then tumbled and crashed into another. *"Shhhh,"* I whispered to Stew Pot, who was used to getting blamed for things I did. "You'll wake the house."

During the time the house was abandoned, a blanket of dust had covered everything. I sneezed at least twenty-six times as I tiptoed across the wood floor and peeked into the next room.

It was a living room. A messy one. Everything had been pushed to one end of the room and piled up, with a trunk tucked under a table and a chair on top of that and a rolled-up rug on top of a couch that was pushed up against two worn leather chairs. Behind the jumble, on either side of a long narrow window, stood two built-in bookcases just loaded with books.

I scrambled over, yelling, "We've got books!" Never mind waking the house. I trailed my fingers along the dusty shelves, calling out, "Paperback Westerns. Mysteries. Romances. Books about Indian history and lore . . . old schoolbooks . . . and what looks like a whole set of old encyclopedias!"

"Mam'll gobble those up," I said in a low voice to Pot. She was always trying to read and get smarter on account of not finishing high school.

With the furniture all jammed over on one end, there was a pathway to a latched double door. It squeaked as I pushed it open. The unfinished log addition was empty except for a wood stove in one corner and a ladder. The logs hadn't been chinked and wind blew through the spaces between them. I quickly snapped the door closed.

Another door off the living room led to a hallway with a room at each end. A tiny bathroom squeezed itself in between them. A hammer, some screwdrivers, and a can of screws lay on the bathroom floor, along with a set of towel racks still in their wrappers.

"We've got a job to do, but not one we can't handle," I called back to Mam, and opened the door at one end of the hall.

On a snow-white floor stood a bed made of aspen, its posts rising up to clouds in a blue painted-sky ceiling. Everything—walls, dresser, chair, and table—sported coats of white paint. Not a scuff mark anywhere to be seen. The room looked as if it had been freshly painted and then barely touched. I twirled into it and plunked down on the quilted bedspread. Dust rose like clouds in the afternoon light.

Poking her head in from the doorway off the kitchen, my mom's mouth dropped open. She stood there blinking at all the whiteness.

I started to shout *Dibs!*, but the word stuck like a frog in my throat. "Dib—adubadu," I croaked instead. "It's perfect. For *you*."

Oh please, *please* let her like it, I prayed.

"We'd be better off in the bunkhouse" was what my mom said. "This house is too fancy for me. You take this room. I'll put my bedroll on the couch."

"Put it on top of the bed, then," I sniffed. "It's not like Mr. Mac didn't tell us to settle in. And anyway, there must be another room down the hall."

And there was, but it was empty, with not a stick of furniture in it. Some cans of paint and a roller and brushes were set out on a canvas floor cloth. A mural of mountains and cliffs had been sketched across all four walls—

around the window and door even—but only one small patch of the mural had been painted.

"No bed in here, so I guess that leaves us the attic," I said, rolling my eyes at Stew Pot as we headed back to the hallway by the kitchen.

Please don't let it be a big empty room, I prayed, as I made my way up the steep stairs. I closed my eyes and didn't open them until I got to the top.

Imagine walls the color of sunrise. Slanted ceilings the same peachy color, and beds—count them, one, two, three—each covered by a yellow, green, or blue blanket. I trailed through the long, narrow room, touching each bed as I passed. *Maybe it'd been the kids' dorm,* I thought, *back when Mr. Mac was a child.* A chest of drawers stood next to each bed. A soft-looking chair and a vanity table with an oval-shaped mirror faced the three beds. The mirror was cracked as if someone had thrown something at it.

At each end of the room was a window. Mountains and canyons filled one. The tin roof of the old homestead cabin sparkled in the afternoon sunlight through the other. Beyond the cabin, the meadows rolled down to the barn.

A hole gaped near the foot of one bed. Good thing an iron grating covered it. I peered into it. Directly below, in the living room, was a bigger grate, obviously above the furnace down in the basement. Somewhere downstairs my mom sneezed. Ha! I had me a secret hear hole as well as a peek hole.

I sat on each bed in turn and bounced, making dust

fly and the brass headboards rattle. The bed nearest the stairs with the blue blanket on it was *perfect*.

I raced down to the cellar and stoked up the furnace while Mam switched on the electricity. The house hummed to life. Upstairs in the kitchen the old fridge gurgled and buzzed, its vibrations warning the mice and spiders and bugs that things soon would be changing. Even Mam seemed to be feeling a bit better about the big house. We pounded on the cushions and then gagged and coughed from the puffs of dust that rose up. We swept and mopped and cleaned mouse nests from the drawers and shook the rugs and blankets and moved things back into place. In a trunk we found sheets and towels and blankets all layered with sage and sprinkled with the dried, faded petals of roses. We stripped and made the beds. In the bathroom we even screwed in the towel racks.

Then I plugged in my radio and the two of us sat in the kitchen too tired to even *think* about going down to the bunkhouse to check out the provisions there. We hauled out my just-in-case box. Mam chose chili while I globbed peanut butter on crackers and topped them with rounds of dill pickles. Stew Pot stuck up his nose and pouted when Mam offered him his choice of chili or pickled herring. He would've much preferred oatmeal or asparagus or carrots. He's pretty much a vegetarian—like me, though Pot will eat stew and I won't. But he loves scrambled eggs and toast. Luckily I'd saved some from breakfast.

It was way dark when I yawned my way up to the

attic. I unpacked my colored pencils and pens and placed them neatly on the chest by my bed. I got out my journal and opened it to a fresh page.

May 9—Day One, I wrote. *Far Canyon Ranch, somewhere over the rainbow . . .*

I yawned. I was way too tired to write more. I fluffed up Pot's beanbag, gave him the biggest hug ever, and crawled into bed. My old teddy bear Grub's black button eye I tucked under my pillow.

Chapter Five

The next morning, I lay in bed and watched as the sun rose and light streamed through the window, turning the peachy walls to pure gold. Then I hopped out of bed, threw on some clothes, and tore down the stairs.

Mam and Stew Pot were already gone, though the sun had only just now come up. My blue-for-me kitchen throbbed to the loud hum of the fridge and the dum-dumming of Indian drums on the radio. My schoolbooks had been laid out on the table. On the stove was the pot of leftover chili. The packets of jam from yesterday's restaurant were piled on the table, along with the peanut butter and pickles and the box of crackers from my just-in-case box.

The sad truth is I snitch things. I've stolen from every ranch kitchen we've ever set foot in. Sometimes the loot won't all fit into my just-in-case box and gets left behind, stuffed in some closet or piled under my bed. I can imagine the puzzled look on the cook's face at the last place when he discovered three jars of pickled beets he'd been missing. Not to mention those six cans of mandarin oranges, four boxes of fish fry, five cans of sardines, and a whole bag of self-rising flour . . .

I tried to tackle a few pages of schoolwork, but I was way too stirred up, so I soon gave it up. I was stuffing my feet into my boots in the mudroom, about to head out to explore, when I heard Ol' Yeller roar up the road.

"Glad to see you're finally up," Mam called from the window of the truck. "We could use you down at the barn." She turned the pickup around as I grabbed my jacket and gloves.

"Been down there since four," she said as we bumped down the road. "I'm going to saddle up to bring in two heifers that are about ready to calve. Stew Pot's helping me. You go help Mr. McCloud."

Mr. Mac had sure gotten himself an early-rising self-starter. As for me, I was no cowgirl like my mom. I was okay on a horse and pretty good at helping to round up the cattle or to check on the cows and calves, and I could even fix fences if they didn't need to be stretched. But there were some things, like branding, that I absolutely, totally hated. I shied away when it came time for weaning the calves and sending them away from their mamas. Mam always said I was overly sensitive and I should just get over it. Easy for *her* to say. Sometimes I figured being overly sensitive was the worst possible trait one could have. Especially if you lived on a ranch.

The cattle on this place were mostly older cows, I'd noticed—a small herd of Black Baldies and Angus and Herefords. The older cows needed little or no help having their babies. But there were also some first-time heifers, and those had to be watched night and day. With heifers there was always the chance of something going dreadfully wrong. A calf might be too large or turned around the wrong way, or it might get stuck in the middle of trying to be born.

"Mornin', Miss Blue," Mr. Mac said when I met him by a stall near the back of the barn. "We've got a sorry situation here. These little twins were born last night out in the willows near the creek. Your mom and I found them at dawn." He crouched on his heels beside two tiny black calves bedded down in some straw.

"They're preemies," he went on, pulling at his neck scarf and scratching the stubble on his chin. "And they're plumb tuckered out by their difficult birth. They're too weak to stand up and nurse. Not that they've got a mother to nurse them—she didn't make it, I'm sorry to say."

I tried not to picture the scene. "Poor little bums," I said—bums are what they call little orphans. I squatted beside them. Their matted black fur was still wet.

I squinted. It was shadowy dark in the back of the barn, but I could have sworn there was a foggy light around the bums. And as Mr. Mac stroked them, pale streamers of bluish light seemed to flow out of his fingers. Each time he touched the calves, the foggy lights around them got a little brighter. When he took his hands away, their lights grew dim again.

I looked down at my own hands and sure as anything, I wiggled my fingers and watched lights flickering out of them.

One thing was certain: I was seeing more light than ever before.

Suddenly one of the calves stretched, and a sparkle of dark reddish light streaked out of its lower front leg.

I frowned. What did that mean? I took a spur-of-the-moment guess.

"Bum's got a broken leg," I said, startling myself by how certain I was of what I was seeing.

Mr. Mac's mouth dropped open. "Words stolen right out of my mouth," he said. Gentle light flowed from his fingers as he reached down and touched the calf's leg. Then it was my turn to stand there with my jaw hanging loose as I watched the light growing brighter as he caringly examined the break.

"The mother cow must've stepped on it not long after it was born. It's a wonder either of these critters survived. They'll need a whole lot of good care and nursing if they're going to make it." He paused. "Your mom says you're real good with animals. Want to take on these critters for me?"

"Sh-sure," I said, bobbing my head up and down before I had time to think, but to tell the truth I wasn't one bit sure at all. I'd helped my mom feed bum lambs and calves plenty of times, but two tiny preemies had never been handed over to me just like *that*—nor had one with a leg that was broken.

Still, my grand list-making mind jumped right into action.

"We'll have to make a splint and get something to wrap the leg with," I said, counting off on my fingers. "And they'll have to be cleaned up, and we'll need some straw or hay to make a bed. A good place would be in that shed in the pen up by the house—that way I can keep good track of them. And we have to have two calf bottles and a bunch of nipples, 'cause I know how calves always chew through them." I thought for a second. "And of course some dry milk starter. And a drain tube to start them off with a drenching, 'cause, like you said, they're way too weak to suck and they'll need some milk in their bellies straight off. Plus we might need a can or two of beef consommé on hand just in case they get the runs."

I took a deep breath. Sometimes I talk as if my brain's overeaten.

Mr. Mac's lights got even brighter as he rocked back on the heels of his worn cowboy boots and laughed. "You're somethin' else, Miss Blue," he said, smacking his knee. "I've got some pipe that would work as a splint." His voice was all smiley as he headed to the tack room in the back of the barn. He came back with a plastic pipe he'd split down the middle and some duct tape and a piece of clean gauze. Then he pulled off one boot and handed me a warm sock. "We'll cut the toe off and slip it over the splint," he said as he did a little dance, tugging his boot back onto his bare foot.

I pulled out my handy pocketknife and held up the sock. *"Eeew . . . !"* I said as I sliced off the toe.

He grabbed the sock. "What? Smells like daffodils," he said, and handed it back.

Between giggles we somehow got the leg splinted and wrapped, being careful not to get it too tight.

"I'll get some hay to bed them down in," Mr. Mac said. "The rest of your list you should find in the tack room. Except for the soup. I'll have to check in the cookhouse for that."

Sunlight streamed through a high window in the tack room, glinting off the saddle racks with their blankets folded over them, striking the bridles and reins and silver-starred spurs hanging along the walls, along with branding irons with the ranch brand of 2M. The shelves were stocked with purple horse tincture and hoof cream and leather cream and calf nipples and milk bottles and shot needles and all kinds of pills and cow medicine. I scratched about and found everything I needed and stashed it in a cardboard box and hauled it out to the truck.

Mr. McCloud had already bundled the calves onto the floor of the cab in his big diesel truck. "Hop in," he said, and I did. We drove around to the side of the house and I jumped out and opened the gate to the pen. Mr. Mac helped me fix up a sweet-smelling nest of hay in the back of the lean-to shed, and then he gathered up the calves one at a time and settled them into it. I fussed over my new babies while he unloaded our stuff. He grabbed the sack of dry milk starter and took it over to the porch and set it there.

"Better keep the starter in the mudroom," he said when he returned. "You get settled in all right? Is the house okay?"

"It's perfect," I said. "*Picture* perfect."

He flung me a look like, "You've gotta be kidding." "It was a mess," he said, his voice full of apologies.

I nodded like I understood. Honestly, we'd lived in places that'd been in a whole lot worse shape, but no matter where we ended up it always took time to make a place feel like we actually lived there.

Grabbing the bottles, I scampered off to the kitchen to mix up the starter. When I came back Mr. Mac was mending a hole in the chicken-wire fence that surrounded the pen. "Don't want some critter comin' by looking for a free supper," he said. "And you'll be on your own after tomorrow. The last of the heifers should be calved out by then, and I'll be heading back to the main ranch."

I could feel my insides clench up. *What? So soon? You can't,* I wanted to say.

But already Mr. Mac was explaining how to tube feed a calf that was too weak to suck, and showing me how to figure out the right length of the tube by measuring the distance from the tip of the calf's nose to the point of the knee on its front leg. And how to make sure the tube got put in just right so it didn't end up in the calf's lungs instead of its stomach. And then we got too busy even for words, me holding on to a calf while Mr. Mac drained the milk through the tube and down into its starved little tummy, and then the two of us switching, with him holding a calf and me pouring.

"I don't know, Miss Blue," Mr. Mac said as we settled the calves back into their nest. "It'll be mighty tricky. They're even weaker than I'd thought. You check on that leg and put a fresh wrap on it as the calf grows. It'll take quite a while for this leg to set." He hesitated. "I'm putting a big load on you. Sure you'll be able to deal with all this?"

I got that nervous feeling again. *What do I know about taking care of a broken leg?* I wanted to say. *Or feeding two bums that can't even stand up to suck?* But what I said was "I can handle it." They were Mam's and my favorite words.

Mr. Mac let himself out of the pen. He climbed into his truck and started the engine. "Now, don't get upset if these bums don't make it," he said. "I don't think they have much of a chance."

"But I do," I said, though he'd already chugged down the road.

Chapter Six

Both bums were black, but one had a white clover-shaped mark on her forehead. I named that one Lucky Charm. The one with the broken leg I dubbed Wonder Baby. It turned out to be just the right name.

I stood with my hands on my hips looking down at my grubby orphans. It was clear their poor mama hadn't had time to give them more than a quick lick and a kiss before she took her last breath. Now that their tummies were full, what they needed most was a bit of a cleanup. I grabbed some old towels from the house, filled a bucket with warm soapy water, and lugged it back to the pen. I wiped their snotty noses and then rubbed their little bodies with the towels.

I was taking a break, watching two crows dive-bomb and squawk at a hawk, when Wonder Baby made a strange gurgling sound and her lights started growing dimmer and dimmer, as if she were fading away.

What was I supposed to do? Give mouth-to-mouth? How? Mr. Mac! Help!

But he wasn't there. No one was—it was all up to me! Frantically I pushed with both hands on her chest. I remembered how the bums' lights had brightened as Mr. Mac stroked them down in the barn. I stared down at my own shaky hands. Could I do that?

They didn't look as if they held enough light to make anything brighter at all.

How do I fill up on light? I took in a humongous breath. It's a wonder my lungs didn't pop, sucking in all that air and space and vacuuming in whole shafts of sunlight. All the while I kept imagining everything churning inside me and turning itself into light, and then with a big *whoosh* I let it all out. "Let Wonder Baby's lights come back on," I whispered, and I stuck both hands on my little bum's chest.

Her body twitched. Her lights fluttered. "Hang in there," I pleaded. I watched as her lights grew fainter and then just as suddenly they flared up the same way a spark does when you blow hard and it catches on fire.

"Yes!" I said.

Wonder Baby lifted her head. *"Maaaaa,"* she said.

I stared at my hands. They glowed as if they were on fire.

The whole rest of the day I spent with my bums, puzzling over what had happened. I didn't go down to the barn or off to explore. I didn't do one page of schoolwork.

The sun was sneaking down behind the high mountains when Stew Pot showed up all droopy and feeling left out. He looked up at me with sad eyes. I touched my forehead to his.

"Stew Pot," I said, "please understand. It's very, *very* important that we take good care of these calves." I rubbed Pot's ears for a long time before I went on.

"I get the feeling there's something really special about this place because for some reason I'm seeing lights all over the place. And today, Pot, I think I used my own lights to make Wonder Baby's lights brighter. I don't know how that happened. But it made me think . . . I think I need to do everything possible to get Mam to stay here awhile."

Pot cocked his ears at the sound of Ol' Yeller rumbling up from the barn, and pretty quick Mam showed up at the pen. She leaned on the gate and peered at the calves and then nodded as if things looked okay. But all she said was, "Clear sky tonight. It's cold in these mountains, so it could drop down to freezing. Better bring your bums into the house."

My mom could be such a pain in the neck, but sometimes I so dearly loved her.

While she stoked up the furnace, I pushed the couch and a trunk and some chairs into a holding pen, right in the living room, beside the warm grate. When Mam came up from the cellar she smiled as if I'd done just right. Then together we carried the tiny bums into the house.

That night I lugged Stew Pot's beanbag bed downstairs

and spread out my bedroll so the two of us could sleep near my babies.

Around noontime the next day I ran down to the barn to catch Mr. Mac before he took off for the main ranch. The last two heifers had calved. He'd spent the morning showing my mom all the ropes, explaining the lay of the land and how the ditches were laid out.

"Little rascals could keep you busy full-time," I heard him telling her as I got to the barn. "Used to have one hand who I'd swear did nothing but set traps, and when that didn't work he'd blow up the darn things with dynamite."

I puzzled over that before it struck me that it had to be beavers he was talking about.

Mr. Mac was already loading his gear into the back of the truck. "I was about to quit raising cattle on this place," he said as he hoisted his saddle over the side. Then he grabbed his rope, tossed out one end of it, coiled a loop, tossed it, and coiled it again. Mam and I stood there silently watching.

"These past few years I turned the place over to the hired hands to handle," he continued, tucking the coiled rope into the truck next to his saddle. "That was the wrong thing to do."

Mam flipped her hair the way a horse does its tail when it's got a bit of an attitude. She stared somewhere around Mr. Mac's middle shirt button.

"No, no, I didn't mean to say that *you* couldn't handle it," he apologized, though of course she hadn't opened her mouth.

"Obviously I haven't been around near enough, as you can see from the state things are in. The beavers are building dams to beat hell and plugging up about half of our water. The ditches are in terrible shape, and the fences are even worse, what with moose and elk and stray cattle fence jumping to get to our irrigated pastures. And then there's the stuff you can't do a thing about, like the drought. Wyoming's been short of moisture for eight years in a row. The creeks are running low, there's not enough feed for the wildlife, and the fire danger—don't get me started on that! We used to clear the ditches by burning the weeds, but not anymore. One spark could set the whole county on fire."

Mam and I followed his gaze as he stared at the mountains behind us. The thick forest of green fir and pine trees was peppered with rusty brown patches of beetle-killed trees. Everyone in Wyoming knew about the beetles that bored into the bark of pine trees and were slowly but surely killing them dead.

Mr. Mac sighed. "So with all that, and now the wolves that are spreading out of the park—not that I've seen any of those around here, at least not yet—well, this might be the last year I try to ranch here."

He turned to my mom. "Unless, of course, things work out and I find the right hand to handle all this."

Mam's eyes moved up from his middle button. For a minute they stared at each other. She said nothing.

Sometimes I just purely wanted to shake her.

"Well, we'll see how it goes," Mr. Mac said, and he climbed into his truck. As the diesel motor rumbled he rolled down the window. "Call if you need anything," he said. "Phone's pretty staticky out here, but it usually works. Stay out of trouble, Miss Blue, and let me know how it goes with those calves. Be sure to keep a good watch on that leg. Don't let it get infected. The cast will need changing as the calf grows. It will take quite a while for a break like that to heal."

He tipped his hat. "Stay safe," he said.

He and my mom looked at each other. I looked away. Pretty quick the truck went lurching across the shaky bridge and in two seconds flat the trees on the other side of the creek had swallowed it up. When we could no longer hear the chug of his truck the huge silence of the place settled in.

Chapter Seven

"Enough is enough," Mam said after three nights of bums hanging out in the living room.

Lucky Charm and Wonder Baby left behind—well, what calves leave behind. Each morning I hauled them back to their pen as soon as the sun wobbled up. A blustery wind had whirled in from the east and at night it got down below freezing, and so each evening we carried them back into the house.

When I came back from the pen that morning carrying two empty milk bottles, I found Mam scraping oatmeal into three bowls. She set two on the table and one on the floor and plunked herself down at the table. Stew Pot stuck his nose in his bowl and then lay with his head on his paws looking mournful. Mam puckered her brow and stared at her bowl.

I handed her a spoon. Placed a carton of milk on the table. "Eat," I said.

Giving me a crooked half grin, she stuck her spoon into the thick gluey concoction. She'd left the pot simmering on the stove when she'd taken off before dawn. I'd been so busy getting the bums out of the house and fed and cleaned up that I hadn't even glanced at the stove. Now here it was, a little past seven, and she'd already been out and about for two hours. Since Mr. Mac left she'd been bustling about as if the world would shatter and break if she didn't get the meadows dragged and the ditches cleared before snowmelt in the mountains, and the fences all fixed before the Indian cows got put out on the tribe's grazing lands. She'd barely taken time out to sleep, much less to cook or to eat. I wished she'd take better care of herself. Sometimes I wondered if all kids who had only one parent worried about that. Like, what would happen to *me* if something should happen to *her*?

"I'd be totally thrilled to help out," I said as I rinsed out the bottles and scrubbed the nipples and then plopped them into the drainer. "I could hike along the fences to see where they're down, or I could clear some of the brush from the ditches."

To be truthful, that wasn't just me being Little Miss Goody Two-Shoes. I was itching to get out there. Caring for the bums and doing my schoolwork had eaten up all my free time. I hadn't had one single chance to go off and explore.

"Not till your schoolwork's mailed back." She said that without a lick of responsibility in her voice.

And just who was it who'd busted me out of school, please?

"But," she added, "the calves are a handful and you're doing a fantastic job."

Just butter me up. "Well, I could at least take care of the housework," I heard myself say. "And maybe even some of the cooking." Which, trust me, wasn't like me at all. Volunteer? For *indoor* jobs? *Cooking?*

Mam brought the glob in her spoon to her mouth. She glanced down at Stew Pot, who still hadn't touched his bowl of oatmeal. She took a bite of hers, wrinkled her nose, crossed her eyes, and slammed her spoon down on the table.

"Deal," she said.

That's how it started. How I began to take over the house.

It was Sunday. With no lessons, and with my bums already taken care of, I got going on windows. All fourteen of them, count them, inside and out, except for the outside of the two in the attic that were too high for the ladder to reach.

I scrubbed and wiped and polished and when I was done I ran out into the meadows and stood with my hands on my hips looking back at the house. No more blank-looking, grimy, sad-eyed windows, no sir. The eyes of *this* house sparkled.

Seeing it with its windows glistening in the sunlight made me wonder why Mr. Mac had left the house.

Whatever the reason, it had worked out for the better for Mam and me. It was as if the house had just been sitting there waiting for us to come bring it back to life.

I wondered if by putting it down on paper, by *drawing* it—this deserted house and the wild landscape around it— by seeing it in my mind's eye so clearly, by imagining it to be solid and real, had I somehow, some way, *drawn* it *to me?*

Could the universe possibly work that way?

It was right then, standing there in the meadow, that I got a really bright idea. Maybe, if I fixed it up a bit, I could make my dream house more—well, more *mine.* More . . . permanent. As in something that lasted for more than two months.

Slowly I walked back to the house. It seemed to have its own faint glow, like a slight shimmer that might, or might not, have been the sun bouncing off the newly washed windows.

I dusted the bookshelves and captured six spiders and carefully put them outside. I danced with the broom to some cool Indian rap and only broke two plates that had been set too close to the edge of the table. I poked about in the drawers and cabinets and pulled out a tablecloth. It was the most gorgeous rose-patterned cloth I'd ever seen. We'd use it just once, I decided. I cleared off the table— schoolbooks and notebooks and encyclopedias and gloves and fencing pliers and a pile of rusty fence staples. I shook out the cloth and spread it, wondering about what special, happy occasions the cloth had been spread on the table like this. When I stood back and smiled at my blue-for-me kitchen, it seemed as if it smiled back.

That afternoon I ran down to the bunkhouse to check out the pantry.

Oh my. Shelf after shelf of all sorts of goodies stared me right in the eyes as if daring me. The freezer was jam-packed full of packages of elk and beef and I even found several gallons of ice cream. But believe you me, I was careful. I brought up to the house only what I thought we might need for a day. Honestly, all I slipped into the cardboard box under my bed were two cans of tomato soup and one small jar of pickle relish. And one little tube of something called anchovy paste.

I wasn't much of a cook, but then Mam wasn't much of a critic. For supper I made spaghetti with peanut-butter-flavored veggie sauce for Stew Pot and me, and a meat sauce for Mam. I even mixed up a cake and spread it with peanut butter and coconut icing. It made it look like a party with everything spread out on the pretty cloth, although my mom thought we'd better put it away again right after supper. Mam said it was the best meal she'd eaten in ages. She also said thanks a lot, but she wasn't so tired that she couldn't do the cooking from now on.

Ever since I can remember the two of us almost never sat down to a meal without something to read. Me, I was deep into a book about Indians, homed in on a part about how they showed how courageous they were by reaching out and touching the enemy, a practice called "counting coup." It seemed like a nifty idea because it would sure take a lot more guts to do that than to just shoot someone from far off. As for Mam, she had her nose buried in an encyclopedia. "I'm going to get through the whole set," she said.

There were twenty-six books. How much time would that give us? When she wasn't so tired that she couldn't see straight she could read a regular-sized book in one evening. I'd already caught her skipping from A to M and then peeking at Z. I'd have to keep track. Not that getting through the set would be reason enough for her to stay in one place. But at least it was something I could pin a few hopes on. "Have another," I could always say. "Surely you haven't yet read all of T. . . ."

Up in my attic, after the dishes were washed and put away, and after my mom had trailed off to bed lugging two heavy volumes, I opened my journal. I'd missed several days, so I searched for the date in the little calendar in the back. *Sunday,* it said. *May 13.*

I jumped out of bed. "Happy Mother's Day, Mam," I yelled down through the hole in the floor.

Chapter Eight

I practically lived with my bums. Some nights I found myself out in the shed, not sure how I got down the steep attic stairs and out the front door without waking. I'd curl up with Lucky Charm and Wonder Baby and wake only when the sun tipped over the mountains and spilled its light into the valley. Then I'd stumble to the kitchen, mix up two bottles of milk, and head back and feed my babies.

Both calves had gotten strong enough to stand up and suck on a bottle. Just try holding a squirming wobbly-legged calf between your knees to feed it. And of course be sure you hold on to the bottle with both hands 'cause otherwise it'll get jerked this way and that and the nipple will shoot off and you'll both take a bath in the calf's milk. Try to keep calf number two from butting in while this is going on—see what happens.

I smelled like sour milk. Even Pot turned up his nose when I passed.

Lucky Charm's lights had brightened up right away. Wonder Baby's—well, her lights had perked up after that first day when I'd been afraid she might not make it. She stumbled and clunked about with her casted leg and even managed a few hippity hops, but then sometimes she'd fall down and stay that way until I picked her up.

I chanted their names as I stroked them, and while I stoked them I concentrated on the light in my fingers. It didn't take long to catch on that I didn't have to puff myself up like a blowfish or even actually *touch* them to make the lights grow bigger. Just holding my hands above them and thinking about what I wanted to do seemed to be enough to make light flow gently out of my fingers.

My hands even started picking up things that my eyes didn't catch. On Thursday morning, one week after I got the two calves, I noticed a prickly tingle poking at my hands as I was checking Wonder Baby's leg. I moved my hands back and forth through the air. That was strange. I could feel bulges and tingles and odd bumpy places. It was the same sort of feeling you'd get if you stuck your hand out the truck window and felt the wind pushing against it.

The thing to do, I figured, was to smooth those rough places out. But how?

I leaned my head down and blew at the airy bumps. I blew till I almost passed out, then felt around in the air above the calf's leg. The bumps were still there. I scratched over them by crooking my fingers and then dragging them through the lumpy air. I noticed that doing that seemed to smooth out the bumps, so I raked and scraped the air above Wonder Baby's body till the lumpy air and the tingles and prickles dwindled away to nothing.

Wonder Baby snored. Somehow, I'd banished the bumps. I'd also put her to sleep, so I slipped off her cast and examined the break. It didn't seem worse, but then again, it didn't seem better. Cripes, I thought. If it wasn't such a long ride to the highway, I'd ask Mam to take her to a vet to get it checked out.

Being careful not to wake my bum, I slipped off to the house. Mam had started keeping a supply of medical stuff in the cabinet above the sink. I grabbed a bundle of elastic bandages and tape and some disinfectant and hurried back to the pen.

I've learned a lot in one week, I said in my head as I wrapped Wonder Baby's leg and slipped on the makeshift cast again. But if I'm going to use this light . . .

My head was swimming. This light. What I'd almost said was this *power.*

My schoolwork would've been almost all done by now if I hadn't had so much other stuff to do. I hadn't even had a chance yet to go off and explore! Sure, I'd taken different routes down to the barn and the cookhouse, and hiked through the fields and along the edge of the woods by the creek, but I hadn't yet climbed one single hill. A long, purplish hill ran along one side of the ranch. Steep cliffs rose up along another side. But the biggest, most climbable hill was behind the house on Indian land, just a short way from the fence line. I could hardly wait to get up it and check out the world from the top.

That afternoon I scribbled a note. *Gone for a hike. Be home before dark.* Then I grabbed my backpack, whistled for Pot, and struck out.

When we got to the fence I stopped. The sign near the road had said "Absolutely No Trespassing." Mr. Mac had said *not* to. But obviously there was no one around to ask for permission. . . .

"I'll tiptoe," I whispered to Pot, "and no one will know I was there."

I trailed along the fence until I found a place where the wires had come loose. By the tracks and the hairs in the barbs I could tell it was where antelope slipped under and where deer, elk, and moose leaped over on their way down to the creek or back toward the mountains. I tugged up the top strand of barbed wire and squeezed through.

Stew Pot loped ahead of me, sniffing under rocks for chipmunks and such. "We're on sacred land," I reminded him. "Behave. Sniffing is fine, but no chasing!" Not that Pot does—he's a ranch dog and knows better.

Halfway up I flopped on the ground to catch my breath—funny how a hill suddenly became so much steeper when you actually started to climb it. I took a detour over to a rocky ledge that dropped into a deep narrow canyon. "Whoo, whoo!" I yelled down to hear what the canyon would answer. The hills rang with echoing whoo-whoos as I turned and hiked the rest of the way up the hill.

"Maybe this is why the top of a hill's called a crown," I wheezed when I caught up with Stew Pot. "It's 'cause you feel like a queen—or a king, in your case—when you finally get there. And this"—I threw out my arms—"this will be my throne."

"This" was a juniper tree, a tree so big it fit the word "majestic." Even before I got close to it I could feel it. A thick field of energy seemed to surround it, like what I'd been feeling around the bum calves. The field seemed much bigger than the actual tree. What I could *see* around the juniper was a fuzzy green haze.

The juniper leaned over the rocky rim as if spying on the valley below. Its roots wrapped around boulders and dipped into and out of the ground as they clung to the rim for dear life. Gnarly branches looped to one side around a twisted trunk to form a shadowy cave. The tree was loaded with greenish blue berries. I grabbed a handful and munched. Tangy and bittersweet. Mam loved them. She said they tasted like gin.

I kissed my finger. "I hereby dub you my very own special tree." I reached down and picked up a small pink granite stone. "My *wishing* tree," I said, and I closed my eyes and made my first wish.

"My dad. Please let him find us. And then everything will be *perfect*." I tucked the stone into a crook in a twisted branch of my tree. "Thank you," I whispered.

From the hill I could see my whole queendom. The ranch tucked in its valley, the house looking as small as a dollhouse and Ol' Yeller like a toy truck parked beside a toy barn. The hills tumbling down to the badlands and far distant mountains. The mountains looming behind. And everything bursting with light, as if the land itself made its own sunlight.

I sank to the ground, slipped off my backpack, and sat still as the tree, still as the rocks and the hill.

First came a chipmunk, creeping across the rocky ground, sniffing at my toes, zipping over my leg as if it were just a bump in its path. A crow swooped down and, tipping its head to the side, took one peck at my jeans and then hopped away and flew off. Two magpies landed on the rocky rim behind me and fussed at each other, acting like I was just part of the landscape. Below me, a herd of antelope slowly munched their way across the hillside. Like the smaller creatures, they seemed to pay no attention to me.

I dug out my journal and pencils. Page after page got filled with golden-brown blotches with long spindly legs. It took lots of practice before I got one that looked halfway like a pronghorn antelope.

Soon I noticed I was drawing one particular antelope over and over. I could pick her out of the herd by the white markings on her neck, since their neck bands were all slightly different. For some reason the lights around her seemed brighter than the lights around the other antelopes. Her belly was big, like the rest of the older does. Soon she'd be having her fawns. I knew that pronghorns usually had twins because having two made it more likely that at least one would survive.

I drew comic-book panels showing the antelope

bowing her neck, kicking her heels up, and sprinting away from the herd. I sketched the big handsome buck that ran up onto a rocky mound and then stood there looking like he was the boss. And acting like it too, the way he huffed and puffed and snorted at her. Next I sketched her being chased by him. I drew her fluffing up her white rump as she ran, and I noticed how the reddish brown ruff on her neck stood straight up when she turned to confront him. I drew him edging her back into the herd. I drew her hop-hop-hopping away from him again, and then looking back and panting with her black tongue sticking out. "So there!" I wrote in the bubble over her head.

I called my comic "The Adventures of Lone One."

By now the rest of the herd had scattered out of sight. I got up and stretched. The lone antelope stared up at me, cocking her head to the side. I mirrored her. I cocked my head. I sprinted and stotted around in a circle on top of the hill, and she was so incurably curious that she looked up and watched the whole show. When I stumbled over my feet and went *splat,* she sprinted off after the herd.

I'd barely noticed the shadows creeping into the valley and filling it up to the rim with deep violet blue. Golden rays spiked up behind the mountains so that for a minute they looked as if they'd just been crowned. Down below, Ol' Yeller was now parked by the house.

I stuffed my things into my pack. "Race you," I said to Stew Pot, and the two of us charged down the hill.

Chapter Nine

A few days later, Mam stomped into the kitchen, ripped off her gloves, and slapped them down on the table. "Mr. McCloud wasn't kidding," she said.

"About what?" I looked up from the math problem I'd just solved and shoved my notebook aside. I'd had it with schoolwork.

"Damn beaver dams." She filled her teapot, switched on the stove, and banged the pot down on the burner.

I cringed and peeked over my shoulder. The teapot was still in one piece. Sure, she'd been working too hard, but all in all everything had been going great. It was perfect, her not having a boss around and no one shouting orders at her. It was almost like having our very own place.

"Yesterday I went to the ponds." She drummed her fingers on the edge of the stove as she waited for the water to boil. "It's a lot of work undoing those dams stick by stick. Today the ditch is bone dry—overnight, the rascals rebuilt their dams. No *wonder* the hands resorted to dynamiting the dams and setting out traps."

"But they have rights too," I said, twirling my hair on a finger, not sure if I should stick my neck out by sticking up for the beavers. "They only dam up the water to make ponds for their lodges. . . ."

"Yeah, so they can have babies and make more dams. Well, the ranch's got water rights too," Mam responded. "No water gets to the ditch that's supposed to irrigate the whole west side of the ranch. It'll be a full-time job undoing those dams. I'll have to go up every other day." She plopped her elbows on the table, propped her chin in her hands, and let out a big sigh. "Unless I try trapping them . . ."

"I can help undo them," I said. There I was. Volunteering again. Undoing the dams would be an excellent excuse. I could disappear to them when that dreaded time came around. *Branding time . . .*

"It's like magic, Blue," Mam used to say, "the way you can make yourself disappear when you want to get out of branding. . . ."

My absolute total loathing of it started when I was six-going-on-seven. Mam had hired on at a dude ranch where the dudes sometimes helped out, but usually just got out their cameras and took pictures. I'd been happy showing off that morning, riding out to help round up the cattle. Then I'd sat on a corral with some kids and watched as the cowboys roped the calves and dragged them to the pairs of calf wrestlers. But as the hot branding iron sizzled the hide of the first calf, I leaped down. To my eyes it looked as if the calf had burst into flames. As usual, back then, when I saw lights that scared me, I took off like a banshee and hid.

But as I jumped to the ground I'd heard my mom's voice. "Blue can help." And she waved me over. I hung back. She yelled my name and I had no choice. I shuffled over.

"They're short of hands, and it's the easiest job," she said, leaning down to pat me on the shoulder. "When the wrestlers call, you just carry over this bucket." She put the pail in my hands, squeezed my fingers over the handle, and ran off to help rope calves.

All the calves got a brand and some shots and maybe an ear tag or some dehorning paste spread on their budding horns. But the male calves got one more thing. I only got called to them.

"Ball boy!" a wrestler would yell. No matter that I was a girl. I'd skitter off with the bucket thump-thumping against my legs. Holding the pail out as far as my little arms could reach, I'd crinkle up my nose and scrunch my eyes shut. But that didn't help. Nothing smothered the smell of scorched hide and burned hair and smoke. Nothing drowned out the clamor of calves bawling and cows bellowing, or blanked out the dark reddish lights flashing up from the hurt calves. And even back then I knew what would be put in my bucket. Knew that a knife was slicing through soft tender skin and that a hand was reaching in, feeling for, and yanking out the calf's little boy parts. I'd dash from one calf to the next and hold out my bucket until it was full.

It wasn't until I threw up in a full bucket that they let me quit. I drifted off to hide in an empty horse trailer, where the smell of manure almost blocked out the smells of the branding.

Much later, when Mam found me sound asleep in the trailer, I wailed, "Why do they have to make the calves bawl and light up like that?"

Mam stroked my head and dusted me off. "You're just overly sensitive, Blue," she said. "You'll get over it. I should've had you out helping before now. And we do have to brand them. That's how we know who the calves belong to, in case they wander off and get mixed in with a neighbor's herd, or if somebody steals them. And if all those male calves grew up to be bulls we'd have a head-butting war on the ranch."

But I never did get desensitized. I still dreamed up things that just *had* to be done so I could disappear when branding time rolled around. Going off to the ponds to undo the dams every day or so—what a *perfect* excuse.

Now Mam gave me one of those looks that said she saw clear through me.

"Really," I said before she could open her mouth. "I'm about ready to send off my lessons to get my final report card. Then I'll have oodles of time."

She frowned at her cup as tea sloshed onto the table. She grabbed a napkin and mopped at the puddle as if she could scrub out the problem. "No," she said, shaking her head. "It's wilder than you might think back there in the woods by the ponds. Mountain lions. Bears. Moose. I'll do it. I'm just going in circles right now, with so many things needing to be done. The ditch will have to stay dry until I find time to go back." She gave a huge sigh. "And I need to get it cleaned out. Mr. Mac said they haven't been burning ditches for a while, and the weeds have almost taken them over."

My insides did a flip-flop. She looked so tired. At this rate she wouldn't last a month here, much less the whole summer. I had to think of something.

I'd undo those dams myself. I'd slip away when she was down at the barn or off fixing fence. By the time she figured out what I was up to, she'd have to accept that I was actually old enough to do some things on my own.

My chance came that afternoon when Mam took Stew Pot and drove off to fix the fence by the front entrance to the ranch. I pulled my rubber boots from my canvas boot bag and wiggled into them. A bit snug but, far as I could see, no holes—if they leaked they were hardly worth wearing.

The beaver ponds got their water from a spring, and they spread from one level down to the next alongside of the creek. A snarl of river willows and wild rosebushes barred my way, but I twisted through them and spotted an animal trail. I could feel antennae sprouting out of my head as I threaded my way through the tangle. Lions and bears and moose, oh my. Not having Stew Pot beside me made me feel like a knight without armor. Out in the sunlight was one thing; in the deep woods things felt positively creepy. I held my breath, tiptoeing on soft moss and black dirt, tripping over rotted tree trunks, dodging spiderwebs and low branches. Somewhere a branch snapped with a *crack!* I froze. Water gurgled. An owl hooted. A squirrel screeched. Something huge glided through the dark fringe of brush.

A scream tore its way up to my throat, but all that came out was a gasp.

Velvety antlers spread from one side of the trail to the other. Not ten feet away stood a thousand pounds of bull moose.

Later I'd remember thoughts flitting by about what a shame it was that I'd never get to see my dad again, and how anxious poor Mam and Stew Pot would be when I didn't show up at suppertime. In the next instant all I could think was, wow—how incredibly awesome. Look at me, face-to-face with a moose!

That was my oh-so-brave thought before the moose lumbered toward me. I blinked up at the huge face. Big brown eyes stared down at me. Wonder rubbed at my fear, nudging it aside as I stared at the soft greenish gold light radiating out of him, a light that mingled and mixed with the greenish blue light of the forest. For a long moment moose and I gaped at each other.

Then I reached out and touched its brown nose.

It couldn't have cared less. I might've been a mouse

or a butterfly. The creature took a step sideways. If a tree sprouted legs and could weave its way through its own forest, lifting and shifting its branches, that's how the moose moved away.

Some part of me felt like it'd flown up and was singing full throttle at the top of the trees. The other part of me danced in a circle on the path and shouted, "I just counted coup on a moose!" The thrill of it filled me to bursting.

I wished I could tell the whole world. But there are things you don't want your mom to hear, not even by way of an echo. A moose moment for sure topped that list.

And then I was in a clearing and the sky was bright blue above me and tiny iridescent blue dragonflies glided around me. I scrambled over fallen tree trunks to the pond. It was bigger than I'd thought, but then again it was plumb full because of the heap of sticks crammed across one end of it. Humped in the middle of the pond was a beaver lodge. Toppled aspens lay scattered all over the clearing, their pointed stumps poking up like sharp skinny fingers.

I stood there twisting my hair, picturing a whole crew of beavers scurrying about and gnawing down trees right and left. I could just see them eyeing the direction the trunks would fall, shouting "Timberrrrrrrr," in beaver tongue and clapping their tails as trees crashed to the ground. What engineers they had to be—to topple the trees and then strip and drag the branches into the ponds and jam them together and dam up the leaks with a plaster of moss, mud, and grasses.

And then did they stand back and admire what they'd done?

I did. Then I scrambled halfway across the dam, crouched down, and slithered into the pond. The icy cold water stung through my rubber boots as I waded past dragonflies and water bugs and green floating scum. I tugged at a stick. With a glop it came out of the icky black mud.

"Sorry, beavers," I said, "but it's my job to undo what you've done."

It was there, with my feet sucked deep into mud and icy water up to the tops of my boots that I had my brainstorm. I stared at the black mud and moss.

This was *chink*.

Maybe I could make something like it to seal up cracks in the new log addition. . . .

My head buzzed. The unfinished log add-on was something I could *really* put my mark on. Washing windows and dusting and mopping didn't make a huge difference, but *this* would. Already I could see it—the cracks chinked, the room livable . . . Why, maybe I could even make some furniture out of these nicely peeled beaver sticks and some willowy red-willow branches. . . . And maybe when I was all done we could have a party and invite Mr. Mac and he'd step into the house . . . I pictured it all, how he'd say, "Miss Blue! You did all this so you'd have a place to call home?" And how I'd nod and he'd grin happily and somewhere in the background my mom would be smiling too. But suddenly the picture got all confused. What would happen if—excuse me, *when*—

my dad came back? I had to believe that he'd find us if only we stayed in one place long enough. That was step one.

One step at a time, I said to myself. And then we'd just see what happened.

Sometimes Mam says, "Anchor down to earth, Moon Child," when I get all hyped up about something. I might never have started on this project if I'd thought any longer about it, but instead I threw sticks left and right and finished up and ran back through the woods to the house and threw my muddy clothes into the washer so Mam wouldn't suspect that I'd been to the dams.

I put on some fresh clothes and rushed to check out the rundown homestead cabin next to the house. Sure enough, it'd been chinked the old-fashioned way. I pried between the logs to see what they'd used back in the old days. Crumpled-up newspapers had been crammed into the spaces between the big cracks. The chink looked like it'd been made out of clay mixed with straw. I rubbed a piece of the chink between my fingers. It was the same color as the hillside not far from the house.

I grabbed a bucket from the kitchen and skipped off to the purple hill. Sure enough, it was the kind of dirt that turned into nice gluey clay. I scooped up a bunch and then buzzed about rounding up straw and old newspapers. I hauled my stash through the kitchen and plopped it on the floor in the add-on.

I made me a sign.

BLOOMING ROOM
PRIVATE! NO PEEKING!

I tacked it onto the door and closed it behind me so Mam wouldn't come in and ask questions. I was ready to start my new project. A gust of wind blasted between the cracks, lifting dust, bits of hay, and newspapers. The wind died down, and I started stuffing the cracks.

Chapter Ten

I couldn't believe it. "No way," I muttered as I felt Wonder Baby's leg once again. No lump. No bump. No airy spike poking my hand. And her lights looking almost *normal*.

"Not even *possible*," I said as I let the calf go and watched as she chased after her twin to the end of the pen.

I wrinkled my forehead, feeling really confused. Maybe Wonder Baby's leg hadn't really been broken. Maybe I had just imagined the bumps. Was it just wishful thinking?

In my head I did a little figuring. Today was the twenty-fourth. We'd hired on at the ranch on May ninth and the bums had been born the next day. So two weeks. A broken bone couldn't possibly heal in two weeks. But if it *had*, then something amazing had happened.

The rest of the morning passed in a daze. How I got the last of my schoolwork done I don't know. What I put down on my tests is a mystery. But I finished up and got everything stuffed into a big envelope and ready to mail back to my school, and then I sat at the table drumming my fingers.

"Something made the bone heal . . . ," I said out loud to the room and the broom and the lightbulb.

"What'd you say?" Mam's words pulled me out of my haze.

"I said I need a hike up the hill." I could feel my face getting red. I couldn't just blurt it out, could I? *Wonder Baby's broken leg healed!* Right. In two weeks? Frankly, I hardly believed it myself—how could I expect someone else to?

"Well, you're done! You deserve a break," Mam said as she picked up the envelope and weighed it in her hands. "We'll go get this mailed off tomorrow. And guess what? We've got a full ditch of water! The beavers are getting lazy, I think. I've actually got a bit of spare time on my hands." She grunted as she lifted her latest, biggest, fattest encyclopedia, the M. "Think I'll grab me a cuppa tea, go curl up with this giant, and see what he can teach me."

A cool breeze made me roll down my sleeves as Stew Pot and I slipped through the fence. I hurried straight up to my tree, shrugged out of my pack, and settled back against the trunk. Stew Pot curled up beside me.

I stared out at the blue-forever sky and listened to the sound of the wind and the creek. Sometimes I felt so full of sky I could burst. *What was happening to me?* I wondered. I seemed to have entered into a whole different dimension from the moment I stepped into this place. Were all the lights brighter here, or was it something inside me that had changed? Had Wonder Baby's leg really healed? Was it something I'd done? Sure, I'd read about miracles happening, but they all seemed to have happened long ago. Which, of course, didn't mean that they hadn't happened . . . But still. I scrunched up my face something terrible just thinking about it all.

I was thinking so hard that I didn't even notice the herd of pronghorns gathering on the hillside below me. *"Shhh,"* I whispered to Pot. I snapped my fingers and pointed to the ground, which was the sign for him to stay low and stay put. Which, being a good ranch doggie, he did. He hunkered right down and lay with his head on his paws, looking straight ahead as if he were pretending the antelope didn't exist.

I reached for my pack and pulled out my journal and pencils. I picked out the antelope I'd named Lone One and drew her staring up at me while the rest of the herd calmly grazed. Then I rummaged through my pencils for the gold one and shaded in the fuzzy light that shone out of her and out of the others. I studied them some more and added a rosy pink to the light around the fat-bellied does.

I squinted. Something else was going on here—something I hadn't noticed before. I could see silvery-blue lines linking each antelope to the next one. And to the next and the next . . . I studied the lines for the longest time and then drew what I saw. It looked like golden antelopes caught in a silvery web.

Lights of the Herd All Connected, I wrote.

Then I drew silvery-blue lines connecting the herd to the sagebrush and to the rocks and the hills and the trees, and I drew shimmering light around all of them and up in a corner I drew a glowing Stew Pot and me and my tree, and then I drew lines linking everything all together.

I concentrated on drawing Lone One. While I sketched I noticed my fingers, how the light streaked out of them, and how just by thinking about Lone One made the light in my fingers grow brighter.

I stared at my hands and then down at the herd. *Really, what is it that I am seeing?* I wondered. The lights seemed to be some sort of energy that flowed from one object or animal to another. If I'd learned one thing about light as I sketched the herd, it was that everything was connected.

Everything Light and Everything Connected, I labeled my drawing.

I'd noticed before that people's lights changed, so it seemed that whenever someone had a new thought their lights changed to match it. I'd seen how the light flowed from my hands to the calves. And if thoughts could affect the lights, could the lights affect how a body felt?

Just thinking about all that made my head swim. I gathered my pencils and journal and pushed myself to my feet. Shadows had crept over the hillsides and the wind whirred through the feathery leaves of the juniper. I shivered, wishing I'd brought my jacket. Down by the creek a coyote yipped and another one answered from the hills. The buck antelope snorted, and suddenly the entire herd and their lights turned as one and flowed across the hillside like a fast-moving golden wave.

Looking down, I noticed a shiny white rock that seemed to outshine its neighbors. As I picked it up I swear I could feel its energy tickling the palm of my hand—a perfect wishing rock. I closed my eyes. *How many wishes can I stuff into one stone?* I wondered. There was the big wish for my dad to find us. And then for my mom to be happy and want to stay for a while in one place. And for Wonder Baby's leg to really, really be healed . . .

I tucked the stone into a curlicue branch. "Thank you," I whispered for what the herd's lights had just taught me, and that was my total prayer.

That night after supper, my mom and I sat hunched over our books at the kitchen table eating peanut butter cookies and drinking some of Mam's medicinal tea (good for relaxing, she said). She'd made the cookies special for me to celebrate getting my schoolwork all done. Above the table, the cobalt-blue lampshade glowed like a lonesome blue planet against our painted-sky ceiling. The kitchen was quiet. The radio had been nothing but static so I'd clicked it off, and the fridge for once wasn't humming. I'd been reading the same paragraph over and over. Finally I pushed my book to the side and leaned with both elbows on the table.

"What would you think if I said I thought Wonder Baby's leg was already healed?" I said into the drowsy silence.

Mam didn't look up from her book. "That's impossible," she said. She took a sip of her tea and kept reading.

"Well, maybe. But I took her cast off today and she's hopping about with no sign that her leg was ever broken."

"How long has it been? Two weeks? I don't think a bone could heal that quickly. I saw what it was like when we brought her in." Mam reached across the table and patted my hand. "It was a bad break. To tell the truth, I didn't think the calf would survive."

We sat there not talking. Stew Pot made little sounds as he dreamed under the table. I pulled my book toward me, but the words still wouldn't stick in my head. I snapped the book closed again.

Mam peered over at me. She stuck her napkin in her book for a place mark. "You've been spending a lot of time with those calves," she said, taking a sip of her tea. "What's been going on?"

"Those lights," I said, wondering how to go about explaining something when I didn't fully understand it myself. "Remember how, when I was little, I used to tell you about the lights around stuff? And we thought it was a problem with my eyes? Well, the lights haven't gone away. Far from it. They've gotten stronger."

Mam rolled her eyes at me. "I remember. You used to look at me sometimes as if weeds sprouted out of my ears. Actually, you still do . . ."

"You've got yellow light sticking out of your head right now," I said, "but I'm pretty sure it's not weeds. Hay, maybe, or straw . . ." I took a breath. "So I see lights around everything and I know you've said you don't see them, but I don't think it's anything wrong with my eyes anymore. I think I'm even figuring out how to—" I broke off. It seemed strange to be talking about the lights as if they were something out of the ordinary. But then a thought occurred. Even if Mam couldn't see the lights, maybe other people could?

I took a deep breath. "I think I'm figuring out how to work with the lights."

"What do you mean?" Mam said, frowning down at her cup.

"Well," I said slowly, "it all began when I noticed lights in Mr. Mac's hands when he stroked the calves that first morning at the barn. Then I looked at my own lights, the ones coming out of my fingers. Later Wonder Baby's lights got really weak that first day after I got her fed and washed up. And it struck me that maybe I could make her lights grow stronger—or maybe I mean brighter—by thinking really hard. Concentrating, right? So I did, I concentrated with my lights, and it must've worked, because pretty soon her lights changed."

Mam wrinkled her forehead but nodded wisely, as if that made some kind of sense. Encouraged, I went on.

"It seemed that the more I *wanted* to heal the calves, and the more I showered them with love, the better it worked."

"Intention," Mam said, waving her cup in the air as if yes, indeed, it all did make perfect sense. "That's like having a goal, a target. Some way to direct what you're aiming to do." Tea splashed on the table as she set the cup down. She dabbed at the puddle and said, "I wish your dad could be here to hear about what you're doing. In spite of his faults, he was good with animals. He sang to the horses as he worked with them, and lots of people said he had a gift for healing."

My heart jumped and I stared at her. She hadn't mentioned my dad since—I couldn't remember. She'd for sure never mentioned that he had—what had she called it? A gift for healing.

Honestly, I hadn't even *thought* of what my dad would think. I'd get this huge ache when I did think about him, so I tried hard *not* to. That worked okay when I was busy, but not at all when I wasn't.

Last time we'd touched on the touchy subject of my dad, Mam had said, "Don't be silly. No way was it your fault that he left."

I was almost five when it happened.

He slammed out the door just as we sat down for supper. "I'm going to get mustard," he said. It was the longest suppertime ever. We waited. It wasn't till the next morning that my mom got the table cleared off. She called the hospitals and the sheriff, but I think in her heart she knew that he'd left. It wasn't long after that when I first noticed my mom's long silences, almost like her words had gotten jammed up in her throat and couldn't get loose.

As the years went by she started making a joke about those mustard words, saying, "What can you expect? He was French, and we were out of Dijon." When I asked her about it once she said it was all apples and oranges. I tossed that around, trying to make sense of it, until she finally explained. "If your dad hadn't left, I probably would have." But something in the way she said it made me think that they were Band-Aid words to cover up a big hurt.

When the emptiness fills my heart and I feel like I don't have a body big enough to hold it, she reminds me that it wasn't me he left. He left *her,* she says, but I can't see the difference. He never did come back. He did write a few letters—at least seven of them actually found us. Mam read some parts of his letters to me, but other parts she kept secret.

"At least he's alive," she'd said after the first letter. "And he says he misses his little mouse."

Back then, when I was five, those words had made me clap and dance around singing, "Papa misses his little mouse!"

Later, when we got the second letter, she'd said, "He says he's coming back!" But with each day that passed and he didn't return she got quieter.

I still remember the long dark nights of that winter, and the days stretching out blank and white as I watched the snow fall and waited, and he didn't come. When the fields turned green once again the third letter came. Mam said, "He says something came up. He's been busy with a new project. When he finishes, he'll come find us. And of course he says he misses his little mouse."

But he never did come back. Maybe he'd come looking for us and we'd already moved on. Or he might've sent more letters that we never got. He might've searched for us and given up when he couldn't find us. I wanted to think that he did. But of course we never left a forwarding address because it was then that my mom started hitting the road. A few more letters did somehow find us, the last one about three years ago. Mam had stuffed that letter into her box of secrets and only told me that he had so many projects going on in his life that he didn't have time for us. It was around then that she had what she later called her "fleeting affair" with a cowboy from New Mexico—the one with a wife and three kids that he somehow forgot to tell her about. It's a wonder she didn't break his head with the skillet she threw at him. She's got real good aim.

With a start I came back to the present. I beamed over at her. "I never knew that about my dad. That he was good at healing. I do wonder what he would've thought."

"He would've been proud." Then, her voice so low that I had to lean forward to hear, she said, "You've got a good head on you, Blue. Don't ever let your heart get in the way of your studies."

"What do you mean?" I stared into my blue enamel cup as if the answer to my question might be hidden in the tea leaves on the bottom.

"Anton rode like a dream," she said—how long had it been since she'd last said my dad's name? "He was the best-looking man on a horse I'd ever seen."

"Love at first sight, huh?" I studied the tea leaves, my nose on the rim of the cup.

"I was only sixteen." She smiled a half smile, and for a minute I thought she wouldn't go on.

"It was my second summer working at that dude ranch up near Cody, cleaning cabins and wrangling, helping to bring in thirty or forty horses from the pastures, then saddling them up for the dudes for their trail rides. He was—" She stopped.

I grabbed the rim of the cup with my mouth and raised my head. I felt like I was two years old and begging for a bedtime story. *Tell me,* I wanted to say. Instead I mumbled into the cup. "He was what?"

"He was fresh from France and living out what he liked to call his 'Western Dream.' Seems he'd imagined being a cowboy all his life, a passion, I suppose, that he got from movies and books. I was too shy to even talk to him, but I liked to watch how he handled the horses. He'd sing to them, and once in a while he'd look up and smile. Back then, I would've walked miles for a smile."

I put my cup back on the table and picked up a spoon and stirred, even though it was empty.

"The reason they'd hired him," she went on, "other than the fact that he rode like a dream and could rope— although that was mainly for show—was his great repertoire of old cowboy songs. He sang those with hardly a trace of an accent. The way he played the guitar and sang for the dudes around the campfire at night made mush out of my insides." She laughed a short, stiff laugh, as if not believing she could've been so taken in.

As if not believing she was actually telling me this.

"It was an honor when later I got asked to sing along with him. They'd heard me singing while cleaning the cabins, I guess." She smiled at the memory. "Someone thought it would be romantic to have us serenading each other around the campfire at night. And it was. The guests loved it."

I reached across the table, lifted the teapot, and refilled both our cups. I folded my paper napkin and unfolded it and spread it out flat on the table and then folded it into triangles.

"Perhaps if his visa hadn't been about to expire," Mam said, "and then everything else . . ."

The "everything else" was the fact that her parents and younger brother had died in a car crash in her next-to-last year of school. It was years before I learned that she'd been driving her family back to their house after a school play when it happened. Her little brother had been dressed as a fat red tomato. He was still wearing his costume when a drunk rammed into their truck.

After the accident, the Frenchman she'd had a big crush on was all in the world that she had to cling to.

"Well, I married him and his visa expired and he got to stay in the States," she said, taking a breath to steady herself. "After a baby and a few rough years, he told me that his dreams had been taken off course by our marriage."

"But that wasn't your fault," I said. Funny how we had to keep telling each other how we weren't to blame.

"No, I know in my heart that it was the booze and the

terrible temper that came out when he drank. And of course I drank along with him." She gulped down her tea in one sip. "Sixteen when I met him. I'd barely turned seventeen when I married him," she said. "Just don't do what I did. Do something with your life. Remember, your lessons come first."

Chapter Eleven

"Come on, Blue," Mam said as she grabbed two of our three bags of groceries. "Your books and lessons are mailed and we can't hang around chatting all day." She shrugged her shoulders and smiled at the storekeeper as if trying to make an apology for my big mouth.

"You go ahead," I said. "I'll get us a newspaper."

It's hard not to be rude when you're trying to whisk your kid out the door. My mom managed. Clyde folded his arms over his chest and nodded at her as she turned and pushed through the door. It shut with a *bam* behind her.

From behind the counter he looked down at me over his glasses and winked. He was almost hidden behind a barricade of newspapers, travel maps, tourist brochures, boxes of bananas and cherries, jar after jar of beef jerky, and racks hanging with beaded Indian earrings and necklaces. Beaded barrettes, moccasins, and belt buckles glittered in the glass shelves beneath the counter while drums and beaded vests hung from the rafters. The trading post smelled of coffee and leather and floor wax. It was a good smell.

We'd hit the morning mail rush, the locals stopping to grab a cup of free coffee and catch up on the gossip. With the tourist season just starting, a steady stream of cars had come by to gas up, get a tire changed, or to get reservation fishing licenses and maps or groceries. My eyes had kept as busy as my mouth, I'd been so distracted watching everyone's lights. If I hadn't had a message to get out, I would've just stood there and enjoyed the light show. It was the first time we'd been out in public and I was wide-eyed at my new ability to see everyone's lights so clearly.

I'd chatted so much while Mam got the groceries that I'd about winded myself. Now, with Mam out the door, I sped to the mailboxes lining one wall. I reached into my backpack and pulled out seven stamped, slightly wrinkled letters. They were all addressed to different towns in Wyoming, but to the same person—my dad, Anton Gaspard.

The night before, after Mam's story, I'd run up to my attic, sprawled flat on my bed, and buried my head under my pillow. Sometimes it hurt so bad, as if I had a deep fatherless hole in my heart that could never, ever be filled. Every little bit I learned about him I had to write down in my journals, as if by doing that I could hold something of him down, and at least keep the wisps from floating away. So after a while I sat up and got out my journal. "Your dad had a gift for healing," she'd said. I wrote that down. Somewhere I thought I had a memory about my dad healing something—but for the life of me I couldn't bring it back up. But it made me shivery just thinking about it. Maybe he'd understand what was happening to me. Maybe . . .

I tore some pages out of my school notebook. He just had to find us. He had to. Maybe I should write an ad like they did for lost pets and put it in the paper. Except Mam wouldn't really go for that. Okay, I'd write letters, that's what I'd do. I'd send them all over the state. It was a big state, but there weren't a whole lot of people in it. Even if he wasn't in a town the letter was addressed to, if he worked at a ranch in that area, why, someone would know of him. At least it was worth a try. . . .

Dear Papa, I wrote (I remembered how I used to say *Papa* with a French accent because that was how he'd said it himself).

> *I miss you so much. I hope you're doing well. I'm well and my mom is too, but she's awful quiet. Stew Pot's well too. I'm writing to let you know where we are because I'm sure you've been looking for us. I know we could be a happy family again if only you'd come back. I have a lot of questions I need answered. I'm sending a copy of this letter all over the state. I'm hoping one will find you.*
>
> *Your loving daughter,*
> *Blue*
> *P.S. I never had a chance to say good-bye. You were already gone.*

I made six copies and stuck each in an envelope and addressed them all to Anton Gaspard. Then I covered the state, writing Cody, Cheyenne, Casper, Gillette, Pinedale, Jackson Hole, or Riverton on each one. "Please forward," I added. Then I very clearly wrote down our address. I left the post office box number blank. We never got mail, but I'd ask Mam to get us our own box. Not like we ever got any mail. My excuse would be that we needed a return address to get my final report card. I got all the envelopes addressed and then stuffed them into my backpack. No sense in Mam knowing about this.

I'd gotten one of her looks when I insisted we needed a post office box, but she'd humored me and asked Clyde to assign us one. Part one of my plan accomplished.

Part two had been to spread the word about who we were and where we lived. I'd made a big point of meeting the storekeeper–post master, Clyde, and of chattering away as Mam filled out the forms for our box. It hadn't hurt that the store had been packed with people getting their mail and morning coffee and newspapers and supplies. I'd made sure everyone heard our name and where we lived. "Shh," Mam had said several times, wrinkling her forehead at me.

So now, after she'd sailed out the door, I quickly jotted down our new box number and the right zip code on each envelope and slipped all seven into the mail slot.

I knew Mam would be drumming her fingers by now, so I dashed back to the counter and grabbed the fattest newspaper, the *Star Tribune* from Casper. I fished in my pocket and slid one of my hard-earned dollars across the counter. "Gotta keep in touch with the world," I said. "We're pretty isolated up there, you know."

"Ain't that the truth. That ranch is 'bout as far back as you can get," Clyde said as he patted the change into my palm. "Sure was good getting to know you."

Two ranchers, both wearing tall rubber irrigating boots, stopped sorting through their mail and looked over at me. "You take care, now," one said, and the other said, "Real nice meeting you, Miss Gaspard."

They'd obviously heard my whole story. That was good. About a dozen other people had been around while I chatted to Clyde. I beamed at the men. "Thanks. Nice meeting you too." I squinted at the fatter of the two men. "Be careful," I said. "Take care of your heart."

His hand shot to his chest. I bit my lip. *Why'd I say that?*

I grabbed the sack of groceries Mam had left on the counter and started toward the door. A young Indian woman with two little boys right behind her held the door open for me. I wanted to reach out and touch her belly; the lights around it were so pretty, all fizzy champagne bubbles and sparkly pink lights. I beamed at her. "Thanks," I said, "and congratulations." The woman ducked her head and smiled back. The two little boys peeked shyly around her skirt. I wondered if they knew about the baby. Her belly wasn't the slightest bit big yet, but boy did it ever glow!

Ol' Yeller was practically snorting, with puffs of smoke putting out his rusty old tailpipe. I heaved the sack into the cab and climbed in, nudging Stew Pot into the middle. Mam gunned Ol' Yeller and the truck backfired as we turned onto the highway.

"Was all that chitchat necessary?" Mam asked, keeping her eyes on the road.

"It's not like I've seen or talked to anyone 'cept you and Stew Pot since Mr. Mac left," I said, twisting my hair into knots.

A long silence followed. We turned off the highway onto our road. The "No Trespassing" sign flashed its tin warning into the bright sunlight. Mam stared at it. The veins stuck up on the backs of her hands as she gripped the steering wheel. "I should've known this place would be too remote," she said. "Did I make a mistake taking this job? Are you feeling too cut off from the world?"

"*No!*" I screeched as we hit a rut. "I mean, I'm just a chatterbox, that's all. Sometimes I talk to hear myself talk." I crossed my fingers. Luck and lies—crossed fingers covered both, didn't they?

Mam shot me a look but said nothing.

Truth was, I'd run on at the mouth to let everyone in the store know our names and where we were staying. If somebody wanted to find you and you *wanted* to be found, wouldn't you spread the word?

But maybe I'd overdone it. Sending the letters was one thing, but Mam liked her privacy. Maybe I'd taken this one step too far. Had I even asked her if she wanted my dad to come back? It'd been my hope and my prayer for so long I'd never even thought of asking her how she felt about it. All I knew about my dad since he left was what she'd read out loud to me from the few letters he'd sent. Some parts of those letters she'd kept secret. Too secret, perhaps.

Chapter Twelve

The first day of June was all shimmery green leaves and blue skies, all bees, butterflies, and gooseberry blossoms. It was larkspur, Indian paintbrush, and wild onions popping up on the hillsides. It was a world gone crazy with birdsong.

It was also a trip back down to the trading post. It was letters in our mailbox.

My stomach did a cartwheel as Mam leafed through the letters. "That's strange," she said. "One's from your school. But 'Return to Sender' is stamped on the other five. Obviously that's *you*. . . ."

I felt a knot in my throat. The jig was up. Now she knew I'd secretly sent them off and was seriously searching for my dad. Of course my plan hadn't worked—what had I expected? I stared down at the floor. Two letters hadn't been returned so I had just a smidgen of hope left. . . .

"If he wanted to find us, he would," Mam said, sticking

the five letters into my limp hands. "Be careful what you wish for."

"But this letter here says you passed," she went on, opening the one from my school and reading it through before handing it over. "Congratulations. You did really well. Tomorrow you can have the whole day to do as you please. I'll feed your bums and I'll even take care of those beaver dams you've been sneaking off to undo."

I should've known it was impossible to get anything by her. One by one I let the letters slip out of my hand into the trash can.

Over at the counter, Mam was setting out the things we had to buy fresh, like milk, eggs, bread, and bananas, and some ranch supplies like salt for the cows and more fence staples and some seeds. Clyde rang them up and then pushed a piece of bubblegum across the counter toward me. "Keep smiling," he said, and I flashed him a lopsided smile.

As the door banged behind us the feeling came over me that maybe *this* was what it felt like to have roots. Maybe it was just someone handing you a piece of gum because they'd watched as you dropped your hopes, one by one, into a trash can.

Mam didn't mention the letters again. Instead, she kept me so busy all day that I didn't have two minutes to brood. We mucked out the barn and fixed the fence around the plot in the yard where once there'd been a garden. Then we dug up the weeds and planted lettuce and spinach and beets, potatoes and onions—things that might stand half a chance at seven thousand feet up in the mountains. I even planted half a sack of sunflower birdseed for the fun of it, and because we'd never hung around anywhere long enough to see if birdseed (or any seeds, for that matter) would grow. "Bloom where you're planted," I whispered to each little seed as I tucked it into the earth.

All day long I thought about what I wanted to do the next day. I got everything all set out for an early start. I had a trail mix of raisins and nuts and a bottle of water and my journal and pencils tucked into my pack. My clothes were laid out by my bed.

I went to bed with a plan. I'd never trespassed farther than my hill. Tomorrow I'd sneak through the fence and explore the big world beyond it.

What I didn't know was that events would knock that plan clear off the map.

On the second day of June I woke to the wonder of cold blue-white silence and the whole world hushed by a blanket of snow.

During the night snow had sifted through cracks in the windowsill and dusted the floor like a sprinkling of powdered sugar. Doggie paw prints tracked from the beanbag to the stairway, so I knew Stew Pot had deserted me. I could see by the light in the room that I'd overslept, but I couldn't tell if it was dawn or ten o'clock. It was quiet, still.

Then from somewhere in the hills came the yip-yipping of coyotes and, from another direction, a sound that rose and held and floated on the air and sent shivers up and down my whole body.

A *wolf*? But they were supposed to be farther to the

west, around Yellowstone. Had they spread clear to *here*? It *had* to be a lone coyote howling to his friends on the opposite hill.

I kicked off my covers, shook the snow dust from my clothes and shivered into them, found my coveralls and boots and tugged them on, decided not to take my backpack, crammed my hair into my blue stocking cap and sprinted down the stairs.

From the hallway I could see into the kitchen through the half-open door. Mam's teacup stood upside down beside the sink, so I knew she'd already gone out. And no Stew Pot. He always dashed out the door with the first one who opened it. In the mudroom two bottles of milk stood by the door—well, at least they'd been filled, but there went Mam's promise to feed the calves on my day off.

I grabbed my jacket and gloves, stuck a bottle under each arm, and plunged out the door.

Startled birds whirled off the porch where Mam had scattered the rest of the sunflower birdseed. It was a white-magic day, the whole world transformed by six inches of snow. Bushes draped in ghost sheets drooped to the ground to make snow caves. It was still lightly snowing, though a pale sun peeked through a gray veil of clouds.

Ol' Yeller's tracks led down toward the barn, so I knew Mam had taken off to feed the cattle some hay.

The day before, my bums had been hopping about on green grass. Now they huddled way back in their shed, *moo-ahhh*ing their little hearts out and rolling their eyes as I brushed the snow off the gate and unhooked the latch.

"Hold your horses," I said as they both lunged for the bottles. "One at a time." I crooned their names as I juggled bottles and bums. One day they'd be back with the rest of the cows and I wanted to be sure they knew their names so I could call them out of the herd. As I fed them I daydreamed that Mr. Mac might let me buy them so I could keep them forever and they'd have lots of babies and none of them would ever, *ever* have to be branded or sent off to market. . . .

I wiped their soft noses, closed them up in the pen, and followed my tracks back to the house. I scooped some snow into the bottles and set them on the porch.

I looked again at the tracks leading down to the barn. I knew I should go see if Mam needed help. . . .

Hills or helping Mam?

No contest.

I pinched up the top strand of barbed wire and held the lower one down with my boot and squeezed through the fence, hooking my coat in the prongs. It took forever to get it unsnagged. My boots made scrunching sounds as I trudged through the snow past white humps of snow-covered sagebrush. I checked over my shoulder, half expecting Stew Pot to come bounding up through the white fields. Not even my own shadow followed.

In the hills coyotes *yip-yip-yipp*ed as they ganged up on a rabbit or—oh *cripes*. It was fawning time! The first week of June, the time when the antelopes would start having their fawns, and some deer fawns would already be out there. . . . I covered my ears. Tried not to think of rabbits and fawns. Tried to blank out the sound of the coyotes.

I was halfway up the hill and already my heart thumped and my throat ached from the cold. I sank down and flopped back in the snow and watched snowflakes float lazily out of the clouds. I closed my eyes for just a minute.

I don't know whether one minute passed, or ten, but when I opened my eyes it was no longer snowing. The pale sun had bored its way through the gray clouds, and patches of blue showed here and there. I scrambled up, wiped my snotty face with my gloves, and hopped up and down to shake the snow from the sticky spots on my coat where it'd been slobbered and slimed by the bums. I wished I'd grabbed my trail mix. I snatched up a handful of snow and sucked on it.

That's when I saw them. If I'd hiked a bit farther I'd have noticed the delicate, pointed-hoof tracks in the snow. They looked as if they'd been made sometime earlier in the morning. I had the strangest feeling that they belonged to Lone One, though they could've been those of a deer. I hesitated, and then decided to follow them. The tracks led down an old animal trail that sloped from the ridge into the canyon. I decided to keep to the ridge, following the zigs and zags of the canyon while keeping an eye on the tracks below. I was almost to the end of the canyon, near where it widened out into a small bowl-shaped valley, when I spotted her.

And yes! It *was* Lone One. I couldn't have picked a worse time to come upon her—she'd just had a fawn! She was cleaning it, licking and licking and licking. Thank *goodness* Stew Pot wasn't with me. *Please,* I prayed as I dropped to my knees and wiggled down flat on the ledge, *don't let me ring any alarm bells to make her bolt and run!*

She was standing in a snowy nest of sorts, with sticks and stones scattered in the snow around her where she'd rooted them out and scratched down to bare ground. And of course she'd already seen me. She was super aware of every single thing around her. Her golden light was huge. It spread so far it seemed to touch the sides of the canyon and even reached up to touch me.

Her dark round eyes fixed on me and she didn't move. She stared up, her head cocked to the side as if she were searching her memory bank and remembering where she'd seen me before. Whatever, I must've looked familiar and not a threat because she went back to licking her fawn.

She was making grunting sounds that seemed to come from deep down in her belly. She licked and grunted and licked and grunted and then another fawn started coming right as she was licking the first fawn, licking it all over and grunting, and I just knew the second one would tumble out and clunk its head on something; she wasn't paying attention—she wasn't paying attention at all. She was licking and grunting and licking and grunting as the next fawn slid out all steaming like a little smoking bundle slipping out from a nice cozy warm dark world into a bright snowy-white cold one.

Within minutes the new fawn was struggling to get to its feet. All the while Lone One licked it and grunted and cleaned up all the signs of its birth. All the while her brown eyes scanned the landscape.

It was amazing how quickly the first little fawn had managed to stand, all tipsy and wobbly on its long spidery legs. It latched on to its mother to nurse—the shortest two-second nip ever—and then tipped over, bobbed up, and tried once again. The second fawn wobbled and rose halfway up and then sprawled back down on the ground. Again and again it tried. Again and again it fell back.

I stared at the fawn. With the mother right over it I couldn't see clearly, but something seemed to be wrong. Lone One made a loud honking sound and nudged under the fawn's belly with her long nose as if she were trying to get it to its feet. It took a step, wobbled, and tumbled back down. The fawn seemed to favor one leg.

The fawn finally tottered up long enough to get its first sip. The other fawn was already happily hopping about trying out its long spindly legs. Lone One seemed anxious now; probably she wanted to move the fawns away from their sheltered nest at the end of the canyon to a safer, clean place where the fawns could hide from hungry coyotes and such. Again she nosed the lame fawn up, almost pushing it out of the nest. Soon the family of three was headed for the nearby bowl-shaped valley, one fawn skipping ahead, the other limping behind with its worried mother stopping to grunt at it and to nudge it along with her nose.

Me, I was a frozen lump of ice stuck to the snowy

ledge. I could just see the headlines: "Ice Sculpture of Maiden Found in the Hills. Sculptor Unknown." I pushed myself up and stood still as a fence post, not daring to move and frighten the trio below me.

When they got to the bowl Lone One ran ahead, as if she wanted the fawns to follow her and climb up the hill. But the lame fawn lagged behind and limped toward a snowy clump of sagebrush at the foot of the hill and dropped down. The other one scrambled halfway up the bowl to huddle between snow-covered rocks. Lone One stared for a few seconds at each fawn's hiding place and then turned and sprinted over the hill. I watched her go. When I looked back, both fawns had melted into the landscape.

And then, because the odds against them were so great, I sent prayers up to the skies to please keep all the coyotes, golden eagles, ravens, mountain lions, and owls away. And to please, *please* keep the poor little lame fawn safe.

Chapter Thirteen

From the ridge I'd noticed Ol' Yeller parked by the barn. It seemed strange that Mam would still be there. As I trudged through the snowy meadows the cows barely looked up. They'd been fed a big round bale of hay, and tractor tracks circled back to the barn. I hopped into the tracks and started to run.

As I rounded the corner of the barn Stew Pot bounded over and thumped his big paws on my shoulder. He whined softly, which wasn't like him at all.

"Hey, boy, what's the matter?" I asked as my eyes zipped across the barnyard.

A dark, muddy gash led to the snowy creek bank and from there down into the rushing water and to Mr. Mac's pet of a tractor. The tractor bucked and swayed as the water crashed and sprayed against its big tires. Its hay fork bobbed up and down as it seemed to claw at the gash in the creek bank.

I sucked in my breath as I ran toward it. Where was my mom? No sign of her. I spun, not daring to breathe. Suddenly, over the roar of rushing water, I heard her voice coming from behind Ol' Yeller.

"I've really gone and done it," she said.

Honestly, it took a moment before I could tell her apart from Ol' Yeller—they both were totally splattered with mud. Mam kneeled on the ground next to the tailgate, holding one end of a chain, which she'd just unhooked from Ol' Yeller. The other end of the chain stretched out toward the tractor. Skid marks grooved through the mud-splattered snow.

Obviously they'd been having a tug-of-war with the tractor. Just as obviously, they'd gotten nowhere.

Mam swiped at her forehead, leaving one more streak on her already-mud-covered face. "I'd fed the cattle, and when I backed up to drive the tractor back into the barn, the bank just caved in," she said, glaring at the tractor as if it'd just bucked her off.

Down at the trading post I'd heard talk about "high-water day," as it was called around here, almost like some sort of holiday. The creeks and rivers would gush over their banks while boulders, brush, and logs hurtled down with the rising water. I'd heard Clyde joking about some rancher who was always saying that if his bridge washed away at high water and floated downstream, why, whoever ended up with it could buy it for practically nothing.

I could almost see the water rising as I stared up the creek, see it churning down from the mountains where snow had piled up and soon would be melting.

See us having to tell Mr. Mac that his tractor had—well, had just floated away.

See us loading up Ol' Yeller.

I was still taking it all in when, above the roar of the creek, I heard what could only have been Mr. Mac's big diesel pickup, still out of sight behind the trees on the other side of the creek. Mam and I locked anxious eyes. After everything had been going so great, without a hitch or a glitch, *now* he came.

Slowly the truck drove across the bridge and stopped. In the half-moons carved into the snowy windshield by the wipers I could see Mr. Mac's startled face. I could see a hand wiping a swath across the fogged window. See a frown. I squinted, half expecting to see a spurt of dark red or maybe a cloud of dark gray sparking out of him. I stared really hard. I could hardly believe when his lights just flashed his usual pretty colors as if saying, "Never mind that monster in the creek."

The truck revved up and swerved into the barnyard. The door flew open. "Are you all right?" Mr. Mac asked as he hopped out.

Mam wiped another muddy swath across her cheeks and just looked at him and nodded. I stood there swallowing and bobbing my head up and down.

Mr. Mac scratched his chin as he studied the scene. "Each year when the water rises it gobbles away another big hunk of the bank," he said in a deep, solemn voice. "One of these days it'll nibble away so much that the bridge will tumble right in. I wouldn't be surprised if the barn didn't take off along with it. Of course I hadn't thought of the tractor diving in, too. . . ."

And then, honestly, he beamed at my mom, his smile almost hooking up on his ears. Of course, anyone looking at Mam would've had a hard time not laughing. Really, she made quite a sight.

Mr. Mac had a plan. We'd pull the tractor out with the winch that was attached to the front end of his truck. "Should be no problem," he said. "This truck's plenty big. Good thing I came by to check up on things after this storm."

From then on it seemed as if everything happened in fast-forward.

I zipped about searching for rocks to wedge in front of the wheels of Mr. Mac's truck while Mam attached pulley cables to the frame of the tractor. Her lights flashed pretty pinks when she brushed against Mr. Mac, but she still didn't say more than, "I'm really sorry." He just nodded and said, "It's okay," and then, "Better get out of the way."

Me, I jumped up and down because I really, really did have to pee, but not wanting to miss one second of all this, I galloped off along the snowy bank to find me a stump to crouch behind. I peeled off layers of clothes and stared spell-bound at water spraying against a small dam up of sticks and brush wedged between rocks on my side of the creek.

I'm sure it was fate that had me there on the bank all tucked in and zipped up when, back in the barnyard, the cable snapped loose. I looked up just as Mam dashed over to hook it back up. I saw her take a step backward, out of the way. Saw her arms whirl as if she were trying to fly as underneath her the bank crumbled and she tumbled backward into the creek.

"She can't swim!" I heard myself yell as I stumbled up the bank above the stick jam and without even thinking I threw myself into the water.

Oh! Shock of water so freezing cold it was boiling! Then over-under rumble-bumping until *smash!* I exploded against the logjam and *crash!* Mam blasted into it too and I was wildly grabbing at her coat, water bashing against us, and then *crack!* Stew Pot hit the jam-up and swirled over it, looking helplessly back as he whirled down the creek. My mouth fizzed with icy hard-hitting water and I couldn't hear myself *think* with the crashing roar of the creek, but I heard a loud screaming, either in my head or out loud, and suddenly a big hand reached out and grabbed on to my coat.

Then we tumbled, all three of us. We slipped and slid and stumbled over slippery rocks and fumbled and flopped onto the snowy bank, where I pulled my heavy sodden self up on my elbows and threw up. My teeth clacked in my head so I could hardly hear the deep voice saying, *Stew Pot's okay. He's a hero and Blue's a hero too.* I looked at the bright light of Mr. Mac's hands as he scooped me up and I thought, *He's my hero*, and I wanted to cry but I didn't.

Mr. Mac carried me to Ol' Yeller. He pulled the door open and plopped sopping-wet freezing-me down on the seat and switched on the motor, turned on the heat, and then dashed to his truck to grab a horse blanket. He came back and tucked it around me, all the while asking was I sure I was okay? When I gulped that I was, he boosted a bedraggled Stew Pot into the truck beside me and ran back to help Mam. I heard her shivery voice saying, "I'm so sorry about the tractor." Then I heard her silvery laugh and something about the tractor being a double whammy, twice causing him troubles, or maybe it was the hired hands causing trouble and not the tractor at all. And Mr. Mac's laughing voice saying, "No, Mam, no double trouble at all."

He helped her to the truck, though I heard her protesting. As he opened the door she coughed and said, "I'm a bit waterlogged, but soon as I've dried off, I'll be back down to help."

Mr. Mac shook his head. "No way are you to come back," he said. "I'll get dried off and have that rascal on dry land in no time. "Git, now," he said, slapping Ol' Yeller's back fender same as you'd smack the rump of your horse.

I shivered and shook all the way to the house, but inside me a warm spot grew, as though my heart had stirred up its own fire. As Mam and I dashed from the truck to the house I burst out laughing. We looked like zany sea creatures, our sopping-wet clothes stuck to our bodies, our hair a wild fright. Mam looked at me and laughed too. Stew Pot just looked at us as if we were nuts.

Chapter Fourteen

Late that afternoon, after I'd tossed my wet clothes into the wash, hopped into a hot tub, devoured three peanut butter sandwiches and two cups of hot cocoa and then curled up with my hero dog for a nap, I heard a truck rumble up to the house. I stumbled down to the kitchen, yawning and rubbing at a sore spot on my ribs. Mam stood by the stove sorting through her stash of medicinal teas as she waited for the water to boil.

"Where's Mr. Mac?" I asked, looking around. "Didn't he come up?"

Mam shook her head. "I ended up going back down. We had quite a time winching the tractor up the bank. He just left to go back to his ranch."

"Bummer," I said, upset that I'd missed the whole show. "Double bummer," I added as it hit me how much I'd counted on Mr. Mac coming up to check on the bums.

"Multiple whammy's more like it," Mam said. "First

the tractor gets dumped in the creek, then me, then you and Stew Pot and Mr. McCloud. Thank goodness the day's almost over."

I slumped down on the couch by the window. Steam from the teapot clouded the panes. I wiped a clear strip and peered out. Was it only yesterday that the world had been spring green and crazy with birdsong? In the yard, ghostly bushes still sagged under the weight of the snow. Blue shadows stretched across the white meadows. The wind swirled around the house with a sound like a flute.

Stew Pot padded over and stuck a cold nose in my palm. I scratched his ear with one hand and sighed. If only Mr. Mac had come up. I'd so wanted to see the surprised look on his face when he examined Wonder Baby's leg, the way his eyes would twinkle as he saw how fantastic the two bums now looked. The way he'd run his hands down Wonder Baby's leg to check it. How he'd reach for the other leg, thinking he'd got the wrong one . . . But now, by the time he returned again (after who knew how long!) the leg would've healed up on its own anyway. What a downer. "Serves me right for wanting to show off," I muttered.

"Well, so much for my day with no chores," I whispered into Pot's furry shoulder. Then, "Guess I'd better go feed my bums," I said loudly, so Mam could hear me over the whistling teapot. From across the room she gave me a half smile as if to say she was sorry my day had been so messed up. She held up a tea bag, like, Did I want a cup? I shook my head. No. Maybe I'd go eat some worms.

I shuffled through the mudroom and out to the front

porch where I'd left the bottles—was it only a few hours ago? Back in the kitchen, I rattled them about in the sink and then shook them till the nipples almost flew off. I let the front door bang behind me.

When I got back, the house was quiet. I knocked on Mam's door and, when she didn't answer, peeked in. She lay in her fairy-tale bed with the rose-patterned quilt pulled up to her chin, one hand resting on the open pages of the book at her side.

I stood in the doorway studying her. The way her tanned, cracked, calloused hand somehow seemed fragile on the white pages of the book. The way her eyes had dark half-moons beneath them. The bright lights that I normally saw spinning about her now seemed sluggish and dim, and I could see darker places where I guessed she'd been battered and bruised by her dump in the creek. I had a few of those places myself. I thought of how she never, ever complained about feeling sick or tired or hurt. How she always smelled slightly of sage, as if she breathed in the land around her and breathed out its essence. I wrote that down in my journal a while back and was real proud of how the sentence came out. Sometimes she had smelled of gin, back then. She hadn't bought any bottles of gin since we'd been at Far Canyon, of that I was certain. No wine, either. She knew she had to be careful. I thought of how I used to worry about her, and how one drink always seemed to lead to another. She always seemed so strong, but with that one thing she wasn't. I crossed my fingers and made a quick wish that no temptations would land in her path. I smiled as her breath came out in soft whistles.

Then all of a sudden it hit me.

She could've drowned in the creek. How had she gotten out of the tractor when it slipped over the bank? It could've tumbled over, she could've been trapped! I could've lost her. . . .

I tiptoed over to the bed. I was so full of love at that moment that I could feel my heart puff up like a balloon. And the light. I could feel it around me, transparent and golden. A rush of energy surged through me, as if I was plugged into an electrical socket with a current of love and light flowing out of my fingers.

I squinted, studying Mam's lights. It was as if her normal patterns had gotten off balance, the way a musician might suddenly hit a wrong note. I let my hands ripple several inches above her body. When my hands were over the places where she'd thumped hard against the jam-up I could feel a prickly pain shooting up into my hands. Even taking my hands away, I could still feel it.

That's weird, I thought. *Am I absorbing her pain? I don't want it!* I shook my hands really hard, and the hurt went away. I took a deep breath. My feet seemed glued to the floor, as if they'd grown roots that were keeping me from floating away.

Carefully, so as not to wake her, I put both my hands on her feet. Then, for the longest time, I just stood there. It wasn't me actually *doing* anything—I just stood there letting the light flow through me and through her. I watched as around the bruised places her lights changed as my light mixed with hers; watched as her lights flickered and fluttered and spun back into their usual bright luminous colors. When her lights seemed more like their normal pattern, I picked Mam's hand up off her book and held it.

Which made me think. I hadn't held my mom's hand since—well, since I couldn't remember.

Mam's eyes blinked.

I slid my hands away.

"Blue?" she said sleepily. "I didn't know you were there."

I smiled.

Mam slid her hand under the cover and felt along her ribs. "I'm not hurting so much anymore. That medicinal tea I drank must've worked wonders."

"It's good stuff," I said.

Mam yawned. "I've been thinking about those antelope fawns you told me about at lunchtime. It's rare to see such a birth. You should feel really privileged."

"I do," I said. "I was just wondering if I should go check on them."

"The sun's about to go down—can't you wait till tomorrow?" She yawned again, stretched, and closed her eyes.

"I'm worried about the lame fawn. But don't worry. I'll be back in a flash, and my hero dog will take care of me."

She was already asleep again as Stew Pot and I slipped out the front door.

A cold east wind lifted my blue baseball cap—I'd lost my knit one to the creek. I jammed it down and pulled up my collar. I'd left my boots on the furnace grate to dry, and my cowboy boots slipped and squeaked in the snow. We followed my tracks to the fence. Holding up one barbed wire with a gloved hand, I pushed down with my boot on the other and scrambled through.

We cut across the hill to the ridge above the canyon. The wind gusted along the rim, spitting snow at us, and after going a short way I turned around and headed back toward the game trail that led into the canyon. Halfway down it, I hesitated. Much as I hated to leave Stew Pot behind, it probably wouldn't be a good idea to bring him along. I glanced around. Near the start of the trail was an overhang that looked like a good shelter from the cold wind. I hiked over to check it out, and then whistled to Pot.

"Stay here," I said, patting the snowy ground. "Stay so we don't scare the babies."

Pot knew the words "stay" and "babies" because he was a cow dog and used to little critters. He was always careful not to spook anxious mothers and their playful calves when he helped Mam, or when we trailed the cows from one range to another. All it took was a whistle or a pointed finger and he'd be off to do what cow dogs just naturally do. He knew all the commands. For sure he knew the word "stay."

That's why I was startled when halfway down I looked back and saw Stew Pot behind me. His eyes didn't leave mine. "Go back!" I said, and he hunkered down but rose as soon as I took a few steps. But I was in a hurry to get to the end of the canyon, so I pointed to the sheltered nook, snapped my fingers, and said sharply, "Stay." He turned and slunk back. "Good boy," I said, and trudged on.

It was creepy down in the shadowy canyon, with the craggy walls leaning in and only a band of sky showing above. I hurried, zigging and zagging my way toward the place where the fawns had been born. Near the far end, where the canyon widened and the sagebrush grew tall, I almost stumbled into it. From there I practically tiptoed. Except in squeaky cowboy boots tiptoeing didn't work very well. The last thing I wanted was to spook the new fawns.

Blue shadows filled the bowl, but the snowy rim gleamed bright gold as the setting sun struck it. A few tracks crisscrossed the snowy valley. I scanned the hillsides but could see no sign of the fawns—either they were well hidden or they'd found new places to hide. I was about to hike up the slope when I heard a rustling sound.

I stopped. Cupped my hands to my ears. What was that?

Suddenly a piercing scream split the silence, a scream so wild, so loud, my heart tunneled into the earth. The scream rose shrilly and broke off in midshriek. All the hairs on my body stood up.

I stared bug-eyed as a black shape streaked across the golden rim of the bowl. Something limp hung from its jaws. The black thing froze, glared at me with yellow eyes, and then loped away with the skinny legs of its bundle swaying back and forth, back and forth. . . .

Another sound, this one a wild, frantic honking, like a goose gone crazy mad, rumbled toward the rim. It was Lone One! She jerked to a stop, saw I was a familiar shape, and tore off again, grunting wildly.

She was going after a wolf!

I crouched and touched the ground with my hands, feeling my stomach heave. *Hang on,* I said to myself. *Don't throw up. It'll only attract . . . wolves.* I swallowed hard. I was still dizzily hanging on to the earth when Lone One came honking back to the rim, her black tongue hanging out, her thin sides heaving. With each grunt her white tag of a tail shot up.

Halfway up the slope, from behind a clump of sagebrush, I saw a small head pop up and just as quickly sink down again—the other fawn!

Up on the rim, Lone One spun and bolted away again. *You're so brave, but it's too late, too late,* I thought as she vanished. I didn't breathe till I heard the sad honking sound returning. The poor mother antelope walked slowly over the rim, breathing hard. She looked down at me and grunted.

This time it seemed as if her frantic grunts were

aimed in my direction. Rightly or not, that's how I heard it. I unstuck my hands from the earth. Stumbled up the slope to the fawn's hiding place. Quick as a flash I reached down and grabbed it.

Oh, poor mother antelope! If a sound could slice a heart in two, then this sound did. It was the same terrified, shrieking bleat as before, so loud and shrill I almost dropped the fawn right then. Legs kicked in all directions. With one gloved hand I tucked its spinning legs into the crook of my arms and clutched the struggling fawn to my chest. The fawn gave one last muffled bleat and fell silent.

I stood there, the two of us trembling and me so shaky I thought I'd tip over. "Hush, baby, hush, it's okay, it's okay," I finally managed to croak.

But of course it wasn't one bit okay at all.

Lone One stared down, her head lowered, her legs splayed apart. She looked ready to charge.

Feeling self-conscious, I made a low, guttural sound as near as I could to her deep belly grunt. *"Eaaaaaaahhh! Eaaaaaaahhh!"* I grunted.

Lone One grunted back. I grunted again. She answered. I took a step backward. Lone One took a step down the hill.

Slowly—step, grunt, step, grunt—I backed toward the canyon like a crab hunched over its treasure. I couldn't turn my back on Lone One. She had to see her fawn. *Follow me.*

Amazingly, one step at a time, Lone One followed.

Her eyes didn't leave for an instant the bundle I held in my arms. She kept a distance of about fifty feet. At the first bend in the canyon I lost sight of her. I walked a short way and stopped, wondering if Lone One followed. Several minutes passed, long enough for me to reconsider what I'd just gone and done.

Long enough to wonder, *What on earth am I doing? Where am I going?* A cold chill ran through me. I'd just picked up a *fawn*—I'd taken it away from its mother. And now, if the mother charged and I dropped it, it'd run like crazy, its mom would chase after it—and what if a whole *pack* of wolves was waiting out there in the hills?

But what if . . . ? What if this was the fawn that'd been having so much trouble walking? What if this was the lame one?

I untucked a thin leg from under my elbow.

I was about to check it out when a long, wailing howl rose from the hills. Another howl answered. I could feel the hairs on my body rising again. I quickly stuffed the fawn back into the crook of my arms.

"Hush, baby, hush. It's okay," I whispered with my mouth on the soft furry head.

I huddled over my precious bundle and kept walking. I was so intent on looking back and trying not to stumble that I didn't see the figure looming above on the ledge of the canyon.

"Ho! You!"

I jumped out of my skin as the sound bounced across the walls of the canyon. The fawn's legs lashed out and I hunched over it, trying desperately to hang on to the windmill of rotating legs as I crooked my head and squinted up from beneath the bill of my cap. A boy on a horse peered over the rim of the canyon. With the setting sun's bright glow behind them all I could see was their dark shadowy shapes.

"Ho! You down there!" the boy yelled. "You know you're trespassing? And poaching too."

Of *course* I knew I was trespassing. And, like any ranch kid, I knew the laws about picking up wild animals. As if I didn't already feel bad enough about what I'd done! I could feel my face catching on fire.

"Could we discuss this some other time?" I hissed up to the cliff. What terrible timing! *Just leave,* I wanted to say. *You're going to spoil everything. If you don't move away, the mother antelope won't come—and* then *what will I do?*

"I saw this dog runnin' around crazylike," he called down. "Going back and forth along the ledge here. I was wonderin' what he was up to."

"That'd be my dog. He was supposed to stay. Listen, you mind if we continue this conversation some other time?"

The boy looked beyond me. His head jerked back in surprise.

Lone One stood at the bend of the canyon.

"Eaaaaaaahhh! Eaaaaaaahhh!" I grunted, my voice startling me by its loudness.

Lone One's eyes didn't leave the figures above as she

gave a short, sharp grunt in reply. Then she spun around and skittered away.

"What's your name—Talks to Antelope?" The boy backed his horse away from the ridge. "Catch you again," he yelled as he rode off.

"Yeah, right," I muttered up to the ridge. "But not if I see you first."

I stood there while the strip of golden light above faded and cold blue shadows swallowed us up. I shifted from one foot to the other. Lifted one shoulder, stretched, lifted the other. Thought about unkinking my arms and re-arranging the legs of the fawn, but it seemed to have fallen asleep. I scrunched my fingers inside my gloves. Arched my back. Kicked at the snow. Tried not to think about that nosy, rude kid. Tried to blank out the dead twin and the wolf.

I focused on the slow thump of my heart compared to the fast beat of the fawn's. At least fifteen minutes must've trudged slowly by before I heard worried honks coming up the canyon. The fawn raised its head. Lone One rounded the bend at a run and came skidding to a stop. I took a deep breath and then, keeping the fawn in full view of its mother, I did my sideways crab walk down the canyon. This time Lone One seemed anxious to follow.

Slowly we retraced my tracks to the trail. And of course there stood Stew Pot, anxiously peering down from the sheltered nook where I'd left him.

"No, Pot," I called up, my voice sharp as a rock. "I've got a baby. Go home, Pot. Go home."

Instantly he dropped and turned his head away so his eyes wouldn't scare the fawn or the mother antelope in the canyon behind us.

"Go home," I pleaded, my voice all choked up and croaky. "Please. Go home. I'll be okay."

But I didn't feel like I'd be okay. I felt like I needed the biggest doggy hug ever.

Pot didn't want to go. His job was to protect me, and here I was sending him off. But he turned and slunk away, his belly brushing the snow. When he got to the fence he darted a look back to see if I'd changed my mind. I shook my head. He slipped under the wires and headed down toward the house.

I stumbled toward the fence. What now? There were two loose wires in the four-wire barbed fence. Both my hands were wrapped tightly around my bundle. How could I possibly get through it?

I took a breath and snaked a leg between two wires, then hunched over the fawn and squeezed through them. I heard a big *rippppppppp* as I pulled my other leg through and took a nosedive into the snow, crumpling into a heap of elbows, knees, foreheads, and little fawn feet.

Of course Lone One again scurried away.

I kneeled there, blinking back tears as I stared down at the snow. I sniffed, trying hard not to wipe my snotty nose on the fawn's furry back. The tears came anyway, and before long I was bawling as if I was hooked up to a hose and the faucet had been turned up on high. I didn't know if I was crying because of what had happened to the fawn, or because of what I'd just done, or just because it had been such a strange day. I was about to drown in a puddle of tears when I felt a soft, warm breeze on my neck.

It was a breeze that smelled strongly of sage and wild onions. It blew in my ear and parted the hair on the back of my neck. Each of her breaths held a deep grunt.

Slowly I got to my feet. Lone One skittered away once again. This time I was sure she'd return. Soon she did.

I grunted at her and took a step down the hill. Lone One followed.

One step at a time took forever, but I'd finally come up with a plan.

Chapter Fifteen

That night I hardly slept. I was restless in the chair I'd pulled up to the window that overlooked the homestead cabin.

Lone One had watched me take the fawn inside the cabin. She'd seen me shove the broken door sidelong across the doorway and then speed toward the house to get out of her way. But the mother antelope must've been confused by the dark shape of the cabin. She'd run back to the fence, slipped under it, and had disappeared over the hills. I'd dashed around the snowy yard breaking off branches of sagebrush and then climbed over the door and into the cabin again. "Here's something to snuggle down in," I'd whispered to the frightened fawn as I bunched up the sagebrush beside it. "Your mama will be back soon. I hope . . ."

"She'll come back," I whispered now to Stew Pot in the beanbag I'd dragged to the window beside me. "She *has* to come back."

I tried not to think of what I'd do if she didn't. It was bad enough to have stolen the fawn from its mother. If Lone One didn't come back, how on *earth* would I keep it alive?

Now, forehead pressed to the windowpane, I stared down at the cabin. With its dirt floor and three windows for sunlight it should make a good, safe place for the fawn. After all, hadn't Mr. Mac said an elk had lived there one whole winter when he was a kid?

I pushed up the window and poked my head out. A huge round moon spread its white silence over the snow-covered fields. I could see the fine, inked lines of the fences stretching across the white hillsides and the dark shapes of cows dotting the fields. Down by the cabin two rabbits hopped by, their eyes flashing red in the moonlight. Above the sounds of the creek and the wind there rose a long, lonely howl. From the hills behind the house came an answering howl and before long a whole chorus sang to the moon. I shivered and slammed down the window.

Beside me, Pot trembled and buried his head in his paws. He'd never acted this way when coyotes yipped in the hills. Why, more than once I'd watched him chase after a coyote and actually nip it. It wasn't unheard of for a coyote to lure a dog off so a waiting pack could attack it, but Pot had never been afraid of a fight. He'd always come home unharmed. But the howl of the wolf must've touched something ancient inside him, some part that said, *This howl is different. . . .*

I scrambled into the beanbag and wrapped him in my arms. "They scare me too," I said. "And thank you, my hero dog, for taking good care of me. You jumped into the creek after me this morning, and I know you would've done something heroic again this afternoon if you'd had the chance. But, sweet Pot, there's no way you could've tackled a wolf and come out the winner. . . ."

Outside, the howls seemed to stretch out as far as the moon. Then the sounds faded. The hills became silent again, and Pot stopped his trembling. I lay beside him scratching his ears till he slept.

I wriggled up and slipped across the dark room. I grabbed a pillow and the blanket from my bed and settled back into my chair. I don't know if it was the bright moonlight, the white landscape, or the fact that it'd just been such an incredibly difficult day, but when I glanced out at the whiteness I thought I saw the wolf running off with the fawn. I imagined I saw the mother antelope frantically, fearlessly, chasing the wolf. My heart started pounding and I closed my eyes. I imagined then that I heard the Indian kid yelling down into the canyon.

"Talk about rude," I snorted out loud. In his beanbag beside me Pot's eyes snapped open. "I sure wouldn't want *him* for a friend" I added, and Pot swished his tail back and forth. "Oh, believe me," I said, jabbing at him with my toe, "neither would you."

Really, that kid could've ruined everything. It was amazing that Lone One had come back after he'd shouted like that. It was even more amazing that she'd followed me clear to the cabin—almost it had seemed as if she'd wanted my help. If only she'd jumped in after her fawn. Now, who knew what might happen. For sure I'd have to keep the fawn safe for more than one night. Because yes, it *had* been the lame one. I checked the fawn's leg as I settled it into the cabin. Nothing was broken. I'd seen calves limping about like that because a leg had been scrunched up in the mother's belly, and usually it was just a matter of time before they'd be hopping about good as new. For sure I didn't want to "humanize" the fawn or get it used to me by touching it any more than I had to. After all, the fawn did have a mother.

Right. It *had* a mother. At least until I came along and took it away from her. I squeezed my eyes shut. *Come back, Lone One,* I begged. *Please . . .*

But what if she *didn't*? What if the cabin seemed too strange—what if Lone One wouldn't jump into it? Would she understand that it was a safe place for her fawn, or would she be frantic and just want to get it out of there? What if she deserted her fawn now that I'd touched it?

Well, there was nothing I could do now but just sit and watch from the window to see if she'd come.

I pulled the blanket up over my shoulders. In the soft light of the moon I could see blue-white light streaming out from my fingertips, like searchlights exploring the night. I wiggled my fingers and lines of light crisscrossed through the darkness of my attic, making patterns along the walls and across its slanted ceiling. I played with the lights, making them flare and then fade and then grow bright again with my thoughts.

While I'd worked on the bums I'd noticed that by imagining certain things I could boost up the power of the light. Now, sitting up straight, I stared out at the bright moonlight. I imagined breathing in all that brilliance and filling myself up with light. After a while I looked down at my hands. I watched as the light in them grew until not just a stream but a flood of golden-white light fanned out of my fingers.

All night I sat in the dark and watched the way the light streamed from my fingertips and lit up the night. I practiced turning the lights red and then blue and then all the colors of the rainbow. Purple was the easiest, after golden or silvery white. The thought of the wolf made the lights turn grayish white, and somehow those lights even *felt* different, all prickly and sharp.

It didn't take much to make the lights change. Just the thought and the—what was the word Mam had used?— "intention." Yes. Zeroing in, being still, and thinking so hard about what I wanted that I could almost see it and taste it and feel it.

When I couldn't hold my eyes open one minute longer, I could still see the lights through my eyelids.

All night I kept watch by the window, dozing off, then waking with a jolt and searching the white landscape for Lone One.

As the first light of dawn spread across the horizon,

she came. One step out of darkness. Two. Lone One stood by the cabin doorway. She froze and stared into its shadowy darkness for what seemed like forever. Then she jumped over the barrier door.

Up in the attic, *celebration*!

"She came! She came!" I yelled, tossing my pillow up to the ceiling, catching it and hurling it at Stew Pot, who'd jumped up excitedly and now barked and nipped at my legs as I twirled across the long room to the stairway. "Let's call the fawn Light of the Dawn," I yelled as the two of us tore down the stairs.

I threw open the door to Mam's bedroom. "Can you believe it? She *came*!"

Mam leaped out of bed. "*Who* came?" She grabbed her jeans off a chair and snatched her shirt off the chest of drawers, sending her book and hairbrush clattering to the floor. "What are you talking about? Who's here?" she asked as she wiggled her clothes on over her nightgown.

"The mother antelope! She's in the cabin. Right now. Feeding her fawn."

Which of course meant I had a whole load of explaining to do.

But before Mam could ask what on earth two prong-horns were doing there in the first place, I spurted it all out—or most of it. She'd still been in bed when I got back from my excursion into the hills, so I'd just called out "Good night" as I rushed up to my attic. Now I told her about the wolf, but I didn't tell her how close I'd been to it. I told her about how I'd picked up the fawn, and how the mother antelope had followed us home. I didn't say one word about getting caught by that Indian kid. She would've agreed with him. Oh yes. I'd definitely been poaching and trespassing too.

"I won't tell you things you already know," Mam said when I finished. "Or *should* know. Especially about picking up wildlife. What's done is done. For your sake, as well as the fawn's, I hope the mother accepts her fawn after you've handled it. As for the wolf—where there's one, there are bound to be others. We'd better keep an eye on our calves." She leaned down and shook Pot by the ruff. "And you stick close by. No dancing with wolves, do you hear?"

From her bedroom window, Mam and I kept an eye on the cabin doorway. I was scared the mother antelope would be frantic about the barrier door, that she'd smash against it trying to get her fawn out of the cabin. But after a short while we saw Lone One sail over the door, stop and stare back at the cabin, and then take off for the hills.

I tugged on my boots, grabbed my ripped coat, and rushed outside. Mam followed. In the sleepy dawn, long blue shadows stretched across the white fields. We tromped through the snow and peeked through the cabin doorway. Tucked under the sagebrush we could see the pearl-gray shape of the fawn.

Mam planted her hands on her hips. "And just how long do you plan on keeping it here?"

"Till the fawn's leg has healed up enough so that it can outrun a wolf," I said, biting my lip. "Two weeks?

Three? Of course it all depends on the mother. If she doesn't keep coming back . . ."

I couldn't go on. We'd just have to wait and see what happened.

The sun came up summery bright and soon turned the snow into slush. Green grass poked up through the white. Birds couldn't stop chattering, and every once in a while we'd hear the cracking sound of branches breaking off under the weight of the snow.

So all morning we gathered branches and stacked them in piles. Later we'd load them into the tractor bucket to take to the ranch dump to burn. Some branches had broken plumb off, but others had just split from the trunk. Mam used a handsaw to finish the job. She got way ahead of me. I reached up to touch each place where she'd hacked. I wondered, Didn't it bother her? Didn't she see the light streaking out of the trees? All the wounded places spurted out a dark reddish purple light. Where the branches once were there was kind of an afterimage effect.

It was midmorning when I glanced up and saw Lone One come sprinting across the hillside. She nosed under the fence and sped toward the cabin. I dashed through the fields to the cabin and then tiptoed to a window and peeked in.

Lone One grunted worriedly as her fawn limped toward her and sank down. The mother antelope tucked her nose under her fawn and boosted it up, and then licked it so hard that it tumbled again. Finally the fawn managed to scramble up again, and Lone One crooked her head and licked under its tail as it nursed. All the while she grunted and grunted.

Four more times that day she came back to the cabin. Each time I breathed a huge sigh of relief.

That afternoon I sat on my bed struggling over the giant rip in my coat. I'm not a good sewer, but no *way* would I ask Mam for help. I mean, you should see *her* coat. I threaded my needle, stuffed the feathers in as best I could, tugged it all together, and jabbed through the layers. *Ouch.* I sat sucking my finger and studying the rip, and thinking about the fawn. It didn't look like I'd have to touch it again. I wondered if there was some way to send healing light to its leg by long-distance. Would that work? I had no idea. All I knew was that I'd have to keep the fawn in the cabin until it was strong enough to outrun a wolf.

Which got me to thinking about that darn kid. I felt my face get hot. What'd he been doing, anyway—sneaking around spying on us? What a jerk. He could've wrecked everything yelling down like that. Spooking me, almost making me drop the poor fawn.

I stabbed at my coat. Okay, so I shouldn't have been out there. I knew better than to slip through someone's fence. Not that that'd ever stopped me. And anyway, what was so special about the other side of the fence? Other than that I'd drawn a picture that looked so much like those mountains that it was totally spooky. And of course there was my special place. My hill. My wishing tree . . .

I thought of that scene in *The Wizard of Oz*, the

one where the house comes whirling to the ground and Dorothy goes to the door and suddenly everything turns into color. To me, the other side of the fence was *color*. Was I supposed to look past the fence at the landscape I'd drawn and *not* trespass?

That kid may have caught me once, but now I'd be on the lookout. No way would he catch me twice.

I tied a knot in my thread and held my coat up for inspection. I shrugged. So I'd mangled it. But out here, who gave a hoot?

It was late afternoon, after my bums had been fed and closed up in their pen safe from the big bad wolf, when Pot and I slipped away. I looked left and right, up, down, all around. No one.

"*Shhh,*" I said to Stew Pot. "Let's not make any noise. Just in case . . ."

It felt almost like summer again—breezy, cool, hawks floating about in a blue cloudless sky, and wildflowers so pepped up by the snow you'd think they'd been drinking caffeine. Most of the snow had melted except in the long shady draws. Pot galloped ahead while I took my sweet time. Near the top of the hill a blast of wind billowed up under my coat, almost sending me skyward like a big fat balloon. I whirled, swirled, I was a bird, a hawk, I could fly! I twirled to the top of the hill. Spun dizzily to my tree.

I about peed my pants. Because there, in the shadowy green cave of the juniper, leaning against my tree as if he owned it, was the Indian kid.

"Thought you weren't coming," he said.

"Well," I said breathlessly, "here I am." Let *him* explain how he knew I'd be here.

I glared at Traitor Dog Pot. I had a dog who hadn't barked to warn me someone was there. A dog who sat wagging his tail. A dog who stuck out his paw to be shook, and *then* had the nerve to look back at me as if he'd just found his newest best friend.

The boy didn't reply. Well, I could play that game. We both stood there, him leaning against the tree, me kind of woozy and light-headed with the wind pushing against me and tangling my hair.

He stood still as still, as if he were part of the tree— *my* tree, by the way. He wasn't fidgety at all, not like the boys I was used to—not that I was any authority on boys, far from it. He had on the usual ranch-kid getup of beat-up jacket and jeans. The toes of his cowboy boots were bandaged with silver duct tape. He was short, but taller than me, and stocky, with short cropped hair. I figured him to be my age, maybe a bit older. And he glowed.

Honestly, I'd never seen anything like it. I must've looked really stupid, standing there squinting and blinking my eyes. Because "glowed" didn't even begin to describe it. He looked like he'd swallowed a star and it was shining out of his chest.

Finally I broke the silence. "So how'd you know I'd be here?" I said, trying hard not to sound flustered.

"Took a chance." He puckered his eyebrows at me. "How's the antelope?" he asked.

"Which one?"

"The one you poached."

"The fawn's down there in the cabin. She's fine."

"You feedin' it?"

"Why should I feed it?"

He scratched his cheek. *Let him puzzle over that,* I thought. I was beginning to enjoy this game. I bent down, picked up a rock, and studied it as if it were the most interesting rock in the world.

"What do you think she's got a mother for?" I finally said, throwing the rock up and catching it in one hand. "She's come down four times already today. I think she's plumb fine with what I did. Taking the fawn. Maybe she's even thankful. Especially after what happened to this one's brother."

His eyebrows went up. "How do you know the fawn you've got is a 'she'? And the other was a 'he'? You can't tell the difference at this early age."

"Well, if you really want to know, I watched them being born. I saw the whole thing. The way the mother licked them—one under the belly and the other under the tail. Anyone could figure it out from that. I watched her through the window today and this one she licked under the tail. This one is the female."

I thought I caught the flicker of a smile. Maybe his mouth just twitched. "You know you were—are—trespassing," he said, his voice stern again. "That is, unless you belong to one of the tribes."

"I don't have a drop of Indian blood in me. I plead

guilty. I'm sorry. But I did what I did and I'd do it again in an instant," I said, putting my fists on my hips. "That fawn didn't stand half a chance. . . ."

I left off. Did he know about the wolf? Or did he just think I'd picked up the fawn for the fun of it? Suddenly I felt confused.

He studied me, frowning. "A pack of wolves has moved into this area. I saw them a few days ago. Five of them. One black, four gray. They got two of my grandmother's calves. Seeing what they did . . ." He let the words trail away.

"Well, I saw what the black one did," I said, "and it wasn't pretty. I suppose it has pups to feed, but still . . ." I shuddered. My heart broke all over again and I couldn't bear to think about what I'd seen. I took a breath to steady myself. "By the way, my name's Blue," I said, just to get off the subject of wolves.

"Blue?"

I shrugged. "Take your choice—deep blue, light blue, sky blue, sad blue, cool blue, blueberries, bluebells, or maybe the blue of these juniper berries."

He looked very seriously at me as if he were thinking over each of my words. "All true blues," he finally said.

"And this is Stew Pot." I shot Pot a look. Forgave him a little.

"We've already met. I'm Shawn," he said, pushing himself away from the tree. He looked Stew Pot in the eyes as if the two of them had a secret I wasn't in on. "So, Stew Pot," he said, "don't let the wolves get you."

Without another word he walked to the other side of

the juniper tree, leaned one hand on the rocky ledge, and hopped over.

Stew Pot and I watched as the shining boy loped down the hill, knocking rocks loose and causing a landslide that startled the black-and-white horse that waited under a pine tree at the foot of the slope. When the slide stopped, the horse trotted toward him, trailing its reins on the ground. Shawn gathered them, put his foot in the stirrup, and mounted. He turned his horse and looked up. "Catch you again," he called.

We watched as they crossed the little valley, climbed the next hill, and disappeared over it. Shawn never looked back.

Chapter Sixteen

The next two weeks passed in a blur as our world dashed madly toward summer. The hills turned green and soft as velvet after the summer snow. Here in the mountains it was hard to believe that the whole state of Wyoming was in the middle of a long dry spell. Down at the trading post everyone said it was just like old times, almost.

"But not quite," Clyde said. "Eight years of dry don't disappear with one snowstorm. I've got a feeling we're in for a blistering summer. There'll be wildfires all over, same as last year, if we don't get some rain." Stone-faced, he'd added, "Why, even with the creeks running high, no one lost any bridges. Or even any tractors, I hear."

"Yeah, but it sure was exciting," I said. "The . . . the high water, I mean," I blurted when I noticed the look on Mam's face as the four ranchers standing there chuckled.

Ignoring them, Mam turned toward the door and studied a notice tacked to the wall. She studied it so long

I was sure she'd learned it by heart. She nodded a quick good-bye to Clyde and the men, and gave a jerk of her head to let me know I should hurry. She slipped out the door as a burly tourist rushed through it.

"This place got a garage?" he bellowed. Reddish black light flashed around him.

I lurched out of the way of his lights and tumbled into a rack full of postcards. I scrambled to gather the cards that'd scattered. Behind me, at the counter, the tourist ranted about having had two blowouts, and how he'd then driven for miles without a single gas station in sight. I stuffed the cards back into their slots and threw Clyde a quick "Sorry!" as I skittered out. Even after the door closed behind me I could still hear the man's furious voice. I'd seen lights flash out just like that. *That's what's meant by "bad vibes,"* I thought.

Mam was more quiet than usual on our way back to the ranch. I started to blurt out that stories sometimes got all bent out of shape as they traveled the gossip wires, but then figured it might be a good time to keep my mouth shut.

Besides, I had my own stuff to think about. Such as the fact that my last letters had been returned. Mam had handed them over without saying a word. I'd stuffed them into the trash can.

Well, I'd tried. Was I going to spend the whole rest of my life going around looking for a father? Or would I just have to learn to live with it? How could I? How do you ever forget something like a *father*, for gosh sakes. I gave a sideways glare at my mom. It was partly her fault. If she'd stayed in one place he would've tracked us down ages ago.

We turned onto the dirt road and jounced along over rocks and ruts, swerving twice to avoid a fox and an antelope. I grabbed the armrest. *Lighten up and slow down,* I wanted to shout. Instead, I slumped in my seat and tried to ride the bumps loose as a rag doll.

Halfway across our bridge Mam lurched to a stop. "Sorry," she said as my head practically rammed into the windshield. In the back, Stew Pot thumped against the rear window. "And sorry about your letters. . . ." She didn't say, "I told you so." Instead she leaned on the steering wheel and stared at the dark mudslide in the bank by the barn where the tractor had tumbled into the creek.

I rolled down my window, poked my head out, and looked down. The creek rumbled peacefully, almost as if it were singing a song. After one good week of wild rushing water it had dropped. I didn't know what "normal" was for this time of year, but judging from the brush and logs washed up along the banks from past high-water flooding, we'd missed that mark by a long shot.

"Beastly tractor," Mam suddenly said.

I ducked back in and stole a look at her.

All of a sudden she slapped the steering wheel and hooted with laughter. "That story," she whooped. "I bet it gets wilder each time it gets told! If they'd only seen the whole thing—weren't we a sight!"

It took only a split second before I caught the bug. Mam always said I cackled like a coop full of hens laying eggs, so now I flapped my arms and crowed and the two of us laughed hysterically. For some reason I had the strangest feeling that our laughing was almost like crying, and once started with either we might never stop. I let myself laugh even harder. It was a long time before our laughing dropped off into hiccups and snorts.

Mam wiped her eyes. "On the serious side," she said—which only set us off again. She tried once more. "On the serious and totally humorless side," she said, "seeing how much the creek has dropped it does seem likely that we might run short of water. . . ."

Her words made us sober up fast. I knew what "running short" meant—use it or lose it. If the water got lower than our headgate on the creek, we'd be in trouble. And the beavers didn't help the situation one bit since the water they kept damming up irrigated one whole side of the ranch. The summer before, we'd been at a ranch where the creek and the well had run dry. I doubted it would be that bad up here in the mountains, but who could predict what would happen if we didn't get any rain?

So that very day Mam and I made a deal. I'd attack the beaver ponds every day with her blessing, while she took on the ditches. We'd irrigate the heck out of those fields. And if we ran out of water later, well, at least we'd have made good use of it while we'd had it.

So, what with running back and forth to the ponds and doing house chores and weeding our garden and working on my Blooming Room and checking every few hours on the state of my fawn and feeding my bums, I kept so busy I hardly had time to even *think* about my dad or that Indian kid.

Or at least I tried not to. But when my hands are busy my mind's usually off doing its own thing.

I'd be peeking through the cabin window, watching as Lone One bent into a comma and licked her fawn as it nursed. Somehow Shawn would wiggle his way into my thoughts.

I mean, this kid had almost bitten my head off. For sure he didn't act like a saint or anyone special, though he'd practically put Stew Pot under his spell. So why did his lights shine as if he had a star blazing out of his chest?

I'd only once seen someone with lights almost as bright white as Shawn's. That hadn't been a priest or a holy person—it was an old gray-haired woman mopping the floor at a rest station. She'd wrung out her mop and looked over at me and smiled. *Pow!* A bright white light flashed across the bathroom. I felt as if I'd been filled to bursting with sweetness and light and something I could only call love.

Shawn's lights had been even brighter. How could that be? I must've seen wrong—had dust in my eyes, or stardust or something.

I'd be at the ponds, undoing the beaver dams and sorting out the neatest beaver-trimmed sticks to take back to the ranch for the chairs and tables I was making. Or trying to make. Then I'd sit on the dam with my boots in the icy cold water and throw sticks for Stew Pot to fetch.

I'd be in my Blooming Room, twisting willows to

nail onto beaver-gnawed sticks to make a chair—okay, a *really* strange-looking chair. And all the while I'd be wondering, *What would it be like* not *to see the lights? Would night be as dark as black ink if you couldn't see the light from your own body or the soft glow of the dog sleeping beside you?*

Do we all make up our minds about people based on the lights that surround them? What if you just saw a body and not the colors rippling and flashing around it?

But how would people know to be wary if they couldn't see warning signs like flashing red lights or dark clouds building up or yucky pea-soup green swirling around certain people? By intuition, I supposed . . . Though even I didn't always act on what I saw. Like with that rancher Mam had worked for at her last job. I'd seen the way his lights reached out like tentacles to touch her as if he were an octopus and she a little fish. I knew I should've warned her about him, but I'd kept my mouth shut because she'd needed the job.

I felt my face turn red. I'd also wanted to just stay *put*. I'd had more than one reason for keeping my mouth shut.

I grabbed my hammer and pounded so hard that the willow sticks I was nailing together split right in two. I grabbed more sticks out of the pile beside me and, using the big garden cutters, cut them to size. I tossed the broken sticks into my trash heap and sat staring at the bits of willows and slivers of bark and sawdust and bent nails.

I'd seen how I could change the colors of the light coming out of my hands, and how I could make the lights brighter. Or not. It amazed me, the lights I was now able to see. But it was scary, too. Bad thoughts seemed to reach out the same way that good ones did. If love reached out to touch a loved one, would hate do the same? And jealousy? Anger? Sadness?

I thought of Mr. McCloud and his nice, bright rainbow lights. Some lights I was drawn to like a moth. Others I tried to steer clear of. Like that blustery man who'd blasted into the trading post.

All of a sudden I remembered. A drawing. I couldn't have been quite five when I'd done it.

I dropped willow sticks and hammer—*clunk*—on the floor, then sprinted up to my attic. I reached under my bed and pushed my just-in-case box aside, making the cans in it rattle. I yanked out my suitcase. In a pocket inside the lid I kept my old journals—six packets of them, each tied with a blue ribbon. I grabbed the lot up and dumped them all on my bed. I picked up the packet holding the two most tattered journals.

It'd been years since I'd untied the ribbon and leafed through them. I'd been hardly more than four when I first started drawing in a journal. Mam had encouraged me to keep at it, and I had. They were filled with squiggly drawings, with tattered leaves and crushed flowers and old rodeo tickets Scotch taped into them. I shuffled through the pages till I found what I'd been looking for—the memory that'd been hiding away in the back of my mind.

The picture I'd been looking for showed a pair of

cowboy boots with stars on their heels. For someone not quite five I'd put a lot of work into drawing the spurs and the fancy stitching on the sides of the boots and their sharp pointed toes. Near the top of the page, the boots were cut off by a long wavy line. On the floor beside the boots was a bottle turned on its side. Angry-looking black and red scribbles covered the rest of the page up to the wavy line and past it.

"Oh no," I whispered.

It was the view I'd had from under the bed. The cowboy boots, partly hidden by the bedspread. The bottle pointing under the bed at four-year-old me hiding there.

It all came back in a rush, as if the picture I'd drawn carried its own scary light. How I'd heard the bottle rolling across the wood floor and the boots stomping and my mom's voice crying, "Don't! Please don't!" And even though I'd squeezed my eyes shut I'd still seen through closed eyelids the red flashes of light and it was all jumbled together with my mom's soft crying as the boots stomped and the door banged with a whoosh of air that'd sent moth wings and dust bunnies flying.

The thing about memories you've blanked out is that there must've been a really good reason why you'd done that. I almost didn't want to turn any more pages. But I did, and I grinned when I saw what I'd drawn.

A bed again. Another little me, but this time a smiley face peeking out of the covers, along with the round teddy-bear face of old Grub. A tall, sticklike man stood by the bed with his arms stretched up over his head. I'd drawn zigzags of blue coming out of his hands and his head was lit up like a bright yellow lightbulb.

It was my dad telling me stories. I'd drawn this after the one he'd told about how I was so special that the whole country of France celebrated my birthday. On my birthday everyone danced in the streets and the night would be lit up with fireworks. Then he'd jump up and excitedly throw out his arms, shaking his fingers and dancing about to show firecrackers exploding up in the sky. I'd seen sparkly lights flicking out of his hands and I'd laughed at his magic.

I flipped the page. A tall stick-figure man with a black hat stood with both hands held out toward a big red shape with four legs that must've been meant for a horse. I'd taken a green crayon and made the hands green, and scribbled green and yellow all around the man and the horse. I must have watched him work on a horse and seen light shooting out from his hands.

I sat on my bed for the longest time feeling all soft and open, like a turtle that had suddenly lost its hard shell. Had I had any idea what I was drawing back then? Because it was only now, since the lights had come back so much more brilliantly, that the drawings made any sense.

Somehow, almost every afternoon I found some excuse to climb up to my tree. Shawn never showed up. I always felt just a tiny bit disappointed.

My tree bloomed, and not just with buds, though it was

loaded with greenish blue berries. It bloomed with the feathers from a crow and a great horned owl and the tiny skull of a chipmunk. It blossomed with long blue ribbons and a tuft of antelope hair and a fossil shell found in the creek, and with some strange shiny oval-shaped stones that I'd found on the hill where I got the clay to make chink.

Each time I climbed the hill as warily as if I had antennae poking out of my head feeling about for what might be lurking or hiding up there. No matter that Stew Pot always ran ahead. How could I depend on a dog who wouldn't warn me if a certain someone was there?

I could always feel the energy of the tree before I got to it. Then one late afternoon I felt something *other*. I crept up, keeping low to the ground.

I saw a hand reach out of the dark shadows of the tree. The hand glowed. It touched a blue ribbon and then fell back into the shadows.

Was Shawn purposely hiding to startle me? I scowled at Stew Pot, who sat panting in the shadows beside him.

I stopped creeping around and marched over. Shawn didn't say hello. He glanced at the ribbon and then at me. His silence only made me feel cranky. Pot's sickly sweet grin didn't help.

Well, okay, and hello to you too, I thought.

"So what is it?" I asked huffily, still out of breath from my climb. "You mad about me trespassing or sticking stuff in the tree, or what?"

Shawn looked startled by my outburst, but he just blinked and lifted one shoulder like, "Take your pick."

I turned away and stared down at the ranch. Behind me I heard him say, "Maybe I just don't like whi—" He stopped.

I spun. "What is it you don't like?" I asked, staring straight into his eyes. "Whining girls? Or *white* girls? White *people*?"

Shawn looked me in the eyes too. "Maybe all three," he said. "It's a problem I'm working on."

"Well, maybe I don't like Indian boys. I've never known one before, so I don't really know," I said.

"I like your dog," Shawn said, his voice very serious, as if this was important. He reached down to scratch Pot's ears just as Pot stuck out his paw.

"Well, my dog's pretty particular. I can't figure out why he likes you. Up till now I thought he was smart."

I blew the hair off my forehead. How was that for a great start? Well, he hadn't exactly been friendly, but my own lousy humor hadn't helped. And it *was* his turf I was trespassing on.

Shawn stepped out of the shadows and, I couldn't help it, I stared. He wore an electric-blue shirt and he glowed like he'd gulped down a star. I watched the show of bright yellow flashing in the colors dancing around him. He had lots of thoughts floating about.

He took a few steps away from me toward the rim. For a moment I thought he was going to hop over and leave, but he turned back and cocked his head and looked at me as if I presented some kind of problem. He kicked a rock around with his boot, then picked it up and tossed it from one hand to the other.

"You live in the big house," he suddenly said. It wasn't a question.

"Yeah, I do," I nodded. "The house hadn't been lived in for several years."

"It'll be three years come August. I know. My aunt used to live there. I did too, for a while."

My eyebrows shot up. He could've said he'd just come down from the moon and I wouldn't have been more surprised. For once I didn't know what to say. "Wi—with your aunt?" I stammered. "You *did*? Why?"

Shawn grew very still. "Because she was married to Mr. McCloud," he said.

I shook my head to clear it. "But . . . why were you with your aunt instead of your mother?" I asked, mystified.

Shawn clenched the rock in his fist. "I don't usually talk about this kind of stuff. Don't ever, actually." He lowered his eyes and then looked straight at me. "But since you asked, my mom had problems. Still has. Drugs. Drinking too much. The usual. So she handed me over to her sister Rose soon after I was born. It's the Indian way. Nothing unusual about that. And later, when my aunt married Mr. Mac and moved here, I came along too."

"So what happened?"

"Nothing. One day she just left."

"Just *left*? Why? Where'd she go? She and Mr. Mac—were they . . . ?"

"I thought they were happy. I guess everyone did. At least till she took off with a sculptor from up on the Crow Reservation in Montana."

"Cripes," I said. "A sculptor. What does he sculpt?" As if that mattered one bit, but I was so flustered I hardly knew what to say.

Shawn shrugged. "Buffalos. Bears. Big stuff. Indian warriors on horseback. Bronzes. Museums are buying them up."

"It must've been really hard on Mr. Mac," I managed to say. "No . . . no wonder he's kind of abandoned the house."

"Yeah," he said.

"And your dad? What about him?" I wanted to know.

"I never knew him. He was in an accident before I was born."

"I . . . I'm sorry," I said, feeling the words as I said them. At least I still had a dad, even if he wasn't around. I thought a moment. "But why aren't you with Rose now, up in Montana with the sculptor?" I asked.

"Because," he said, his voice husky, almost a whisper. "Not long after she married Mr. McCloud, well, my grandpa died. So she handed me over to my grandma. My grandma's not well. I help her take care of her cows. And sometimes I go stay with my other grandma or my uncle at the fort or my relatives who ranch out by the Owl Creeks."

I plopped down on the ground and hugged my knees to my chest. Shawn crouched on his heels. I felt like I should give something back in return.

"My dad took off, same as Rose," I said, feeling my voice get all flat. "Only I don't know the reason why he left. I was almost five. He sent a few letters saying he was coming back, but he never did. It's been a long time now since we've heard from him. 'Course my mom hasn't exactly made it easy. She changes jobs about every two months. And I know something about alcohol problems too. My dad's got one, I think, or at least he used to, and my mom has to be really careful because if she takes one little drink she's hooked. . . ."

My babbling trailed off. We sat there, two kids and a dog on a hill. Grown-ups could really complicate things. Mess up your life real good if you let them.

I picked up a rock. Shawn did too. I sat staring at mine while he tossed his from one hand to the other and then lobbed it over the hill. Mine was pinkish white, sparkly, and way too pretty to throw. I tossed it to Shawn. He snatched it, examined it, and stuck it into his shirt pocket. Then he nodded at me and stood up.

"That antelope fawn," he said. "She okay?"

I got up too, brushing off my jeans and pushing my hair out of my face. I tucked the wisps under my cap. "She and her mother are both fine," I said. "I'm worried though. I don't know if I should let the fawn out yet. Its leg doesn't seem to have gotten much better. What about the wolves? They still around? Did they get any more of your grandma's cows?"

"They got one of her dogs. That's what I came here to tell you. Watch out for your dog." He reached out, gave

Pot's ear a tug, and walked to the ridge. Pot trotted after him. At the edge of the hill Shawn nodded at me and then put one hand on the rocky ledge and hopped over.

I watched as he loped down the steep, rocky back side of the hill. He had a chunky way of running, his feet hitting the ground hard, not light-footed at all. Rocks tumbled down to where his horse waited. Again the horse trotted to meet him, and he climbed on. As they galloped off Shawn looked back over his shoulder.

"Catch you next time," he called.

Mam was already eating, an encyclopedia on the table beside her. She barely looked up when Stew Pot and I burst through the door. The kitchen smelled suspiciously of onions and garlic and something else. I pinched my nose.

"Stew's on the stove. Elk meat. It was in the freezer down at the cookhouse. Don't worry, it's mostly potatoes and carrots," she said, and bowed her head again over her book.

"I made a friend, sort of," I said, spooning the veggies into my bowl while trying to steer clear of the meat. "An Indian boy I bumped into up on the hill."

I didn't mention that I'd run into him twice before and that he hadn't exactly been friendly. Or that he didn't like white girls, or whining girls, or white people, or whatever.

"Oh? That's good." Mam put a finger on her place and looked up. "I'm glad you found a friend. I didn't think there was anyone around here for miles. And miles and miles . . ." She smiled. "He live around here? What's his name?"

"Shawn, and I think he must live south or east of this place. His grandma has cows out on the tribal lands and he looks after them."

"Sounds like a nice kid," she said. She stuck her nose back in her book

I took a bite of stew and pushed a hunk of meat to one side of my mouth. I held the lump in my cheek. Pretended to swallow. Coughed and spit the lump into my napkin. It's a trick that never works. Mam looked up and frowned.

So without thinking I burst out with the news.

"I also found out that Mr. Mac was married to Shawn's aunt. Her name was Rose, and she used to live here in this house. They must've been fixing it up, painting and making the house bigger by adding on to it. You know what? I bet they were planning to have a baby, because that's what that other bedroom with the half-finished mural and those paint cans in it would've been for. And then she just up and left him"—I snapped my fingers—"like *that*."

Mam put her hand to her head as if something heavy had fallen out of the sky and hit her. "How awful," she said. "He must've been so . . ." She let the words trail away.

Heartbroken, I thought. Of course she knew how Mr. Mac had felt. I remembered how, after my dad went away, the silence had grown until it filled the room and then our whole universe.

"I don't know . . . ," she said, staring up through the ceiling and out to someplace far beyond it.

I stirred my bowl of stew, lifting a spoonful of the mush of brown potatoes and carrots, eyeing it suspiciously. I couldn't think of any words to fill up the long silence without making things worse.

"It hasn't been easy, living here," she finally said. "The worst part is that we're so far off the road and, except for that boy you just met, you don't have any friends. I wouldn't want to just run out on Mr. McCloud, leave him in a fix, but I don't know. . . . This place somehow just seems so . . . sad."

"But it's been a long time," I said, my words tumbling over each other now in their rush to get out. "Almost three years since the house had been lived in, that's what Mr. Mac said."

"I don't know . . . ," Mam said again. She put her elbows on the table and her face in her hands.

"But I do," I said. "I'm sure of it. I'm already fixing up the log addition. Next time Mr. Mac comes out, we'll surprise him." *If only he'll come in,* I thought to myself.

Another silence filled the room. My mom's rough hands fiddled with the pages of her book—the old, out-of-date encyclopedia she studied so hard, trying to make up for the schooling she'd missed. A lump grew in my throat that had nothing to do with the stew.

"We'll stay till you finish what you're doing. After that, I can't promise. It all depends on . . ." She bit her lip. "Never mind," she said.

Depends on what? I wondered. Mr. McCloud? Her own loneliness? Or the possibility that my dad might miraculously find us? Or was it just that we'd about reached the end of her staying point, the time when she almost automatically started to think about moving on.

I slipped my bowl under the table. Pot cleaned it up. I made me a peanut butter and banana and honey sandwich and took it up to my room. It was my favorite thing in the world. Comfort food, Mam always called it.

Chapter Seventeen

That night I woke to the sound of cows mooing and stirring about. I ran to the window to see what was disturbing them, but clouds hid the sliver of moon. Nothing howled, nothing cried out, so I slipped back into my dreams.

I woke before sunrise and crept barefooted down to the kitchen. No Stew Pot, no Mam. I figured they'd already gone out. I grabbed my radio and headed for the log add-on and turned on the light.

Rising from the scraps of beaver-peeled sticks and river willows stood two rickety chairs and a small table. The table hardly wobbled if I propped it up in a corner. There'd been four chairs, but the first two had collapsed.

No wonder. It wasn't as easy as I'd thought, making furniture. Especially trying to get all four legs to touch the ground, and making it strong enough to actually use. The hardest thing was trying to keep things more or less square.

I thought I'd weave some feathers into the backs to

pretty them up, and some treasures too, like a few white bones or some of those shiny smooth stones from the hill where I got my chink. I still had a lot to do.

And the chinking was really coming along, although you could tell where I'd started, not sure of what I was doing, and where I'd finally more or less figured it out.

I slopped water into my purple-clay-bits-of-straw-chink-mix and stirred. Only half a wall left to do! But why hurry? We'd stay at Far Canyon until I finished the room. That's what Mam had said, right?

I should take my time, then. We'd been here six weeks plus a day—but then, who was counting? I wondered if not wanting to let Mr. Mac down was enough to make her stay on. "It all depends," she'd said. "No promises." Each time we'd left in the past, she'd given me not one word of warning. I knew better than to count on promises. Frankly, I'd thought she'd been really lucky to get this job like she had, and if I'd been her I'd have hung on to it tight as I could. It was a wonder any ranch ever hired her, what with no references and no recommendations at all. Sometimes, from the sideways glances we got when she drove into a ranch looking for work, I suspected the word had been passed along that she was a fantastic hand but not one to be depended on for the long haul.

I wiped at the dribbles on the line of chink I'd just finished. On the radio the flute music stopped and a steady fast drumming started. I threw down my trowel and skipped barefooted outside. The sun was just peeking over the hills and the sky was the color of raspberries.

"Wake up, world!" I shouted. "It's the summer solstice, the first day of summer, and the longest day of the year!"

"Part of the world has already been up for hours." It was my mom, tromping around the corner of the house wiping her forehead with her sleeve and looking as if she'd already done a day's work.

"We've got a fence down," she said. "I've already put out six strays and brought back a few of our own that got out. I put them in at a gate, but I suspect the break's up at the top of that hill." She pointed toward the hill where I'd found the clay for my chink. "Get your chores done and we'll head up there. I'd like to ride but that's not a hill for a horse."

Pretty quick we were winding our way up the hill, me clutching fencing pliers and a sack of staples and Mam hoisting a small roll of barbed wire and the stretchers. I'd never climbed this hill. Trees lined the top of it, but on the side nothing grew. It looked like a moonscape with its steep twisted slopes and purple-and-cream-colored clay. I skipped ahead, drumming a tune on the staple sack with my pliers.

"You look like you're floating on a cloud," Mam said as she scrambled up the hillside behind me.

And I was. I was in heaven, up here in the Winds, as these mountains are called, as if they're some wispy place in the sky.

"Always do some detective work when you're out fixin' fences," I said when we got to the top and spied the downed fence. By the look of the hair in the wires and the scat, a big herd of elk had passed through.

I whistled and Mam hummed while we worked, while Stew Pot sniffed about trying to scare up some rabbits and chipmunks. We gathered up the broken ends of the wire and spliced them together. I handed Mam staples and she hammered them into the wood posts as we tightened the drooping wires. We strung out more wire where the old fence couldn't be mended. The sun scooted halfway up the sky and then seemed to sit there, not moving. All around us the world glistened and glowed.

We got the job done and were halfway down the steepest part of the hill, checking the fence that ran practically straight up and down, when I suddenly stopped. I looked around at the ground and then pried out two staples from a wood post and loosened two wires instead of making them tighter.

Mam glared at me as if I'd lost my mind. "What on *earth* are you doing?" she asked.

I pointed to the bare earth. A trail used by wild animals passed along the steep hillside and then under the fence. "I'm just making it easier for the animals to get through," I said.

"We've got a fence that didn't need fixin' and here you've taken it apart."

"But the trail here glows!" I said. "Don't you see the way this trail is *different*?" A hazy line of light floated on top of the trail like the silky thread of a spider, only thick and gauzy and the color of a smoky crystal. It stretched out straight past my hill and on into the mountains. Other straight silvery trails joined with it, and they all met and formed a shimmering star. Other lines headed west and I lost them, though from a faraway canyon I could see light shining up from what appeared to be a huge star. Whatever these lines were, the animals knew about them because some of their trails closely followed the lines.

Mam scratched her head as she stared at the animal trail. "Can't see a thing," she said, "except for that fence you just mangled."

"It's like fairy trails across the landscape that meet up and make a big star. I don't know why I've never noticed them before," I said, waving my hand. "Maybe these lines can be seen only under special conditions. Maybe it's something about the light today on the summer solstice. . . ."

Mam rolled her eyes. "What I think is that you'd better fix that fence back like it was, young lady," she said.

Somewhere, I remembered reading about something called "ley lines." They were lines of energy that led to power centers, or to ancient sites. I stared at the place in the mountains where the lines all met up. If I never got to see them again, at least I'd remember the high pink sandstone cliff near where the lines formed a silvery star. A gray landslide scarred the pink cliff. In my head I marked where the star blazed up from the valley off to the west.

Now, even as I looked at them, the lines lifted and faded like fog in the sunlight.

That afternoon clouds gathered and hovered like spaceships over the badlands. Pot and me, we squeezed through the fence like old pros. It was late, but it was the longest day of the year. We had oodles of time before dark.

Ravens exploded from my tree as Stew Pot loped up the hill. I picked up their gift of a long blue-black feather and stuck it into my pocket. I had my feelers out for Shawn as I climbed, but they only picked up my tree. I was glad. Today I just wanted to sit on my hill and *think*.

I'd searched through the old encyclopedias and found out that the word "ley" was connected to light, or to a meadow open to the sun and therefore filled with light. It said that the ley lines were series of straight lines that linked all of the Earth's various landmarks into a network of ancient tracks. So I wasn't the only one who'd ever seen them. Maybe I really wasn't plumb out of my mind. . . .

The lines had reminded me of the bluish white light that streamed out of my fingers. As I'd loosened the fence wires up on the hill I'd noticed a faint, cool, smooth-feeling energy pushing up against my hands. So even if I could only see the lines when the light was just right, I figured I might be able to *feel* them if ever I wanted to explore this some more. Those lines had to mean something.

I sighed. For sure the lines led to special secret places. I'd probably never get to explore them, since all I'd seen just happened to be on Indian land. . . .

The ley lines were long. I wondered how far my own light could reach. I stuck out my hands and pointed my fingers toward the badlands. I concentrated as hard as I could on making my light stretch out farther and farther. After a while I could see the light from my hands stretching out in a line toward the horizon.

I was so intent on waving my hands about and watching the light that I didn't hear Shawn come up behind me.

"You doin' some kind of sign language?" he asked.

"Cripes!" I yelled. "You 'bout scared the living daylight outta me!" Then I slapped my hand to my forehead. Ohmygod! *Living daylight* was what I'd just seen!

"What kind of sign language was that?" Shawn asked.

"None of your business," I snorted. "Maybe I was just talking to the hills and the trees. Maybe I was signing to those alien spaceships hovering over the badlands."

Shawn didn't answer to that. He twisted his mouth in a smirk and reached down and scratched Pot's ears. Who of course acted as if he'd never gotten a pat on the head in his whole entire life.

"What do you do all day out in the hills when you're not busy sneaking up on people?" I snorted. "You and your horse. What's his name?"

"Tivo. We just ride. Look about." Shawn scratched at the dirt with the toe of his boot and then reached down and picked up a rock.

I picked one up too. We looked at each other. Shawn took a step toward the ridge and stretched his arm back. I did the same. He nodded, and we lobbed the rocks as hard as we could. They arced in midair and nearly collided and then hit the ground with just inches between them.

I reached up a hand and we hung a high five.

For some reason I could feel a happiness fill up inside

me. I swallowed it down and then asked in my most serious voice, "You look about. For what?"

Shawn shrugged. "Nothing. Well, okay, something." He scratched around for another rock. Swooped it up. "A rainbow, okay? I'm looking for a rainbow, if you gotta know."

"Oh, right. You're out there looking for rainbows. Of course. And a pot of gold, maybe?"

"I shouldn't have said anything. Forget it." He dropped the rock like a hot potato and turned and walked toward the ridge.

"Because," I said quickly to his back, "if you're looking for rainbows, I see them all over."

"Yeah, right," he said, and kept walking.

"Really. Like you, for instance. You're a rainbow. For such a grump you're amazingly bright."

But then he turned and stared at me. I could see him weighing this. Wondering if I was making fun of him, or what. "What do you see?" he asked.

"You really want to know?"

"I asked, didn't I?"

"Well, I see lights. Mostly around people, but they're everywhere—trees and rocks sending up fat waves of light. . . ." My voice trailed off. I'd never talked to anyone except my mom about them.

Shawn had gone still as a fence post. "Auras," he said. "You actually *see* them? You're kidding."

"I've always thought of them as just the 'lights.' They're everywhere. Seeing them is nothing special."

"The living daylight . . . ," Shawn said almost to himself.

I gave him such a big grin that my cheeks hurt. "That's exactly what I see. What do you know about it?"

"That's the name my great-grandmother gave me. 'Sees the Living Light.' But I don't. I don't see any kind of light, living or dead. She—" Shawn stopped.

I could sense that he was close to clamming up, so I made a big fuss about finding the right place to sit, trading a big rock for the ground and then for a twisted juniper root. Then I sat really still, just looking up at him.

Shawn lifted his shoulders and let out a huge breath. *"Whew,"* he said. "I've never talked about this."

"Well, me neither, so we're even," I said.

"Okay. My great-grandma," he said slowly, as if choosing his words very carefully, "she was a full-blood Shoshone who married an Irishman. She used to tell stories. Before she died, when I was six, she told me . . ." He stopped and sucked in his breath, as if he'd suddenly realized he was telling all this to a white girl. He searched my eyes.

"It's a long story, okay?" he went on. "So my great-grandpa was a white man, a sheepman, but also an amateur geologist and archaeologist. He and my great-grandma would go and camp out with their sheep. He'd climb and explore the mountains while she gathered herbs for her medicines. She knew all the plants, and what to tell people to take if they were sick. People would come from all over to see her. She could tell at a glance where they hurt and see what was wrong with them."

I nodded. "You probably won't believe this, but I can do a little of that too," I said. "See where there's a hurt place, I mean. I don't know a thing about herbs."

"I wouldn't tell you this if I didn't believe you," Shawn said.

I nodded. The silence grew until I could almost hear the grass growing.

"My great-grandma went places most of us don't," Shawn finally said. "The places where spirits live. We don't go there out of respect. White people go there because they don't understand or respect these places." He frowned at me, but I didn't say anything. I knew this was true.

"So she went with her husband, and he'd go exploring and sometimes they discovered things she'd later tell stories about. Sometimes she'd have dreams and see into the future. There was one story she told only to me. It was about my name. She said one day I would see the same way she did. But it wouldn't happen, she said, until I came to a certain place of power, a place of the spirits, she called it."

I was so stuck on his words my eyes must've been huge as an owl's. "So that's what you're looking for?" I asked.

"Yeah," Shawn said. "It's a rainbow. A petroglyph of one, actually. But even the elders don't seem to know of it, or if it really exists." He glanced quickly at me and then down at the ground. I could tell by the way his lights had flared and then shrunk back close to his body that already he was thinking he shouldn't have opened up like he had.

I didn't know what to say, all I knew was that I felt as if I'd been hit in the chest. I was half scared I'd cry.

Cripes, why'd I get snivelly at the least little thing? Actually, it wasn't little—it was huge, what he'd told me. For sure the biggest secret his heart held . . . I sniffed and wiped my nose on my sleeve.

A shadow had inched over us as we talked. The clouds over the badlands now looked like triple-decker scoops of peach ice cream.

"I'd better be gettin' back," Shawn said.

"Yeah, me too," I said.

I pulled the raven feather out of my pocket and held it up to him. "Ravens fly all over these mountains. They must know things we don't," I said. "I don't understand what this rainbow is that you're looking for, but if it's out there, you'll find it."

Shawn took the feather from my hand and studied it as if it really might hold some secrets. Then he carefully tucked it into his shirt pocket. He gave me a "thank you" kind of nod, scratched Stew Pot under the chin, and turned and walked to the ridge.

"Catch you next time," he said. "Friend."

Chapter Eighteen

Brandings don't just sneak up on you. I should've suspected something was up when I came down off the hill and found Mam practicing roping. She'd made a steer's head out of a tin can stuck on a stick and jammed into a hay bale. After supper she whipped up a batch of fresh, hot, melt-in-your mouth peanut butter cookies, handed me two, and packed the rest into a sack. But my head was so full of what Shawn and I had talked about on the hill that somehow none of this set off alarm bells.

So I was caught totally off guard when, first thing the next morning, Mam spouted out, "We're branding today."

I clomped my elbows on the table and screwed up my face.

"I didn't tell you last night," she said as she spooned out three bowls of oatmeal and put one on the floor. "I knew you wouldn't sleep if I did."

"Yuck," I muttered. In my head I was screeching, *No*

way! I've got plans! The beavers have gotten ahead of me—I've got dams to undo! The weeds are taking over the garden. I should clean up the mess in my room. And besides, this is the day I was going to let Light of the Dawn go. . . .

Not one bit of this hit the sound waves.

"Mr. McCloud is sending a crew, but an extra hand's always handy," Mam said into my thoughts.

I looked wildly around the kitchen as if some excuse to escape would pop out of a cupboard. Then suddenly out of nowhere I got this incredible thought. I could use *light* to heal things. Maybe I could be a veterinarian or a doctor one day . . . or maybe even something that doesn't yet have a label. It was almost as if I heard a voice booming out of the sky saying, "Okay, Blue Gaspard. Now's your chance. Get out there. Prove you can do it."

"Count me in," I said.

Mam's eyebrows shot up in surprise.

"But I've got a few things I've got to do first."

Her mouth twisted. She'd expected excuses.

"No, really, I've got to feed the calves and let the fawn out. . . ." I stopped. She was right. With my history, she knew I'd find a way to get there when they'd just about finished. The fawn could wait. The calves couldn't.

I whizzed out to the mudroom, dumped milk starter into the calves' bottles, dashed back, poured water into the bottles and shook. Pot's eyes zipped up and down with my hands—sometimes the nipple popped off and he got the spilled milk, but not this time.

"Don't be long. We'll be short-handed, I reckon.

Mac . . ." Mam didn't go on. She rinsed out her cup and carefully sponged off the counter and then picked up the sack of cookies. "He's bringing lunch for the crew," she finally said. "I'm taking these down for a snack. I'd better go saddle up." Her lights flushed the rosy pink color of sunrise as she slipped out the kitchen door. Pot padded after her, but she'd closed the door without even looking at him.

I rolled my eyes. "Now, don't go getting your feelings hurt," I said. "I can't remember when she ever lighted up like that just at the thought of someone."

I tried to picture lights the color of sunrise around her back when she'd been with my dad, but somehow all I could remember were the colors of dark rainy days.

But time was wasting. Even before I got to the pen I could hear Lucky Charm and Wonder Baby mooing, their noses already up to the gate. "It's a good thing you're not little bulls," I said as I sidestepped to keep from getting stomped on. "I'll cross my fingers that you're still too little to brand," I said when I closed my babies back up. But I knew I was kidding myself. They'd almost caught up with the other calves, and now I couldn't use Wonder Baby's broken leg as an excuse for her not to be branded. I only hoped Mr. Mac would come up and not send one of his men to brand them.

I ran back to the kitchen and carefully rinsed out the bottles. I should wash the breakfast dishes too.

I took a deep breath. I'd have to face it. There was no getting around it. Somehow I'd get through the branding.

I'd try really hard to do a good job, even if it was just carrying a bucket.

The cows had already been rounded up and the calves sorted when I got to the corrals by the barn. The bawling calves, and the cows left with them to help settle them down, stirred around in a holding pen that'd been set up beside the corrals. Three horses stood pawing the ground, their reins tied to a horse trailer hitched to a pickup. I didn't see Mr. Mac's big diesel truck.

I climbed over the high corral fence and hopped down beside a man who was crouched over, scratching both knees. He slowly unfolded, putting one hand on a knee and the other on a hip as bit by bit he stood crookedly up. I wasn't surprised to see spurts of light streak out from all sorts of places. I was pretty sure there was hardly a space on his battered old body that hadn't been busted or broke.

"Mornin'," he said. He tipped a hat that looked as if it'd been run over by a herd of stampeding cattle. "I'm Slim John Aikens."

He jerked a hand missing half a thumb at a man who limped across the corral. "And that's Jakey Jones," he said. Jakey turned and waved at me. He was almost but not quite as crooked and sparkly as Slim John.

"And that there"—Slim John gestured toward a younger cowboy checking out the propane burner he'd set up near the loading chute—"that there's Dingo Malone." Dingo smiled over at me and then stuck two branding irons on the fire. He stood back as he watched them get yellowy hot. A bucket stood next to the burner. Beside it was a long red wooden medicine box.

"I'm Blue," I said. "Blue Gaspard." I stuck out my hand.

Slim John grabbed hold of it. "Gaspard, did you say? Is that French?"

I nodded. Everyone's eyes swerved to my mom on her horse, watching every move as she carefully coiled her rope.

Slim John squinted at my mom. "Jakey and me, we thought we'd be ropin'. Boss said he had a good hand up here. Girl help, he said. Didn't know she could rope like a man."

"Yeah, and probably better," I said, a little sharply.

"Myself, I lost that ropin' a steer." Slim John held his hand up for me to inspect. "Thumb caught in a rope when I dallied up. Danged if it didn't get plucked up by a magpie before it hit the ground."

"Gee, thanks," I said. I managed a smile as Mam built a loop. She and her horse moved quietly through the calves. They sidled up to a calf. Quick as a frog snitching a fly on its tongue she tossed the loop, roped the calf's spinning hind legs, twisted the rope around the horn of her saddle, and dragged the calf toward the fire.

Slim John was muttering to himself. "Dang it. Gaspard," I heard him say. "Now, where'd I hear that?"

"Huh?" I blurted. A sudden cold feeling crept up from my boots to the back of my neck. I reached out to grab his arm. But Jakey was waving his hands at us. "Quit your gabbin' and git over here," he yelled, and Slim John winked at

me and darted off, spritely in spite of his limps. Everyone scrambled, Slim John plunking down on the ground and grabbing the calf's front legs while Jakey tackled the back ones. The calf bellowed and banged its head on the ground and Dingo got out his knife.

The calf was a male. I swallowed and ran for the bucket.

"Can you vaccinate too?" Dingo called after me. "We're short on help."

"Sure thing!" I tried to make my voice sound—well, *sure.* I'd watched my mom doctor calves. Mostly I'd turned my head when she gave them their shots, but if I was going to be a veterinarian, I'd have to learn how to do this. Right?

I flipped open the medicine box, grabbed a syringe, stuck the needle in the bottle of vaccine, pulled back the plunger, filled it, and dashed back to the calf. Slim John noticed the look on my face as I knelt beside him. My heart pounded so hard I was sure he could hear it.

"I lied," I said under my breath.

"Just pinch the skin up here, under the front leg," he said out of the side of his mouth. He held tight as the calf struggled. "Go ahead," he said. "Quick while I got a good hold."

I took a deep breath, jabbed, and squished the plunger. With everything else going on the calf hardly noticed. I let out my breath and gulped my thanks toward Slim John, but already Dingo was slicing into the tender underside of the calf. I reeled back, remembering I was bucket boy too.

I grabbed the bucket and held it by Dingo's hands as he squeezed the calf's flesh. I swung the bucket and set it on the ground as Dingo pulled the 2M brand out of the fire. The calf bawled and struggled to kick as, with a twist of the iron, the red-hot brand scorched its hide. Slim John yelled, "Hang on, hang on," while Jakey muttered, "Ol' man, I got as good a hold on it as you do."

With smoke and dust everywhere I felt sure no one would notice if I held my hands over the scorched patch on the calf's side. By the way its lights changed, I sensed it didn't hurt quite so much. Beside me Slim John was saying, "Git on there, little critter," and the two wrestlers let the calf go.

Mam had already neatly roped the next calf. I knew I could get through this next one. And the next and the next and the next.

Slim John never stopped chatting. He'd squint and tell me to pinch up that skin a bit tighter. Then, "Gaspard," I kept hearing him mutter. "Gaspard."

Suddenly, just as I was about to give a shot, his watery blue eyes peered up into mine.

"Got it!" he said. "Now I remember!"

Inside I was like a thermometer rising and falling. Hot. Freezing cold. Hot again.

"Pinch that skin up," Slim John said, but my hand and my brain had stopped working.

"Do it," Slim John said, and I jabbed and squeezed the plunger. Reeled back and grabbed the bucket. Held my hands over the calf's burned spot. Shook off the burning sensation. No time to talk. Just the numb feeling inside me. And the questions. *What do you remember? Who? Where?*

And then suddenly Mr. Mac was there, rushing to take Slim John's place wrestling calves. I noticed how his lights flickered rosy pink as Mam breezily roped a big calf.

I absolutely will not *snoop on their lights*, I said to myself. I tucked my head down so I couldn't see them.

"Look's like you've got a real knack givin' shots," Mr. Mac said. I gave him a lopsided smile.

Lopsided. That's how I felt. Partly tipped forward, dying to know what Slim John had to say, although deep inside I was sure I knew. Partly tipped backward, wanting—*this.* To be right here, right where I was, even if it was helping with branding. For nothing to change.

The rest of the branding passed in a blur. It was almost noon when we finished.

Slim John sank down on the back of the trailer and tugged off a boot. "Ol' foot's drivin' me crazy," he said as he tried to wiggle his toes. They lay in his sock still as a rock-hard dead fish.

Without a concern for what he would think, I kneeled and cupped his old toes in my hands. *Please may Slim John's foot be healed* ran through my head. Then, as if I had opened a door to bright sunshine and let the light flood right through me and into Slim John's old toes, I saw the dark reddish black lights around his toes change. After a few minutes I let go of his toes and looked up at him.

Slim John's watery blue eyes met mine. He wiggled his toes. "Well, I'll be," he said. "That was quite a foot rub you gave me. I swear these ol' toes already feel better." He reached down and bent his toes back and forth. "Couldn't do *that* before," he said, now peering at me as if I were some kind of really strange critter. "Thank you."

"Thank *yourself*. Slim John," I said, "what was that you were saying about . . . well, about my name? Gaspard. You said you remembered. What?"

"Oh, that. Well, I was just tryin' to recall where I'd heard the name. Not too long ago, either. Met a man in a bar, quite a talker he was. Had a bit of an accent."

"Where? When?" I could barely get the words out, barely breathe.

"Well, let's see. The bar. Now it might've been in Lander or maybe it was Riverton. Could've been Dubois. Easy to get things a bit mixed up. Can't say rightly, but it weren't too long ago."

"And the name . . . did the man say his first name?"

"Can't rightly recall. 'Gaspard' just sounded familiar. Get to be my age, things sift through the ol' brain like it's got holes."

"Thank you," I whispered.

My world tilted. It wasn't much to go on, but more than I'd dared hope for—an actual, real-life sighting! Maybe . . . But could I depend on an old man's memory? I walked slowly back and gathered up the used medicine bottles and all the shot stuff. One of Mam's rules was to always tidy up neat when you'd finished a job.

I couldn't trust something like this to chance. Still holding a syringe, I ran back to where Slim John sat tugging his boot on. He looked up. "I really don't need a shot," he said. "That rub got the cricks out."

"No, great, listen, there's something I'd like to ask of you." The words tumbled out. "About that man with the same name as ours. If by chance you see that man again, maybe you could say something about us living up here?"

Slim John looked startled by my outburst. "Why, sure . . . ," he said.

"Thank you," I whispered, and ran back to finish my job. Halfway there I stopped and yelled back, "Promise?"

Slim John tipped his hat. He pointed to his hair. "Same color," he mouthed.

Same color? His hair was almost pure gray! I shook my head at him. Really, he was losing it. I started to run back to question him, but already Mr. Mac was standing by the medicine box, lifting it, and carrying it to his truck.

"Good, our shot giver!" he said when he saw me come running up with the syringe still gripped in my hand. "We'll give those bums of yours their vaccinations, but, what with that broke leg and them being preemies, I doubt they'll be big enough to brand. Let's have a look, shall we?"

I nodded dumbly and followed him to his truck. Here I'd been, daydreaming about Mr. Mac coming up to see what a good job I'd done. But now I wondered, *Have I done too good a job with the calves? Please don't change your mind when you see them!*

Stew Pot eyed the free ride. Mam had snapped her

fingers and pointed to the ground when she rode off to check the calves we'd let back into the fields with their mothers. They didn't need a dog doggin' them, she'd said. Not after what they'd been through. So I let down the tailgate. Stew Pot jumped up but didn't quite make it. I gave him a boost. Not long ago he'd have been able to jump up on his own.

"You okay, Blue?" Mr. Mac asked as I climbed into the cab and leaned back and squeezed my eyes shut.

"Just . . . tired, I guess," I said, my voice shaking a little. I should've been thrilled that I'd just gotten through a branding with flying colors. I should've been floating on air with the thought that my dad might be out there, somewhere, not too far away.

What on *earth* was the matter with me?

"Anything I can do?" Mr. Mac's big calloused hand touched my knee. "Things goin' all right?"

I tried hard to keep them back. Why did tears seem to have minds of their own? "Don't know why I'm carrying on so," I muttered, brushing my cheeks with both hands. "I've never been so happy. Never in my whole life. Everything's perfect."

"Sometimes we cry when we're mixed up about things. I'm like that whenever I come out here. It's my favorite place in the world, and yet . . ." Mr. Mac's words drifted off. "Happy-sad, I guess that's how I feel," he said.

"Yeah. That's it exactly," I said, my voice barely a whisper. I wished I could tell him what was the matter, but I couldn't understand it myself. And I wished I could ask him about what'd happened with Rose, but I knew from experience that asking questions about stuff like love got you totally nowhere.

We bumped up the road to the house and sat while the dust rose around us and then settled back down. I don't have any idea how long we sat there, both of us lost in our thoughts. In the meadows, the mother cows mooed comforting sounds to their calves. The horses nickered. Crows cawed. The wind and creek mixed up their sounds. Everything was *perfect*.

"I'm okay now," I said at the same exact time as Mr. Mac asked, "You okay?" He grinned. "Well, let's get those calves of yours checked out, shall we?" He lifted the medicine box from the back of the truck and helped Stew Pot out while I unlatched the gate to the pen.

"Lucky Charm! Wonder Baby!" I called, but they'd already scurried over to slather me with slobbery kisses.

"Don't believe I've ever seen such grand calves," Mr. Mac said as he set the box down. He scratched his chin. "Now, which one had the broken leg?" He felt both calves' front legs. "That's strange. I honestly can't tell which calf it was." He felt all four front legs again. "I give up. Which calf was it?" he asked.

I pointed.

He carefully felt Wonder Baby's leg again. "Not a bump anywhere. Miss Blue, that's amazing. . . ." He smiled down at me.

Me, I was beaming so brightly that for a moment I

could see my own lights flash against the dark shadows in the back of the pen. I saw my lights come back closer to my body as he put his fists on his hips and studied the calves.

Was he thinking they were big enough to be branded?

"What if . . ." He paused and put a hand on my shoulder. "What if we just gave them their shots and an ear tag?" He opened the box and pulled out two small purple tags. "We could print their names on the tags, along with the 2M." He handed me a black marking pen and the tags.

I beamed up at him. *Lucky Charm,* I wrote on one tag. *Wonder Baby,* I squeezed onto the other. On the other side I put the 2M. Then I reached for a red marking pen and around each brand I drew a red heart.

"Earrings," I said.

"Won't that be pretty?" Mr. Mac's eyes twinkled. "Okay, watch how I do this. See these veins in her ear?" He rubbed Lucky Charm's ear with a finger. "You don't want to hit one of those, so the key's in positioning it right."

I listened and watched. He gave the calves their shots and I paid close attention. I can honestly say that in one day I learned I could do stuff I never, *ever* believed I'd be able to do. If I hadn't been so muddled by what Slim John had told me I'd have been puffing my chest out with pride.

"Won't be long before they'll be wantin' to go play with their friends," Mr. Mac said as he packed the box back into his truck. "I've been worried about you not having friends close by. You can get pretty lonesome living out here. And your mom. She should have more of a life than just working from morning till night. I can tell she's been awful busy."

Down below, in the meadows, we could see my mom on her horse as she rode through the cattle, checking to be sure the calves were okay and that they were all mothered up.

"Yeah, she does keep busy," I said. "She's okay, though. She likes being her own boss. And I do have a friend. Sometimes I meet him up there." I pointed to the hill.

"Oh, you must mean Shawn Lightfoot. I think he's the only other kid livin' out this far. He's a good kid. Quiet, serious, slips about in the hills like he's on some kind of mission. His family, some of 'em are considered to be healers. One of his grandmas was pretty well known. I always figured that one day Shawn would follow along in her footsteps."

"Yeah," I said. To myself I said, *If only he doesn't get too discouraged. . . .*

"Of course, he could follow after one of his aunts, who's a tribal attorney, or an uncle who's a doctor, or—"

I cut him short. "Rose? Was she a . . . ?" I bit my tongue. "I'm sorry, I didn't mean . . ."

"No, that's okay," he said. "So Shawn must've told you something about what happened. But no, Rose . . ." Mr. Mac cleared his throat. "She was the artist of the family. A grand one too, least I thought she was. Evidently others thought so too."

"I can tell from the house, the way it's painted. The kitchen, the bedrooms . . ."

"Well, she didn't quite get it finished. Or *we* didn't . . . But you probably noticed the walls. They're pretty blank, except for that mural she'd started. When she left, she took all her paintings. They covered the walls. She did leave one painting behind. I have it at the ranch. It's hard for me to look at."

I swallowed. "All my dad left behind was his guitar."

Mr. Mac reached over and laid his hand on my shoulder. "Your mom never said anything, so I've never asked. But I kind of figured . . ."

I felt myself melting, as if his hand was a sponge sucking up sadness and hurts. We stood there watching my mom, not talking, listening to the sounds of crows and cows and the creek.

"Well, enough of this. Let's go eat," Mr. Mac finally said in a really soft voice.

"I can't," I said without thinking. "I mean, I've got something I've got to do."

Suddenly all I wanted was to be by myself. There was no way I could face Slim John's questioning glances, or just sit there and eat without smothering him with questions. And Mam would be close by.

No. Better to leave things as they were. I'd have to trust that Slim John would keep his mouth shut about what he'd told me.

Mr. Mac climbed into his truck. "Don't know how we'd get along up here without your mom," he said. As the motor revved up he tipped his hat and winked. "And without you, Miss Blue."

Chapter Nineteen

Soon as Mr. Mac drove off I wished I'd gone with him. I stumbled into the house feeling all prickly and raw. If anyone had even *looked* at me funny I think I'd have bawled. I grabbed a few slices of bread, opened a jar of peanut butter, and then stood staring into the jar as if it would magically jump onto my knife. One thought alone filled my head. *My dad has been seen somewhere close by.*

My hands shook as I fixed my sandwich and the next thought—the terrible one—washed through me.

And if he finds out we're here, will that ruin everything?

How could I even *think* those things? All I'd wanted for *years* was for my dad to come back. What on earth was the matter with me?

No way would my sandwich go down. I slipped it under the table for Stew Pot. He followed me up to my attic, where the two of us curled up in his beanbag. I fell asleep with him licking my ears.

It was midafternoon when I woke. From the window I noticed that the horse trailer that'd been parked by the barn was no longer there. I groaned. I should've gone down to have lunch with them. I should've asked Slim John more questions. Now I'd lost my one chance. . . .

Below me I could see the dark hole of the cabin doorway. I couldn't put it off any longer. It was time to let the fawn go.

As Stew Pot and I rounded the corner of the house Lone One came sprinting down from the hills. Without me saying a word, Stew Pot loped back and hunkered down beside the house. Lone One ignored him. He was something she'd gotten used to and wasn't the least bit afraid of. That was how she usually acted toward me.

But not this time. Her round eyes narrowed. Her neck ruff bristled. The white patch on her rump flared. She pawed the ground, lowered her head, and charged, slamming her head into my belly.

"Hey," I yelled as I skidded backward. "We're in this together, remember?"

Lone One tossed her head and butted again. Thank goodness the little black knobby horns on her head weren't big enough to do any harm! I knew that she could rise up and stomp me with her sharp pointed hooves. I spread my legs, trying to hold my ground as I fended her off with my hands.

Behind me I heard a low, rumbling growl. "No," I said loudly without taking my eyes off the antelope—the last thing I wanted was for Stew Pot to attack her!

Lone One took a step back.

"Stop!" I held my hands up in front of my chest. "Lone One, it's time. I'm letting your baby go."

The antelope gave a snort. She ducked her head, but this time her long slender black nose slid down my leg. She sniffed at my boots and then, with her nose going a zillion miles a minute with speedy quick huffs like a train chugging up a steep hill, she smelled her way back up my legs. Then she took a step back and studied me. I wondered what she saw: the faded, torn jeans, scuffed boots, and old T-shirt with the logo "Go Blue Jays." My sad greenish brown eyes and my tangled dark reddish brown hair. She stopped her high-speed sniffing and crinkled her nose. Her eyes changed, softening, it seemed, and she spun, grunted loudly, and sprang into the cabin.

My breath was coming in quick huffs too as I stepped to the doorway and watched the fawn nurse. I bit my lip. If only I'd had as much luck with the fawn's leg as I'd had with the calf's. Every day I'd stood by the window and imagined light healing her leg, but it hadn't seemed to do any good. Maybe some things just *were*, and no matter how hard you tried, no matter *what* you did, you couldn't change them.

Slowly I slid the old battered door away from the entry. Lone One's eyes hooked on to each movement.

"It's up to you to keep her safe now," I said.

I slipped over to wait beside Stew Pot. "You think of the fawn as one of your charges, don't you?" I whispered. "Like with the calves, you're Light of the Dawn's protector, her guardian angel. And mine . . ." Pot stiffened, and I looked up.

Lone One stood frozen in the doorway as if puzzled by the strange new hole.

One thing I was learning about antelopes—they kept track. If one tiny thing was out of place, Lone One noticed it. If I added a fresh bunch of sagebrush to the fawn's sleeping place, or if I'd left my cap or my gloves on the dirt floor, Lone One would freeze when she saw the new object. She'd stare for five or ten minutes before deciding if it was harmless. Sometimes it seemed as if she had the whole landscape memorized and stored up in her head.

So it was a while before she took a hesitant step outside and then crooked her head up as a shadow swept over the ground. A hawk circled above us. She kept her eyes glued to it until finally the hawk flew out of sight. Only then did she honk for her fawn to follow her out of the cabin.

Light of the Dawn blinked in the bright sun. She sniffed the ground and looked up at her mother as if asking a question. Suddenly she gave a stiff-legged leap into the air, but when she came down her leg wobbled and she almost fell. Her mother grunted and nudged her, the same way she had when she pushed her out of her birthing nest. Then Lone One took a few steps toward the hill. Light of the Dawn's little white rump flared as she saw her mother leaving. She looked at the cabin, then over at Stew Pot and me, and then hobbled off after her mother.

I watched the two antelopes walk slowly away. The fawn stuck close to her mother as they twisted their way through the sagebrush and up the hill toward the fence.

"Stay safe! Watch out for the wolves! Come back and visit! I looovvvve you!" I wailed as they slipped under the fence. Like two bronze statues, they stood looking back. Then slowly they drifted toward the ledge of the canyon where the fawn had been born. I watched till the big lonely spaces swallowed them up.

Stew Pot and I headed up to my hill. "You'll see them again—don't you *dare* cry," I kept muttering to myself as I climbed. If I'd looked up instead of down at the ground I would've seen Shawn standing at the top waiting for me. At least this time he wasn't sneaking about or hiding in the shadows of my tree.

"See you branded today," he said when I came up to him. He waved his hand toward the meadows. Even from up here you could tell, if you knew anything about cattle, that the calves weren't exactly frisking about through the fields.

"Yeah," I said. "Mr. Mac came out with a crew."

"I would've helped out if I'd known."

"Gee, thanks," I said, meaning it. "But I didn't know 'bout it till this morning. I have this thing about brandings. The smell, the hurt-looking lights—" I broke off.

"Guess that might be kinda scary. Or sad. Seein' auras around calves at a branding."

"*Uh-huh*. Sometimes I wish I didn't see so much. . . ."

Shawn grinned. "Here I'm wishin' I saw more. Wanna trade?"

I laughed. "Why don't we share, half and half. Here," I said. I held my hands out as if offering him an invisible platter.

Bursts of bright yellows flashed around Shawn's head while a burst of rosy pink showed up near his chest. But he didn't move, and after a few seconds I dropped my hands. I turned my head so he wouldn't see my eyes. The only sound was Stew Pot gnawing away at something that'd gotten stuck in his paw. I made a move toward Stew Pot, but Shawn beat me to it, kneeling and examining Pot's paw and then pulling out a prickly cactus spine. It wasn't till then that he spoke.

"I'd take it," he said, "if I could. I'm about to give up. I've looked everywhere for that place my great-grandma told me about." He gave me a crooked, sad smile. "It was just a story, anyway. When I was little, I thought all stories were true. This one, that whoever found the rainbow etched in the cliffs would be able to see rainbows, I believed. I still do, sort of. But maybe it's time I grew up and stopped believing that those stories were more than just something told to teach lessons."

"If I could help . . . ," I said lamely. "I mean, not that I know anything about any Indian places, or even what a place of the spirit might be."

I looked around at the huge space around us. I wouldn't have any idea where to start if it was my search. Maybe I'd just follow the strange lines of light, the ones that'd seemed to meet up in a star. The ley lines.

"Except," I said, my mind racing now. "I did see some pretty weird lines . . ."

Shawn broke in. "It's my own thing, you know? I don't ask for help, not even from my family or my uncle who's a medicine man."

"Then I'll just tell you what I saw. Take it or leave it. They were lines of light. They stretched from down there"—I pointed toward the badlands—"to up there, under that cliff, where they met in a big star." I gestured toward the pink sandstone cliff in the mountains behind us. "And other lines went over the hills and it looked like all those met up in a valley because even though I couldn't see where they joined, that star was incredibly bright."

Shawn sucked in his breath. "You're kiddin'," he said.

I shook my head.

"You're right on, then. Both those are places of power. The one over there"—he pointed to the cliff—"we'd usually stay away from—there's a big cave there. The other, I know what's there, but it's not a place you go unless you're asking for a vision or preparing for the Sun Dance. I've been there with my uncle. It's a place of very big medicine."

"Yeah, I could tell it was something really special," I said.

Shawn took a step back and looked at me. For some

reason I thought of Lone One, the way she'd sniffed me all up and down and then stepped back and studied me. Like with her, I didn't move.

"The petroglyph I'm looking for," he finally said, his voice so low I had to bend forward to hear, "maybe it's so old it's crumbled. Or maybe the weather wiped the rainbow away. Maybe it got chipped off by some artifact thieves. Whatever, I haven't been able to find it."

"Yet," I said.

"Right. Yet. Though it seems as if I've been searching for it all my life. Like it's all I ever wanted . . ."

I just bobbed my head up and down. I mean, what could I say? I knew a little bit about searching and that feeling of wanting something you can't quite put your finger on. That feeling you get in the middle of the night almost like when you're really hungry, only a hundred times bigger than that, and there's nothing, not a peanut butter sandwich or a hot fudge sundae or the biggest chocolate bar in the world that'll fill up that big, empty feeling.

As we stood on the hill the clouds seemed to blow through and around us. I shaded my eyes with my hand. Shawn's eyes followed mine.

"Your friend?" he asked.

I nodded. "I just let her fawn go. It's still lame. I hope the wolves don't—" I couldn't finish. Hoping was about all I could do now. Sometimes it seemed as if my life was just one big crossing of fingers.

"Wolves haven't bothered my grandma's cows again. The fawn'll be okay."

"Hope you're right."

"Yeah," Shawn said, "me too." He bent down and scratched Stew Pot's ears. I knew he'd stand and nod good-bye to me, and he did. Sometimes it seemed like we didn't need words. When he got to the ledge he stopped and looked back.

"I've got to go help my relatives for a while. Out there, by the Owl Creeks. Coupla weeks. But I'll catch you when I get back." He nodded again and hopped over the ledge.

I stood there already missing him.

Chapter Twenty

It's a wonder I got through the next three weeks without driving myself and Mam bonkers. Every time Stew Pot barked or the wind rattled the door, I jumped up to see if someone was coming. I don't know quite what I expected—my dad to come merrily driving up to our front door? Knocking politely, tipping his cowboy hat, and saying, "Excuse me, do I have the right address?"

But that wasn't what happened.

Nothing happened.

I stuck a calendar on the wall by my bed. I crossed off the days since the ninth of May when we'd come to the ranch. Every day I searched for signs that Mam had come to the end of her stay-in-one-place rope.

It staggered me how much she'd already done. The fences didn't lean crazily and the wires weren't all droopy and snagged, and the ditches all carried water—well, thanks a little to me and my beaver-dam project. We hadn't lost one single cow or calf to illness or anything else, and the barn probably hadn't been cleaner since the day it got built. And of course the house was now totally livable.

So what now? Would my mom figure it was time to pack up? What would happen if I told her my dad had been spotted close by?

No, I couldn't chance it.

Mam buzzed about full of her own private thoughts. I got more words out of Pot than her. At suppertime we turned the pages of our books and said "Please pass the salt" or "Would you like ketchup?"

When I worry I always seem to drop back into old habits. I stashed away a sack of flour and ten cans of tuna fish and three jars of honey and two cans of jellied cranberries. Just in case.

I searched through the bookshelves and carried piles of books up to my attic. There were so many I hadn't yet had a chance to read, like the ones full of stuff I'd never been taught at school. The ones telling the *other* side of the story. The ones from the viewpoint of the Indians instead of the white men. At night I couldn't turn off the movies running wild in my head.

But some nights Shawn rode into my movies. Those were silent, like the olden-day films before sound. He'd show up out of nowhere and beckon to me, and I'd follow him into mysterious rocky landscapes where we searched day and night for a rainbow.

The nights had turned almost as hot as the days. I

tossed in bed, fanning myself with my sheet. I kept the windows at both ends of the room wide open.

For three afternoons in a row, dark stormy clouds had built up over the badlands. In spite of the wild show of thunder and lightning, not one drop of rain touched the ground. Clyde the storekeeper had been right. Eight years of dry hadn't disappeared with one snowstorm. It was hard now to imagine all the snow we'd had back on that wintry day. I wished we could've saved a bit for later and spread it out like butter on this dry, burned toast of land.

Every afternoon Stew Pot and I sneaked through the fence. Each time I crossed my fingers, hoping that Shawn had returned from helping his relatives out by the Owl Creeks. But he hadn't—or else he was avoiding me. Maybe, I thought, maybe he was sorry he'd let me in on his secret. Maybe he'd decided I was too nosy prying out secrets he'd kept to himself until I fished them out of him.

I stuffed my tree full of wishes. Only my wishes were more like demands. Commands. Statements of fact. *My dad is coming,* I said. *He's on his way. I know he is. Thank you.*

On the thirteenth of July I crossed off the day on my calendar and hopped into bed. Tomorrow was the fourteenth of July. Tomorrow I'd be thirteen.

I pulled my journal and box of colored pencils off the chest by my bed and sat twisting my hair into knots. I picked out Metallic Violet and wrote, *To Papa.* The tip broke. I chose Electric Blue and started writing. Halfway through my poem I smashed that tip into the page. I finished the rest with True Blue.

Which was exactly how I felt. As if I was finally getting the truth out.

To Papa
I was four when you walked out the door.
"I'm going to get mustard," you said.
Must've stuffed your chaps and lariat ropes
Into the back of your truck, along with your
    spurs
And the silver-tipped saddle that wasn't yours;
    it was Mam's.
But you forgot your guitar,
Forgot Stew Pot and me.
Your lights that night, I remember them now
As sparkly red arrows darting out of dark gray.
I said, "Papa's gone off in a dark thundercloud."
I remember you calling me "ma petit Bleu"
And how I thought you said *blur*, like a smudge,
    a mistake.
I remember the way you pinched my cheeks
And said I was small as a mouse.
You were tall as a house, and your silver belt
    buckle
Shone like a star when I stood on your shoes and
    we danced

And when I rode on your shoulders I lifted the
    sky.
I was four when you walked out the door.
What can I say? We were out of Dijon.
But you forgot your guitar,
Forgot Stew Pot, Mam, and me.

Chapter Twenty-one

The fourteenth of July I lay in bed fanning my sheet up and down. It was hot, even with the windows wide open. The morning sun struck the peachy walls and turned my attic to gold. Downstairs the radio belted out an Indian song about fry bread.

"It's my birthday," I said. "I'm *thirteen*!" I shouted, expecting sloppy wet kisses. None came. I reached down to pat Stew Pot and stirred empty space. I'd been deserted. Mam had already gone out.

Well, no matter. It was my day, and she'd promised to take care of my chores. I stretched, thinking about how my dad had made such a big deal about the fact that I was born on the French Fourth of July, as if that somehow made me more French or more his daughter. But I wasn't going to think about him—no, today I'd just boot him out of my thoughts. I yawned. Maybe I'd stay in bed all day and catch up on my reading. Maybe I'd go sit on my hill and do nothing. Maybe I'd sleep in for once. I closed my eyes.

Thrummmp! Something crashed onto the floor. I bolted straight up. A rock? I kicked off the sheets and flew to the window.

There stood Shawn, looking up, aiming another rock at my window. "Wanna go lookin' for rainbows?" he called up.

I raked my fingers through my tangle of hair, grabbed the jeans and shirt I'd worn the day before, then tossed them aside and fumbled through the measly choice of clothes hanging in my closet. Suddenly I stopped. What was the matter with me? I'd never cared a hoot about what I wore. Was it because overnight I'd turned into a teenager? Or was it . . . ?

My heart did an actual cartwheel, as if it'd turned head over heels and dumped me in some curious, far-off place. I almost didn't want to go down the stairs. I almost couldn't wait. . . .

I threw on whatever and shot down the stairs. In the mudroom I stopped, twisted my hair up, grabbed my cap, screwed it down, tucked in my shirt, pulled it back out, took a deep breath, and stepped onto the porch.

"Catch!" Shawn pitched a rock at me.

I grabbed it and clutched it to my chest. Shawn had on black jeans and a T-shirt as white as his teeth. He was smiling. He glowed.

I examined the rock. Had he chosen it because it looked like a heart? I stuffed it into my shirt pocket, but it poked out like a pointed breast so I snatched it back out.

Shawn flashed a big grin. I about threw the rock back at him, but his face suddenly got all serious. "Think you can get the day off?" he asked. "I'll take you to some of the places where I've already searched. Then maybe the two of us can figure out where that rainbow is hiding. . . ."

"My mom's already gone off, but I'll leave a note. I'm sure she won't mind." I started to say it was my birthday, so getting out of chores was no problem. But I already felt so *birthday-ed*, so *gifted*, that I just flashed a huge smile and dashed back into the house. Honestly, my brain wasn't working. I should've invited him in, should've taken more time brushing my teeth and asking what he'd planned for the day, fixed a lunch or something, but I didn't. I hurried, scribbling a note saying, *Gone with Shawn. Be back late afternoon. Don't forget to feed my bums!*

I stared at the rock I'd put down on the table. It was almost perfectly heart-shaped. But maybe it was just what it was. A rock. And just because I was suddenly flooded with all kinds of new feelings didn't necessarily mean that Shawn felt the same way. . . .

I drew a heart on the note and stuck the rock on it. *She needs a token of love as much as I do,* I thought.

Shawn straddled the fence, then pushed one strand of barbed wire down with his boot and held up the top one so I could slip through. We didn't talk as we circled the hill, hiking along the ridge and heading toward the bowl-shaped valley. I wondered if he was thinking about the time when he'd yelled down at me for trespassing—when was it, about a month and a half ago? How on earth had I gone from being so furious at him to *this*? My heart pounding, my feet barely touching the ground, me practically *floating* on air just being next to him!

In my head I was chanting a prayer I'd found in a book I'd just read. *Where I walk is sacred, sacred is the ground. Forest, mountain, river, listen to the sound. Great Spirit circle, circle all around.* Over and over I chanted to myself as we hiked. Suddenly I felt my face getting red. It was an Indian prayer, and I'm white. I thought of the times when I used to play cowboys and Indians with other ranch kids. Sometimes I'd be a cowboy, but usually I'd be an Indian so I could sneak around real quiet and carry a bow and a handful of stick arrows. This time, though, I was with a real Indian, so that meant I was the cowboy. Somehow, after all the stuff I'd been reading, that made me feel ashamed.

Tivo waited in his usual place in the hollow behind my hill. I hadn't thought too much about how we'd go on this search. Maybe I should've saddled a horse? I raised an eyebrow at Shawn.

"He'll take two easy," he said, "given you're not much bigger than a gopher."

I grabbed a handful of dirt and flung it at him. He dodged and stumbled and slid the rest of the way down the hill on his rump. For the first time in what seemed like ages, I laughed. Shawn brushed himself off and bowed. Tivo neighed and trotted up to him. He ran a hand along the horse's flank, swooped up the reins, slipped a boot into the stirrup, and swung into the saddle. Then he reached down, hooked my hand, and lifted me easily behind him. He'd folded a blanket and placed it on top of the saddle blanket as if he'd been sure that I'd come.

I stared at Shawn's back. What was I supposed to do with my hands? I'd ridden behind my mom or some cowboy plenty of times when I was little. I'd always just grabbed ahold of them without thinking. Now I felt very self-conscious. I touched his sides with just the tips of my fingers as we rode across the small valley. But as Tivo reached the next hill and started to climb, Shawn reached back and pulled one of my hands around his belly and squeezed my fingers as if to say "Hang on tight." I felt a shiver go through me.

"You okay?" Shawn asked.

"Yeah, why?"

"You're shaking."

"I'm just . . . excited, I guess."

I closed my eyes and moved with Tivo's rhythm, filling my lungs with the smell of horse and sweat and sage-scented air and the warm-boy and soap-smell of Shawn. On the flat tabletop of the hills Tivo galloped, gliding over sagebrush, sidestepping boulders and prairie-dog holes, following along barely visible animal trails.

I smashed into Shawn's back as we swooped down a steep slope. At the bottom, spiky buffalo-berry and gooseberry bushes scraped our legs as Tivo brushed his way through to the creek. At the shallow crossing he snorted, spread his legs, and guzzled.

"Creek's lower than I've ever seen it," Shawn muttered as Tivo waded across it.

We climbed out the other side and rode on. Soon we were at the edge of the mountains where the foothills turned into jagged cliffs and rock outcrops and deep forests. A herd of cows and calves scattered as we slowly rode through them. We stopped while Shawn stared at an old cow, checking to be sure her calf had been nursed. Satisfied that it had, we went on. We skirted the forests and outcrops and galloped steadily along until we clattered to a stop at the edge of a towering cliff.

I slid off Tivo's rump, sank to my knees. I crawled to the jagged edge of the cliff. Looking down made my head spin.

Far, far below, a sea of white rocks flowed across the valley, smashing up against pink cliffs that held it in on both sides. The land seemed to gush back and forth; I could almost hear the deep ocean sounds of waves curling and crashing.

Shawn crouched beside me. "This is where the ley lines meet up, isn't it?" I said.

"That's why I brought you here," he answered. He pointed toward a cliff on the other side of the valley. "The dreaming rocks. That's where we come to fast and to have us a vision."

On the other side of the valley, pink cliffs rose out of a milky-blue lake. Clouds hovered around the cliffs, but for a quick moment they parted. Even from this distance

I could make out that the cliffs had been used as a drawing board. They were covered with petroglyphs, some of them huge. Strange-looking figures, some circled by zigzags and dots and long wavy lines, had been chiseled high up in the cliff walls. Then, as if I'd been allowed just this one glimpse, the clouds settled back over the cliffs, hiding them behind a gossamer curtain. I shivered.

"It's the most incredible place," I said, "but I'm glad we're up here and not down there. It's spooky. For some reason I get the feeling I'm being watched."

"I should've told you," Shawn said, giving me a sideways look. "This land is protected. The little people guard it. Only the medicine men and their helpers can go into the back country around here." He touched my arm. "You're shaking again. I've got a jacket in the saddlebag. Want it?"

"I'm not cold," I said, even though goose bumps ran all up and down my whole body.

"Those wavy lines around some of the drawings, some say they're water, and that those are the water ghosts," Shawn said. "When people trespass, when they go where they're not supposed to, things happen. I've heard of folks being pulled into the lake by the water ghosts. Sometimes their truck batteries go dead. Or worse, they break a leg or something. Or a huge storm will come up out of nowhere, with black clouds and thunder and lightning."

"Well, they did a good job of keeping things hidden today. At least the sky's blue and cloudless up here, so let's hope it's a good sign. And I *have* read about places being guarded by spirits—like the pyramids, right? But those wavy lines . . ." I paused. "Could they also be auras? Because that's almost the same way I'd draw them. . . ."

Shawn flung me a look. "Lucky you," he said. He stood upright, held out his hand, and pulled me to my feet. "This isn't a good place to hang around." He looked at Tivo, who seemed to pick right up on Shawn's thought because he snorted and trotted over.

We rode back along the edge of the mountains the same way we'd come. This time I noticed all the reddish brown beetle-killed trees mixed in with the green ones. I got the impression of trees shrinking into themselves as if each tree flinched away from its neighbors. I wondered, *Do the trees near the dead or dying ones sense that they might be next? Do they somehow know about the deadly beetles?*

After a while we stopped. I pushed off Tivo's rump and stood with my hands on my knees, feeling the kinks of not having ridden for a while. We walked, with Shawn holding on to the reins and pointing out places along the cliffs and on the rocky outcrops where he'd already searched. "It's big country," he said. "I'll probably be old and gray before I stumble across that rainbow. *If* I ever do . . ."

"You'll find it," I said. But just looking about, it seemed it would be almost impossible to find something just scratched on a rock. And like he'd said, it might've been erased by the wind and the weather, or been chipped away. Or it might never have even existed. Maybe it was just a story. I mean, if you thought seriously about it, how could it be anything *but* just a story?

Or maybe it was just the search, and the *wanting,* the *yearning* his great-grandmother had known would build in him to do something with the gift of healing she knew he had. I mean, she'd seen auras, hadn't she? So she'd seen that he had that amazing light about him. Because even if he never found the rainbow I felt sure he'd use the gifts he already had.

I stopped in my tracks and screwed up my face. That was it! Shawn couldn't see his own lights. He didn't have any idea that he already had the power. He already could do anything and everything he wanted to do. I wanted to shout, *Why are we searching these hills when the light's already right there inside you? Why are you looking outside for this rainbow?*

"What?" Shawn asked huffily.

The words almost shot out of my mouth. The look on his face made me stop. This was *his* quest. He'd invited me along, but for sure he'd never say another word to me about it if I said it might really be only a story.

"Nothing," I lied. I looked at the ground instead of his face. I walked a few steps and then pointed to a rocky ledge that poked out above some trees. "Have you looked up there?" I asked brightly.

"Yeah. No rainbow, but it'd be a good place to have us a picnic." He headed toward the trees, tugging Tivo behind him. When he reached the shade of the trees he dropped the reins and pulled a sack out of his saddlebag. He waved for me to follow.

It was way past noon. I hadn't realized how hungry I was. I scrambled after him.

It was an easy climb up a slope covered with fir trees and then up the big outcrop. On top, the perfect picnic spot! We sat on the ledge dangling our legs. Shawn handed me a can of pop and a sandwich. It was cheese, pickle, and baloney. I peeled the baloney out of mine and handed it to him. He smiled and stuffed it into his sandwich. For the longest time we sat eating and staring out at the huge landscape.

Little dots far below would be cows. I could see where Far Canyon Ranch was, though the buildings were hidden by trees and the hills. To the east of the ranch, maybe two miles from Far Canyon as the crow flies, another ranch huddled in a valley surrounded by reddish pink hills. No road connected the two places, though tracks wandered off here and there and then lost themselves in sagebrush or gullies. I could barely make out a small house and some sheds and a barn. A bright blue truck stood out among rust-colored trucks that looked as if they'd melted into and belonged to the landscape.

"My grandma's place," Shawn said.

I nodded. The silence around us seemed too big for words. We sat for a long time not talking.

"My people say that when we talk we can't hear the earth," Shawn finally said.

It seemed a good time to ask. "Your people," I said. "You never told me what tribe you belong to. I mean, if it's okay to ask . . . ," I stammered, wondering if that was the kind of question you didn't ask, like asking a rancher how many cows he had, or how big his place was.

Shawn answered with a smile. "I'm Shoshone, Arapaho, and Lakota. And Irish."

"Well," I said, "then maybe we're related somewhere. I'm Irish too. And French. Or at least the parts that I know of."

"I made a mistake," Shawn said. "A whopper."

My heart lurched up like it wanted to jump out of my throat. I closed my eyes. *Oh no,* I thought. He's sorry he opened his mouth, sorry he told me anything. Sorry he brought me here . . .

"I've been thinking a lot about something. Why I said what I did. About not liking white girls." Shawn broke off a piece of sage, smelled it, and pressed it into my hand.

I buried my nose in it, eyes still clenched closed, not at all sure where his words were leading. All I knew was that my heart had sunk somewhere down close to my feet.

"It's hard to explain," Shawn went on. "It's a whole lot of things. Like being angry because of stuff that took place long before I was born. Things that happened to my people because the white people came and changed everything. And the fact that the white people will never be able to admit that they live on stolen land. Or that they took our words from us. Our languages. Words are sacred. As sacred as this land."

I licked my lips nervously. Even after reading all those books about the horrible things that'd been done to the

Indians, I couldn't say, "Yeah, I know how you feel." No, I didn't. Not really, not deep, deep down where it mattered.

Shawn scattered some of his scraps and we watched as ants came and carried them off. "Sitting here, not talking. That's good. White people seem to talk a lot, maybe to fill up the silence. Like at school, in the lunchroom. We Indian kids sometimes just sit there. Makes the white kids nervous. But we listen and learn what's going on in their heads. Or their hearts."

I managed a twisted smile.

"But with you, it's different," Shawn went on. He bent toward me. "It's like we're on the same wavelength. So I apologize. I made a mistake. You're white, and I like you, so maybe I do like white girls. Maybe I've got to learn to give people a chance and not judge them, the same way I don't want to be judged."

Somewhere, down by my feet, I could feel my heart picking itself up and dusting itself off. Feel it climbing back up to my chest, where it swelled out so big I had to take a huge breath to hold it. I looked at Shawn and he looked back at me. We stayed like that for a long time. More than anything I wanted him to bend forward and kiss me.

But he didn't. Instead, he dumped the crumbs out of the sack for the ants to gobble up, and then scrambled to his feet. He put out his hand, but I'd already jumped up and started back down the outcrop. He followed. At the foot of the outcrop Tivo neighed and trotted over to Shawn, who mounted and pulled me up behind him. This time I held on with my fingers barely touching his T-shirt.

We climbed into and out of a gully, and on the top of a ridge we stopped.

Shawn was the first to speak. He pointed toward a pink cliff where a rocky landslide showed up as a gray mass of rocks. "It's there, the other place where you said the ley lines met up," he said. "I was going to take you there, but it's getting too late."

I shielded my eyes with my hands, trying to remember exactly where the star of light had met up. If only I'd seen them more than just once!

"I told you there's a cave near there," Shawn said. "You have to come to it from above or you'll miss it. A creek runs down and into the cave, but it's just a trickle by midsummer. Some people go there to have them a vision. My grandma always told me to stay away from caves, which isn't hard because I think caves are spooky anyway. But if the lines you saw met up there, maybe there's more to that spot than I thought."

I wanted to say, *Hey, let's go check it out. I'm not afraid of the dark because I always can see my own light.* But I swallowed the words. No boy I'd ever known appreciated a girl telling him *she* wasn't afraid of the dark.

"Some other time, then" is what I said instead. "You're right. It's getting late, and my mom's probably starting to worry."

We weren't far from the ranch. Tivo carried us back across the tabletop of hills to the creek, through the tangle of berry bushes, and up the hill above the bowl-shaped valley. There I told Shawn to leave me.

I slipped off Tivo's rump and reached up my hand to Shawn. He bent and grabbed hold of my fingers. I could feel my heart thumping and everything suddenly went blurry. I tried to focus my eyes. He was just a dumpy kid on a horse. No. He was a pillar of blazing light floating on top of a dimly glowing, tired horse.

You're something else, I wanted to say. *Whatever it is that you're going to be, I'd like to be in on it.*

"Yo, *ni hinch,*" Shawn said. "Catch you next time, my friend."

I couldn't talk. I just swallowed, squeezed his hand, and nodded.

My head whirled. If my thoughts had been whisked in a blender they couldn't have been more mixed up. I climbed up the back side of my hill, over the rocky ledge, and headed straight to my tree. I leaned against its shaggy trunk and gave it a hug. Its bark felt cool on my face. I picked up a stone and closed my eyes. For the first time I didn't even think about wishing for my dad to come back.

Instead, I tucked the stone into a branch and sent out a prayer for Shawn that the rainbow really existed. And that he'd find it.

I loped down the hill to the house. It wasn't till I rounded the corner that I saw the dusty brown pickup parked alongside of Ol' Yeller. I stared at the license plate. Who'd we know from Montana? I walked into the mudroom and stopped at the kitchen door. Put my ear to it. My heart thumped so loudly I could hardly hear the man's voice. Was it—no, it couldn't be. My dad?

Chapter Twenty-two

"It wasn't my fault," the man was saying. "You hid your trail as good as someone brushing their tracks with a broom."

"I waited," my mom's soft voice replied. "I couldn't believe you'd walked out on us. Then we got those letters saying you were coming back. Do you know what that did to me when you didn't? What it did to Blue? So I moved on. And on . . ." There was a long pause. "What'd you expect? You think it's been easy, this life?"

"It wasn't a piece of pie for me either. I was, how do you say it, fed up? Yes. Full to the top with arguments, fights."

"It was partly the booze," came my mom's voice, so soft I could hardly hear it. "Your drinking. As well as mine."

"Well, I'm back. You're still my wife. And our daughter, she's still my little girl."

I touched the doorknob as if it would bite. Flicked the door open.

I stared at this stranger. His eyebrows met at the top of his nose like a ram getting ready to charge. A scar ran down one cheek, giving him the dashing look of a pirate. He stood so straight he looked as tall as the sky, so tall he could reach up and grab stars, or at least touch the ceiling. How handsome he was—no wonder Mam's insides had turned to mush when he sang for the dudes by the campfire. And yes. His greenish brown eyes and dark reddish brown hair were the same exact colors as mine.

"Bleu?" he asked, making my name sound like a blur and a question.

"Papa?" I said.

"Happy Bastille Day! Your birthday! My little girl! I thought you'd be tall like me, but look at you! You're still small as a mouse."

I'd already dived into his chest as if it was the deepest ocean, thinking, *I'm home. I'm home. My dad's back after a zillion trillion prayers and wishes.*

But when I floated up from that plunge what I felt was pure anger. *How could you?* I wanted to yell. *Why did you do that to us? And by the way,* I wanted to say, *I've grown a whole bunch since you last saw me.* But I just stood there letting the waves continue to wash over me while his big silver belt buckle grated into my side.

Mam's wide eyes told me she'd been as shocked as I was. On the table, on top of a pile of books, lay a bouquet of red roses still in their cellophane wrapper. She turned and rattled through the kitchen cabinets, holding up a brown pot, then a glass, and then a squatty glass vase. Her nostrils flared as she made a face at the choices. Then she rolled her eyes at the junk on the table. She reminded me of a spooked horse.

"I'll help," my voice squeaked, sounding in my head as if I were sinking and calling for help.

Already my dad had let me go. He stood in my blue-for-me-kitchen as if it was the most natural place in the world for him to be. His black cowboy hat lay crown down on the table. He pushed aside the rock that lay on the note I'd left on the table that morning. Touching the note, he bent to read it. He frowned.

Usually when I'm nervous I chatter nonstop, but now all my questions bunched up in my throat like a big wad of feathers. So I whizzed about, opening a cupboard and having no better luck than my mom at finding a vase for the roses. I grabbed an armful of cobalt-blue bottles off the counter and held them up to see if they'd do. Mam nodded, relieved, and took them from me. The bottles clinked in the sink as she nervously filled them. She unwrapped the roses and stuck two in each of the six blue bottles.

The fridge suddenly roared into action, its motor thrumming and filling the silence. I whipped the books off the table, along with a stack of newspapers, a pile of fence staples, a pair of gloves, a can of nails, a pair of pliers, and my note and the pink rock. My dad's hat I carefully put on a hook in the mudroom.

"Boyfriend already?" my dad asked, pointing to the note.

My face burned. "Just a friend," I said, and felt my heart flutter.

I snatched up a dishcloth and swabbed at the table while Mam shuffled through drawers to find the pretty rose-patterned tablecloth we'd used only once. I grabbed one end as she flipped it, and we smoothed it down on the table. The cobalt-blue bottles she placed in the center, under the cobalt-blue lamp. The three of us stood back and stared at the roses as if they were the stars at a show. I almost expected them to bend their red heads and bow.

Stew Pot had been strangely absent. He hadn't even come bounding to greet me after my long day away. Now he came out of the living room and stood in the doorway with his head tipped to the side and his ears cocked.

"Hey, boy," my dad said. "Don't you remember me?"

Why should he? I wondered.

Stew Pot wagged his tail, tipped his head the other way as if he was puzzling over the matter, but didn't come to him. I hurried over and gave Stew Pot a hug.

"I bet you wonder where I've been," my dad said suddenly, and as he spoke the fridge stopped its humming. The kitchen got quiet with a silence as huge as the years full of wondering exactly *that*. I held my breath, thinking he'd start with day one—the day he'd walked out of our life. But no.

"Last place was up in Montana," he said, jumping over the years as if they didn't exist. "Hollywood's taken over up there. Did a bit of acting myself. *Drums of the West,*

Saddle Up, Sally. You see those? No? Well, those cinema folks aren't anywhere near as impressive when you have to saddle their horses and then watch them comb their hair and put on makeup while they ride. I have had it up to here." He slashed at his throat, around which a red silk scarf was neatly knotted. "No more dudes and dude ranches for me. I got out of there before the tourist season got started. No, I've been scouting around for something new."

He rubbed his hands till I thought they'd smoke, and grinned as if waiting for us to ask excitedly, "What? Tell us!"

This was the storytelling dad I remembered. But neither Mam nor I spoke. I was suddenly reminded of how sometimes my own volley of words seemed to bowl Mam over, leaving her totally speechless.

"Voilà!" he said. "I will make my own film. I will call it, *A Frenchman Roams the West to Find Its True Essence*." He bowed.

Mam looked down at the pot she was stirring. I just stood there blinking my eyes.

"We will celebrate now, yes?" My dad bowed himself out the door.

Mam and I didn't speak. She'd fixed me a birthday dinner; probably she'd worked all afternoon on it, before my dad showed up. From the shocked state she was in I figured he'd arrived not long before I came back. I wanted to ask her, *What do you think?* But she busied herself at the stove, blindly stirring the pot of what looked like already-very-mashed potatoes. Suddenly she stopped and looked over at me.

"So. Are you happy, Blue?" she asked.

"I'm . . . of course. I'm thrilled out of my mind," I said, thinking, *I'm so confused I don't even know how I feel.*

Mam nodded. She blinked at the pot as if it'd suddenly come into focus. She put the spoon down on the stove and sighed. "I'm glad you're happy. You deserve to be."

What about you? I wanted to say, but she'd turned and walked into her bedroom.

My dad was gone so long I peeked out the kitchen windows. He wasn't by his truck. I ran into my secret room and looked out the back windows. I was about to run outside when I spotted him clear up the hill behind the house, up by the fence. He seemed to be poking something into the ground. Is he planting a little tree for me, for my birthday? I wondered. He turned in a circle looking at the landscape, and then he walked briskly down. A few minutes later he burst into the kitchen carrying a really big box under one arm and two bulging paper sacks in the other. He let the box slide onto the couch by the window and then juggled the sacks onto the table. He took three bottles of wine out of one sack. "Voilá!" he said, rubbing his hands briskly together. Then he narrowed his eyes, looking around the kitchen as if setting the stage for something. Without a word he rummaged through the cupboards for glasses, pushing some aside until he got to some wineglasses hiding in back. He held them up, made a horror-struck face, and took them to the sink and washed them. He grabbed a dish towel, snapped it in the air, and then held up each glass and inspected it as he dried it. Then he poked around in a drawer and found a corkscrew and opened a bottle of wine. With a grand, sweeping gesture he poured out three glasses.

"To the birthday girl!" he said.

Mam murmured that I wasn't anywhere near old enough to drink and that she wasn't drinking anymore, but he covered her words with, "Don't be silly! She is thirteen! We must celebrate! I have found my little girl. And"—he bowed toward Mam—"my runaway wife."

It was weird how when he said that it almost seemed true—almost as if the reason he'd been gone all those years had been Mam's fault and not his. It was all so unreal I felt as if I'd tumbled down a rabbit hole when I stepped into the house.

My dad picked up his glass and held it toward me. I picked mine up and tapped his with mine. He held out his glass toward Mam. Her hands had gone to her chest and she stared at the glass on the table as if it might bite. My dad picked up her glass. Held it out to her. She hesitated. Slowly she wrapped her fingers around it. Slowly she reached out and clinked her glass against his.

I almost put mine down. Almost shot a hand out to stop Mam from taking a sip. But I didn't. It was my birthday! My dad had come back! I stood there and watched as Mam held her glass up to the light. I watched as the light shining through the red liquid glimmered across her face as she drank.

I took a sip. It tasted like metal. My mouth puckered. Honestly, grape juice would've been a lot better. I set my glass down and watched Mam. She glanced at me. Slowly she put the glass down. Her hand shook. She picked it up again and took a sip without looking at me.

I almost couldn't blame her. If she'd ever needed a drink, I'm sure it was now.

But my dad was all fun and games, pulling a loaf of French bread, several kinds of French cheeses, and three cans of some kind of French spread and a big box of chocolates out of the sack like a magician pulling rabbits out of a hat. Mam set out the vegetarian chili she'd made just for me and the salad from our very own garden, along with those mashed potatoes that were now totally gluey.

And there we were. My mom, my dad, and me. Sitting around the kitchen table like your regular, totally normal, typical family.

Except nothing was normal at all. I couldn't swallow. Mam pushed her food from one side of her plate to the other. Only my dad ate as if there were no tomorrow. And all the while he talked. We listened. Listening was easy because he hardly even asked about what had been going on in our lives all this time. When he did ask, it only reminded him of his own stories, and he'd spin off into some other tale.

"He had the gift of gab," my mom had once told me.

"He could turn things around till you felt so dizzy you couldn't tell if you were coming or going, or if what he said was the truth or a lie." That was something I just remembered, and if my dad hadn't been there in our kitchen, I'd have run up to my journal and written it down.

The only thing I managed to squeeze into the conversation was the question, "How did you find us?"

My dad frowned at my mom. Then he turned to me. "It was very curious, how do you say? Strange. Yes. I am driving along, going west to Jackson Hole, when my truck suddenly has big troubles. Smoke. I think I'm on fire. I am! Lucky I have just passed the only gas station around for miles. I walk back and they tow it and fix it. I pay with a check."

My dad did a pantomime of someone taking a check, pushing their glasses up, and holding the check out at arm's length.

I could feel my mouth drop and my eyes grow huge. I could just see the man—Clyde! I wanted to shout, *Can you believe it! It worked! My plan worked!*

But already my dad was going on with his story. "Yes, so this man says, 'Gaspard. You related to that pair up at Far Canyon?' And so I know where you are. I go on to Jackson Hole and do some business and shop for you and plan this day. One week ago, he told me. Good timing, yes?"

Timing? The whole thing was fantastic, but I wondered what I would've done if I'd been the father. I think I'd have sped up that road so fast that my truck would've caught fire once again. For sure. But then I wasn't my dad.

I hardly ever paid attention to Mam's lights I was so used to them, but now I noticed how they spiked up around her like a porcupine. I think if my dad had touched her he'd have felt spines going right through his hands.

As for my dad, I couldn't keep my eyes away from the space surrounding his head as it blazed like yellow-orange fire and then exploded into bright blues and purples and then switched back to yellows again.

All evening Stew Pot hovered under the table, nuzzling my feet. I scraped my scraps into his dish, along with Mam's. I felt bad that the two of us had eaten so little because the dinner she'd fixed had been super, except maybe for those potatoes. I told Mam it was a wonderful dinner and my dad kissed his fingers to the ceiling and declared he'd never eaten anything better. That was nice of him, since I'd noticed he'd mostly eaten the stuff that he'd brought.

My mom bit her lip nervously and said nothing. She disappeared into her room and came out carrying a cake decked out with swirls of pink icing that said, "Happy Birthday, Sweet Thirteen." She gave me a quick, brave smile.

"But your presents!" my dad exclaimed. "I've brought you a beauty. Is it not time to open?"

"First things first," Mam said, striking a match.

My dad grabbed the matchbox. "My job! Fire maker!" he said.

The match in Mam's hand burned down to her fingers as my dad lit the candles. I wondered if their life together had been like that, him taking over and her not saying a word.

I bent low over the candles, almost expecting my dad to help blow them out. But he burst out into the birthday song and soon my mom's sweet voice joined in, and I closed my eyes and thought, *Thank you, thank you.* I couldn't understand why, when I should've been totally ecstatic, I wanted to cry.

Mam brought two presents out of her room and set them beside the big box on the couch. Hers were wrapped in newspaper comics. My dad's, in silvery paper as fragile as butterfly wings. I reached for one of my mom's. A pair of hiking boots! "Just what I needed," I said, tugging off my cowboy boots and putting them on.

"Open, open this one," my dad said, but I'd already started ripping the paper off Mam's other present. "Just what I needed," I trilled as I held up a blue shirt and a pair of blue jeans.

My dad pushed his present toward me and bent over my shoulder as I slid the card out.

"To my little girl. Kisses, your papa," I read. "Thank you, Papa," I said, and opened the box. A doll dressed in a long pink satin dress stared up at me. On her head was a shiny tiara. I swallowed. "She's . . . amazing," I said. "Totally . . ."

"A princess for my little princess. And for all the birthdays I did not get to spend with my little girl," my dad said, looking reproachfully at my mom.

I kept my head down as their looks collided above

me. Stew Pot padded over and sniffed at the doll. The hair on his back bristled.

"It's a doll, silly," I whispered. I lifted her out of the box—she was at least three feet tall—and sat her on the couch, fluffed her long skirt, examined her silver slippers. She was Sleeping Beauty laid out in her casket, waiting for the prince's kiss. She was so *not* me. My dad beamed as I reached up and gave him a kiss. "She's . . ." I gulped. "She's . . . incredible. Thank you. . . ."

"I thought of you when I saw her. I am so happy you like her. And now for the even bigger surprise. Outside, everyone, please." My dad waved his arms and shooed us out of the house. Then he disappeared into the darkness.

The dark night was quiet except for the call of a hoot owl. The moonless sky glistened with stars. Mam clutched my shoulder as we stumbled across the yard. "It better not be . . . ," she said. "I hope he didn't . . ."

I held my breath. "No, of course he wouldn't. Not when everything's so dry. . . ."

Stew Pot streaked under the porch as a whistling sound broke the silence. With a soft *crackle pop!* a star burst apart in the sky. Silvery sparks fluttered down to the ground while already another star flew up and popped. Comets hissed and spit as they whizzed up and burst into white and red blossoms. And then it was over and the night settled back into silence.

I couldn't help it. I clapped. My papa had come back and lit up the night just for me! It was just like old times! And no harm done. . . .

Beside me, Mam stood stiff as a fence post. "Well, that wasn't too bad," she said. "Looks like the sparks all landed in the green meadows. And at least he didn't shoot off any loud ones, or the horses and cows might've bolted. Still, you'd better go check on your bums."

Mam was right, and I headed off to see if the ruckus had freaked out my bums. But then a loud bang stopped me in my tracks. Evidently the show had only just started.

Now my dad brought out the big guns. I clapped my hands to my ears as machine-gun explosions *rat-a-tat-tatted* across the hillsides and echoed up and down canyons. Rockets flared and exploded. Mortars shot into the sky and boomed with thundering crashes. The air screamed as slowly but surely my dad blew up the night.

Chapter Twenty-three

Later, I couldn't sleep. Every once in a while I'd leap out of bed, my heart pounding, and run to the window to stare into the darkness, expecting to see a red glow. I'd stare until my eyes watered and then stumble back to my bed. But as soon as my eyes closed I'd picture a wiggling red snake slithering under the sagebrush, sneaking across the hillside, and creeping silently up on the house. Then I'd shoot out of bed and rush to the window again.

All night I heard Mam bumping into stuff in her room as she, too, checked on the hills from her window.

I'd never seen her as furious as when that first loud machine-gun blast tore into the sky. She'd stormed up the hillside to where my dad was busily setting off fireworks, while above us whizzers whistled, rockets roared, and the whole night sky exploded.

At the first really loud blast I'd run straight to the front door to let a shivering Stew Pot inside, and then I'd dashed to the pen where my bums trembled and stared at me wide-eyed. "It's okay, it's okay," I assured them, hugging them, thinking, *Cripes, everything was so perfect. Why'd he have to go and do that?*

Between crackles and bangs I could hear my mom yelling and my dad shouting back, and then above it all rose a shriek that sent a cold shiver of dread running through me.

Fire!

I burst out of the pen as if something dangerous had broken into it. Forgot the gate, whirled, yanked it shut, and then kicked it open again with my foot. *What if the fire got my bums?*

In the black night a thin line of orange crept up the hillside.

I ran, stumbling up the porch stairs and into the kitchen. I jerked the mop bucket out from the cupboard under the sink and grabbed two saucepans off the stove, crashing a stack of plates onto the floor as I dashed out. Fast as I could with bucket and pots clanking at my side I clunked up toward the ditch that curved along the base of the hill—thank goodness it still carried water! Mam ripped the bucket and pots from my hands, so I flew over the ditch, stripping off my brand-new shirt as I ran, no matter that the buttons popped off. I frantically slapped my shirt at the sparks and stomped on the glowing embers with my brand-spanking-new boots. In the darkness I could hear my dad cursing in French, and his panting as he shoveled dirt onto the fiery patches.

I don't know how long we were at it. It took forever, it seemed, before we thankfully got the fire out.

We were sooty and breathing so heavily we might've just run a marathon and boy was my mom ever mad. "You could've burned the place down," Mam yelled breathlessly over her shoulder as she poured one last bucket of water onto the last still-smoking patch.

Not a spark glimmered anywhere, but who knew what little troublemaker might lay there silently smoldering, just waiting to start up again during the night.

"I aimed toward the irrigated meadows," my dad said stiffly. "That is why I chose the spot by the fence."

Mam said something inaudible under her breath.

"All I wished was to celebrate my little girl's birthday. And yes, Bastille Day. Other than this little fire, was it not magnificent?"

He nudged me on the shoulder and I couldn't help but smile into the darkness. "It was stupendous," I said. "Out-of-this-world fantastic."

I didn't dare look at Mam.

"So little damage," my dad went on. "A dry hillside. So what? The grass was no good anyway. Only scrub. Sagebrush."

Honestly, I thought Mam would explode and take off whirling across the night sky. Sparks flew out of her, something I'd never seen happen before, at least not with her. "Only!" she sputtered. "*Only*? This is the ranch I'm in charge of! You could've lost me my job! And I still might lose it . . ."

"The way you move around, what would that matter?"

I wanted to throw myself in between them, yell *Stop. Please. Stop!* I could feel my world crumbling, feel everything falling apart. We'd just had a fine dinner. Just watched a spectacular show. Just kept a disaster from growing much worse . . .

But my mom had streaked off ahead of us. My dad and I trudged silently back to the house. I was trying hard not to cry.

"Now what?" my mom said when we shuffled into the kitchen.

"Now what, what?" my dad asked.

"It's late. What do you plan to do?"

There was a long, sticky silence.

"I will sleep under the stars in the back of my truck. That way," my dad said, winking at me as if it were all a big joke, "I can keep an eye on things. Don't you agree, little mouse?"

I wished I really was a little mouse. Wished I had a mouse hole to creep into.

My dad stayed for breakfast. He even fixed it.

"No one cooks eggs like ze French," he said, wiggling his eyebrows as he searched through the cupboards. "What? No hearts of artichokes? No anchovies? Not a snail in the house?" He twirled an imaginary mustache. "No frog legs? How can I cook?" He opened the fridge and sifted through our leftovers, holding up each new find as if it might bite. I giggled, and even Mam seemed to be trying hard not to smile.

He niftily chop-chop-chop-chopped an onion, holding up a knuckle as he pretended to have sliced off a finger. He cracked eggs with one hand and talked ten miles a minute as he stirred them. Holding one hand behind his back, he flicked the pan and flipped the omelet over. He made each of us our own. It was so wildly weird and wonderful to have an actual dad cooking up a meal in our kitchen. Mam was an okay cook, but she didn't do tricks.

No one said a word about the fire.

My mom was awfully quiet, but then when wasn't she? My dad told a story about a horse he'd trained at a ranch where he'd worked, how he'd taught it to do tricks so that it appeared that the horse could add and subtract and whisper things in his ears. And about how the horse had gone on to make its real owner a gigantic fortune.

"He can still charm the skin off a snake," Mam said when my dad stepped outside for a smoke. She folded her napkin and sighed. "I just hope he doesn't slip the skin on and turn into one. . . ." She looked at me and sighed. "I'm so sorry," she said. "I shouldn't talk about him like that in front of you. But the next thing you know, he'll be sweet-talking me, saying that what happened last night was nothing. But it wasn't just this ranch that could've burned to the ground. It was the whole countryside. Our Indian neighbors . . ."

"But maybe he's changed," I said, flinging her a warning look as the floor in the mudroom creaked.

"I am so sorry for the little problem last night." My dad leaned on the doorframe, filling the space. "What can I do to help?"

Mam and I glanced at each other. I wiggled a finger. "Told you so," I mouthed.

"You've done more than enough," Mam said. "I don't need help. I've managed for years without it."

My dad looked at his watch. *He must have important things to do somewhere,* I thought.

"I could use help." I piped up. Obviously it was all up to me now. If I didn't find something to keep him around, for sure he'd take off before they'd had time to make up. I'd take him out to help me with my bums and then send him back to spend time with my mom. I rushed about filling bottles, then steered my dad out the door. Luckily the calves were still there—I'd plumb forgotten to close up their pen after I'd kicked the gate open just in case the fire had spread.

When I'm nervous I chatter away nonstop, and now I went on and on about how little the bums had been when I got them and how Mr. Mac hadn't thought they'd survive and yet he'd handed them over to me the very first morning, and then how he'd been so surprised to see how great—and I suddenly stopped in midsentence. My dad's mouth had turned down and he'd puckered his eyebrows.

"This 'Mr. Mac.' He must be very, very nice, yes?"

"He's all right."

"He lets you have his big house. This is a bit strange, no?"

"No one had lived here for ages. . . ."

My dad kept at it. "Does he spend much time here?"

I shook my head. "We hardly ever see him. He never comes out." I had to change the subject real fast. "But tell me, Papa," I blurted. "Do you still heal horses?"

Suddenly he got all sunny again. "So you've heard about that! Ah, *oui,* I have—how do you call it, a knack." He shrugged. "It was to my advantage when I worked training horses, but I no longer spend my time doing that. It was for me a matter of—how do you say?—directing my attention to one thing. The same way I had the great desire, the big dream, when I was a small child in Paris, to go to the land of the cowboys. I put all my attention on teaching myself to do rope tricks. I learned English by memorizing all the old cowboy songs. I had a good success with horses, but I got very bored working with animals so I am finished with that. Now I put my mind to other things. Like the film. Yes?"

I fed and groomed my bums as he went on about the film and the cameras he needed to buy and I don't know what all else because I started thinking about what he'd said about directing his attention to one thing. Maybe we had that in common, this knack of centering in on something and making our dreams become real. I just hoped that I didn't ever get so bored with something I was good at that I just up and left.

He was still talking as we walked out by the homestead cabin. There, he turned in a circle as he looked at the landscape around us. I took a deep breath, as if I could somehow breathe in this land of enchantment and beauty, and by breathing it in, hold it inside me. *Isn't this place out of this world?* I started to say when he spoke.

"Do you not get bored out here? Are you not lonely in this desolate place, so far from shopping, from restaurants and theaters?"

I didn't know what to say. I shrugged. "You've lived on ranches," I said. "Did you get lonely?"

"Ah, that was different. Dude ranches, there is always someone around, people coming from all over the world, and they all want to be entertained. But out here . . ." He shook his head and then lit a cigarette. "Your mother. She must get lonely," he said as he blew out a long sigh of smoke.

I shrugged. "Same as me, I guess. You'd have to ask her. She's up at dawn and in bed when the sun goes down. She studies a lot, and we read at the table. She doesn't talk much. But she's so good at what she does. And," I added, looking up at the sky, "she really likes being her own boss."

My dad's eyebrows crashed into each other. "So she likes being the boss, huh? Well, there is only room for one pair of pants in *my* closet." He tossed his cigarette into the dirt and ground it out with his boot.

I pinched my lips together. Shoot. What'd made me say that? Maybe . . . maybe I was testing the water to see if I could really dive in and swim off with this father whom I barely knew. Not, of course, that he'd asked me to come with him. And not that he'd even mentioned some kind of future together.

We looked up as the front door slammed. "I'm heading down to the barn," Mam called when she saw us.

"Go with her," I said. My dad shrugged and held up his hand for her to wait.

"Same old pickup," I heard him say as he climbed into the truck.

I don't know what my parents talked about. They were gone a long time, but when they came back they seemed to be getting along just fine. My dad whistled a tune and my mom's eyes didn't hold the angry glare they'd had almost the whole time since he'd been here. I squinted, trying to catch some pretty pink lights floating around either one of them. I thought I caught a quick glimpse of rosy light around my mom, but as soon as I saw it, it changed.

I'd fixed a peanut butter and honey sandwich while they were gone. Now my dad teased me. "Even when you were small as a mouse, you loved peanut butter," he said. "With honey it must be very good, but have you ever tried it with chocolate?"

Maybe if I could do things over, I wouldn't have had what I had for lunch. Because then my dad wouldn't have decided to give me what he called a "taste treat" by grating some chocolate onto my sandwich. He wouldn't have exclaimed that I hadn't *lived* until I'd tried the European version of peanut butter. It was something called Nutella, he said. It was just like peanut butter only so much better because it was made with hazelnuts and dark chocolate.

And I wouldn't have said, "Oh, I'd love to try some of that!"

And then he wouldn't have gone off to try to find some. Wouldn't have grabbed his hat, given Mam a long, steady look as if trying to memorize her, or to see if she cared that he left. His colors swirled around him with bright pretty yellows and blues floating up over his head, while Mam's lights suddenly turned spiky. My dad kissed my forehead and said, "I'll be right back, little mouse." And then he walked out the door.

Chapter Twenty-four

If a raven flies by my window by the time I count to fifty, my dad will come back today.

I lay slumped in my bed, counting, dragging the numbers out. At forty-nine a black bird flew by. I raced to the window and poked my head out. It *was* a raven! I plopped back onto my bed, blew my hair off my forehead. "He'd better come back," I muttered to myself. "If he doesn't . . ." I punched my pillow with my fist and turned it to the cool side.

It was the morning of day six since he'd left.

The first couple of days I'd buzzed about expecting his truck to come rumbling up any second. By day three I'd started dragging about, barely lifting my feet off the ground. It felt like a heavy gray cloud had settled around me, turning the world dreary and taking its colors away.

On the next bed, the doll stared wide-eyed at the doorway as if expecting her prince to show up any minute. "Don't get your hopes up," I muttered, punching my pillow again.

Why'd he saddle me with a doll as big as a barrel, for cripe's sake. How could she possibly fit in our pickup? She'd take up half the seat, and a princess is way too fancy to stick in the back. I bet she cost a small fortune. What was he thinking? Hadn't he kept track of the years that'd gone by since he'd left us the first time?

The first time. What kind of dad walks out the door *twice*? I could feel the anger inside me growing and filling me up. I tried to remember what Mam had said before I stormed off to bed last night. "It's just the way he is. . . . Don't take it personally."

But I did. I was furious. I'd about driven Mam mad with my raging and stomping about. It didn't help that she seemed to keep her own anger all bottled up deep inside. I wondered what would happen if ever she came uncorked.

Downstairs the door banged as Mam headed out. Stew Pot opened one eye but didn't budge from his beanbag.

Was my buddy getting old? I counted backward. Eleven? Twelve? I'd read somewhere that big dogs got older sooner than small ones. Lately he'd been having trouble jumping up into the back of the truck. I felt a big lump grow in my throat. What good did it do to worry about stuff I couldn't change or do one thing about?

Like my dad being the way he was. *Don't take it personally,* I thought. *It's just how he is.* Yeah, right. I lay in bed trying to think of all the good things about him. Like the bubbly way he told stories. And the stuff he came up with, like setting off fireworks—though of course that'd almost ended in disaster. But then the comical stuff he did—why, even Mam hadn't been able to keep a smile off her face as she'd watched him do that funny French chef act. And he was so handsome it made my heart ache.

That's what he did to me. Made my heart ache. My tall, handsome, heartbreaking dad. And he'd done it so easily. Just breezed in and then out the door. Had he gone clear to France to find that stupid chocolate stuff? I spit out the word. "Nutella." It made me gag. Same as the word "Dijon." Maybe I hadn't understood what was going on when I was little, but now!

I could feel the anger building up like a big fire burning inside me, feel myself getting so hot I thought I'd explode. *WHERE ON EARTH ARE YOU?* I wanted to scream at the top of my lungs. *How could you walk into my life again and then turn around and walk out?*

I stared at the cracked mirror across from my bed. Someone really angry must've thrown something at it, but I bet they'd been nowhere *near* as furious as me. I shoved my hand under my bed and jerked out my just-in-case box. Grabbed a soup can. "TAKE THAT!" I yelled, and I threw it as hard as I could at the mirror. Pot gave a yelp, shot up from the beanbag, and dove to the far side of the room. He crouched by the wall, his worried tail *thump-thump*ing apologies on the wood floor

"Oh, Pot, I'm so sorry," I cried. "I'm not mad at *you!*" I patted my bed and he bounded up into my arms.

I looked at the mess I'd made. Jagged pieces of mirror lay scattered across the wood floor, along with the dented soup can. I hid my face in Pot's furry shoulder and begged him to forgive me for scaring him so. The horrible thing was that my huge, hungry *wanting* was ripping me right down the middle. I felt so divided. I mean, how could I want something so *much*—for my dad to come back—but at the very same time regret it now that he *had*? What was it that I really wanted? And Mam? Yesterday I'd watched her pick up the telephone and then stand there staring at it. I was sure my dad hadn't left her a number or else she would've called him by now, so she must've been thinking of calling Mr. Mac. But she hadn't. She'd held the phone to her chest, sighed, and then put it back down.

And as if things weren't bad enough, she'd drunk up the rest of the wine. Two bottles, all by herself. I hadn't made it easier. Even poor Stew Pot had slunk about hiding under the table or the couch or in the bathroom, anywhere to get away from my ranting.

Every afternoon I'd hiked up the hill, my heart leaping ahead of me, fingers crossed, hoping and praying that at least one happy thing would happen that day. Stew Pot would lope ahead of me wagging his tail expectantly. And then the big letdown for both of us. No Shawn.

I'd walk past my tree and jump over the rocky ledge and then climb partway down the back side of the hill. I stared down by the pine tree, checking for a pile of manure or some hoof marks that would mean Tivo had been there. He hadn't. I'd climb slowly back up and walk to the other side of the hill and stand there with my hand shading my eyes, searching for some sign of my dad. No dust rose on the long road to the ranch. No one traveled it, no one at all.

Now, in my bedroom, I looked over Pot's shoulder at the slivers of glass and the dented soup can. A pool of tomato soup had spurted out on the floor. It looked like blood. I shivered and hugged Stew Pot so tightly he coughed.

At noontime Mam stomped into the kitchen. "Turn down that drumming and singing," she said, throwing her gloves on the counter. "Doesn't it get on your nerves?"

I got up from the table and clicked off the radio without saying a word.

She picked up her latest encyclopedia and slammed it down on the table. All my dad's roses let go of their petals at once. We stared at the blackish red piles. Mam jerked the stems out of the cobalt-blue bottles and stuffed them into the trash can by the sink. Then she turned on the faucet and reached for her white china teapot. Both of us winced as she banged it down in the sink. For a minute I thought she might cry.

"We've had this forever," she moaned, holding the broken pot to her chest like a kitten. "I was going to make some ice tea. . . ."

"I'll . . . I'll buy you a new one," I said softly, though what I really wanted to say was *Please, please don't cry, 'cause then I'll start crying too . . . .*

I watched her set the broken teapot on the counter, then carefully, slowly, scrape the pieces out of the sink. She placed them, sliver by sliver, next to the teapot. She gave a huge sigh and then scooped up the slivers and dropped them into the trash with the roses.

"Never mind, Blue," she said. "It's all over and done with."

I sucked in my breath. Was she talking about the pot or my dad, or us being at the ranch? Cripes, how I hated those huge, heavy sighs and what almost always followed. It's all over and done with. . . . Would she pack up and take off just to pay my dad back for what he'd done? Would *she* disappear? Would she do that to him? To *me*? To *Mr. Mac*?

"After all these years," Mam said, startling me, her voice as cold as ice. "Just like *that* he shows up." She snapped her fingers. "And with no excuses whatsoever except that it was my fault for not leaving a forwarding address. Shows up with wine and red roses. Fireworks and fancy French food and a doll. Gets me thinking about how it was, and how it might be again. Gets me looking at a bottle of wine again as if it holds all the answers." She opened the fridge, stared into it, and then slammed the door shut. The fridge hummed. She glared at it as if it'd talked back.

"I've half a mind to pack up and be out of here

before he comes back. *If* he comes back. Let him come back to an empty house."

I could've sworn my heart stopped beating.

"I didn't want you to get hurt. Not again, not ever again . . ." She slid a piece of china out of the sink and held it up on the tip of her finger.

"Maybe we can glue it back together," I said. The words came out raspy. "Or get a new one. Off with the old, on with the new, right?" I felt light-headed, crazy, as if everything had gotten all scrambled up and nothing made sense. Was I talking about the pot or our lives or my dad or Mr. Mac? Or all of the above? I mean, this was the way we lived, right? Here for a month or two and then gone in an instant. Why should things be different now?

The sink gurgled, making a sucking sound as if something was stuck in the drain. I wanted to run over and stuff the plug into it. Because sure as sure, my whole world, everything I'd ever wanted, everything I'd dreamed about, was now headed straight down the drain.

Without a word Mam started taking everything off the table. She pulled off the pretty tablecloth, took it onto the porch and shook it, and then folded it up and put it away again. It so reminded me of the time when the dishes had finally been cleared from the table, back when my dad left before. Neither of us said a word. Mam warmed up some leftovers and then sat with her chin cupped in her hand, staring at her book but not turning the pages. Me, I wanted my comfort food. I dribbled honey over a peanut butter sandwich, giving the bottle such a squeeze that a big glob oozed out. *Ha,* I thought as I took a huge bite. *If my dad comes back this very minute carrying a whole box full of Nutella, I won't even touch it. So there.*

Mam looked over at me. *She better not dare say anything,* I thought. I frowned down at my book. *If she decides to pack up Ol' Yeller, I'll hop up in the truck and throw everything right back out. I'll chain myself to the table. Or I'll run away. That'd show her. She couldn't leave without me, could she?*

What about those rosy-pink lights that always showed up when Mr. Mac came around? She had feelings for him. But she probably thought she wasn't good enough—that she was just the hired hand, and she hadn't finished high school—my mom was so full of old hurts. But she'd proven she was more than *just* a hired hand. The ranch had been in such poor shape and all on her own she'd turned it around. Maybe I'd helped a little. But she'd done it. She'd repaired all the fences and gotten those ditches running again. And just look at the house!

I glanced at her out of the corner of my eyes. She hadn't eaten a bite, hadn't turned a page, and was sitting with her chin cupped in her hand, her eyes all faraway looking.

"Just tell me one thing," I said. "Did my dad say anything about—anything? Our future, what he wanted . . . ?"

"I wish I could tell you what you want to know," Mam said, "but he never said what his plans were, and I didn't ask. It seemed that all he could talk about was that darn film he wanted to make."

"I was sorry that he wasn't doing anything with that

gift of healing you'd said he used to have. I tried to find out about it, but he brushed it off as nothing."

Mam sighed. "All I can say, Blue, is that he didn't value the things he had. Neither the gifts nor the people."

I pushed back my chair. *I will not cry,* I thought. "Think I'll work on my room," I managed to say. "A few touch-ups and it'll be ready for the grand opening."

Mam looked at her untouched plate and then gave me a lopsided smile. "I can hardly wait. Secrets are hard to live with," she said.

If we were just two hairs from splitting this place, I'd at least get the room all tidied up and make it nice for Mr. Mac. And the room did look kind of pretty, with my funky creations with their feather and birds' nest surprises. They were weird and definitely wobbly but quite fantastic, if I did say so myself. Maybe I should have a little ceremony. Ask Mam to call Mr. Mac to invite him to the grand opening. A two-in-one party, an opening and a closing at the same time . . .

Maybe if Mr. Mac came, it'd make my mom change her mind.

I swept and mopped and then raided the rest of the house. I grabbed some books from the bookshelf and arranged them on my table. I took two turquoise pillows from the kitchen and placed them in my chairs, and then I swiped four cobalt-blue bottles and three stubby candles and placed them on the wide windowsills. It was all just too pretty for words. Then I latched the door and straightened the sign. Soon I could tear it off.

Mam's door was closed. I wrote a note. *Please call Mr. Mac to come out tonight to see what I've done with the room.* I tucked it under the salt shaker. I doubted she'd call. It seemed even more unlikely that he'd come.

I could've spent all afternoon with my bums, but time was running out. *Why hasn't Shawn come by to see me again?* I wondered as I fed my bums and looked up at my hill. It was hot, and one bottle each wasn't enough. They wanted more.

"Hang on," I said. "I'll give you doubles this evening, I promise."

It was a promise I wouldn't keep.

Chapter Twenty-five

Clouds stacked up like cups and saucers on top of the Owl Creeks. In the Winds, soft gray clouds smothered the mountaintops. *We could sure use some rain,* I thought, *but we'd probably just get dry lightning.* From my hilltop I searched the landscape for—what? Dust swirling up the road behind a pickup? Tivo galloping over the hills? No such luck. I counted on my fingers the days since my dad had left. Six. And seven since Shawn and I had ridden into the mountains on Tivo.

I wiped the sweat off my forehead. Beside me, Stew Pot lay panting. His black coat soaked up the sun.

I don't know what I'd expected—maybe to find Shawn sitting in the shadow of my tree, or to see him come galloping over the hills heading for our meeting place. Each day that went by I'd felt less sure about everything. He could've left a note by my tree. Thrown a rock at my window . . .

I could run over to his grandma's place. It couldn't be

more than three miles, though it might seem like more with all the gorges and hills in between. But how could I go panting up to his door, saying, "Excuse me, but why haven't you come by to see me all week?"

It was pretty obvious he didn't share my feelings. Didn't give a hoot that I even existed. For sure he was sorry now that he'd ever opened up to me, the nosy white girl. He didn't want to see me again. That was all there was to it.

Maybe it was a good thing Mam was about ready to pull out. At least now it wouldn't be quite so hard. . . .

My chest heaved. I leaned my head against my tree and spread my arms around its thick shaggy trunk. The bright sun made the shiny stones and tiny white bones glisten. I remembered when I'd spied Shawn's hand reaching up to touch the blue ribbon that now looped down by my cheek. I reached up and untwisted it from the branches. Tugged it out.

What good had they done, all my prayers and wishes? What good at all?

I stared out at the huge landscape. No dust billowed up. No horse came galloping over the hills. If this was the end of our stay at Far Canyon, I'd better find Lone One and Light of the Dawn to tell them good-bye.

I let the ribbon flutter to the ground. "Come on, Stew Pot," I said. "No use wasting what little time we have left. . . ."

Stew Pot followed behind me as I climbed down the back side of the hill. At the base, I checked one last time for signs that Tivo might've stood around waiting for

Shawn. He hadn't. I straightened my shoulders and held my head high and hiked on.

No antelopes in the bowl-shaped valley.

Often, at this time of day, the pronghorns would be taking it easy, the moms sitting around chewing their cuds, the young ones playing or sleeping. Lone One was a real loner, and I'd only once spotted her and her fawn with the herd. I wondered if Light of the Dawn got picked on because she was slower and limped.

"Cripes, but it's hot. One more hill, and if they aren't there we'll go back," I promised Stew Pot. Poor panting doggie. I should've made him take a drink of water before we took off. Should've taken a drink myself.

We'd barely climbed out of the valley and up to a rounded rim when we spotted her down in a shaded hollow below us. Lone One had heard us come clattering across the rocks and stood stiffly at alert, ruff up, her white rump flagging alarm. Stew Pot hunkered down. I froze. After a moment Lone One's alarm system melted, her ruff and white flag lowered, and she turned her attention to scratching at the ground with her hoof. She tugged at something with her teeth, jerked her head back and forth, and yanked a root out of the ground. She ate it like I eat spaghetti.

On the rounded hill above her, at the base of a rocky wall-like ridge, Light of the Dawn suddenly popped up. She shook her head furiously and scratched at an ear with one tiny black pointed hoof and then she sank quickly back down.

I swatted at a fly. They bothered me too. Down in the hollow, Lone One folded up her front legs and then her back ones. She didn't close her eyes, but they seemed to glaze over as she sat there and chewed on her cud.

What good had it done to find the exact place I'd drawn, and someone there who was nice to me and my mom, and a boy who'd become more to me than a friend, and then to have my dad come back—what good had it done? *None at all.* It would've almost been better if *none* of what I'd wished for had ever happened. At least then it wouldn't hurt nearly as much as now, when everything was crumbling away.

I stared up at the sky. I wished I could just be swooped up there, become a little cloud, drift about, and then *poof!* Vanish. No hurts, no memories, nothing.

It was the stillest, hottest afternoon ever. I closed my eyes. Beside me, Pot snored.

None of us, not even Lone One, saw it or heard it.

Stew Pot must've been the first to sense the wolf, the first to spy it slinking over the rocky ledge toward the fawn. Under my hand I felt the hairs on his back stiffen. I felt the growl in his throat before I heard it, and then felt him spring up, his growl ferocious as he sprang down the hillside toward the fawn. I jumped up and grabbed a chunk of dead sagebrush and bounded after him while the loudest scream ever screeched out of my throat. A small tan blur rushed past me and I was somehow aware of two antelopes dashing by as I flew, yelling and waving my stick, charging after Stew Pot toward what now was a whirlwind of ferocious snarls and deep growls. "NOOOOOOOOO! NOOOOOOOOO!" I screamed, and suddenly the wolf streaked back up and over the rim.

The fight couldn't have lasted more than five seconds.

But on the hillside, a furry black mound lay still.

"NOOOOOOOOO! STEW POT!" I cried as I crashed to my knees beside him. "DON'T . . . NO! YOU CAN'T!"

My hands worked their way under the mound, under his head, and around the thick ruff on his neck. On the back of his neck I could feel a warm stickiness. I stared at my hands. Blood. A small puddle had already pooled on the ground.

All shivers and jitters and prayers and pleas, I looked up at the sky and asked, "Please, please, what do I do? HOW?"

In my head I heard, "Don't panic, don't freeze."

Already my hands must've been running on automatic, one clutching the front of his throat, the other pressing against the deep bloody gash on the back. "How could I live without my best friend?" I sobbed, and then I took a huge breath. I gulped down all the sunlight around me and then sent the light rushing into my hands. I heard high-pitched moans coming out of my mouth as I bent over my sweet hero dog.

The light pouring out of my hands grew stronger.

The tiniest mewing yelp slipped out of Pot's throat. His eyes opened and then closed again.

Somehow my hands kept going, tugging at my

T-shirt, trying to rip it, then tearing it and leaving a ragged band that barely covered my chest.

"The wound is closing up, it's closing and sealing up," I repeated over and over while my shaking hands wrapped and tucked the bandage around Stew Pot's neck.

A shadow floated over us. Two ravens circled. "*Shoo! Go away,*" I cried. The ravens flew higher but still slowly circled above us.

"Sweet Pot, I need to run to get help," I whispered as I looked wildly around. But how could I leave him? Those ravens would fly down and begin picking away at him as soon as I left. And what if the wolf came back? My chest heaved.

"Oh, Stew Pot," I wailed. "I can't do it. I'll never be able to carry you all the way home. But I can't leave you, so what do I do?"

Stew Pot's tail swished once.

I looked up at the ravens, and suddenly, out of nowhere, something popped into my head from a book my mom used to read to me after my dad left. Something Christopher Robin had said to Pooh Bear. "Remember this," he'd said. "You're braver than you believe. And stronger than you seem, and smarter than you think."

I took a deep breath. Let my arms go limp, and tried lifting Stew Pot. "This won't hurt," I said, but it did, and he whimpered as I tried to lift him. I couldn't do it. I took a deep breath and tried again.

He wasn't as heavy as I'd thought. I staggered to my feet.

Each step down into the hollow where Lone One had dug up her root—when was that, fifteen, twenty minutes ago?—and then up and over the rim where Stew Pot and I had snoozed, and then down into the bowl-shaped valley and into the sheltered canyon where the fawns had been born . . . It was like the repeat of a horrible nightmare.

Again I found myself trying as hard as I could to find the tiniest soft spot in my heart for the wolf. This one had been gray, and smaller than the black one that had taken Lone One's other fawn. If it'd been the big black one it would've gotten Light of the Dawn for sure, and just as surely Stew Pot wouldn't have survived the attack. I might not have even been able to scare him away with my shouts and my stick.

"We're lucky, really lucky," I said into Stew Pot's furry ruff. But in spite of the heat, I shivered.

How many times I slumped down onto a rock to rest my arms and catch my breath, and how many times Pot squirmed so uncomfortably that I set him down on the ground, I don't remember. But somehow we made it to the trail that led out of the canyon and then down to the fence. Somehow I eased Pot to the ground, slipped through the wires, then reached through it and pulled him to me.

"Mam'll be there," I said into Pot's furry ruff, "and she'll rush us off to the vet in Dubois."

It wasn't until I rounded the corner of the house that I saw the brown pickup. My heart did a somersault in my chest. My dad had come back! I'd been wrong! He'd come back!

It didn't strike me right away that Ol' Yeller was missing.

"Somebody, help!" I yelled as I fumbled to open the front door, and then the next one into the dark hallway, and the one into the kitchen. "Help," I said as I stumbled into the kitchen. No answer.

I pressed my mouth against Stew Pot's furry head at the sight of the empty wine bottle on the table. The two glasses, the plate with a few crackers and some slices of cheese in it. They'd been sitting there not long ago. Where were they now? Where were they *ever* when I needed them? My arms felt like mush. I hunched over, Stew Pot's legs almost dragging the floor as I staggered across the kitchen and through the living room toward the bathroom. I thumped against the door with my shoulder and edged in.

My breath was all short hollow puffs as I shifted Pot's weight to keep from dumping him on the floor. My knees crumpled as I laid him down on the rug. I yanked the bath towels off the rack and settled his head on them. "Stay," I wheezed.

As if he could do anything *but*.

Wiping the sweat off my forehead, I dashed back into the kitchen. What was I supposed to do now? Where *were* they? They'd probably gone off to the bunkhouse to find something for dinner. Maybe they'd gone to the barn? But Stew Pot needed help, and he needed it now.

What did I need? Penicillin. Mam kept it stored in

the fridge. I flung open the fridge door, swept milk and juice bottles aside, grabbed the bottle, stared at it blankly, then searched through the cupboard over the sink for the syringes and antiseptic. What else? Roll of bandages? I frantically searched through Mam's stash of medical supplies. What? No bandages? The box clattered to the floor as I dashed up the stairs to my room and grabbed two T-shirts. I glanced at my blood-smeared self, grabbed a fistful of clothes, stumbled back down the stairs, swept the medicine onto my pile, and skidded into the bathroom.

I turned on the faucet. As the tub filled, the room filled with steam.

Later I'd remember the whole bathroom scene as if it had happened inside a gray thundercloud, and how the constant booming sound could've been rushing water, my heart pounding, or Pot's shallow breathing. Somehow bloody bandages got taken off and the hair around the ugly gash clipped with Mam's pair of nail scissors. "This won't hurt," I remember promising, and then Pot's startled, hurt eyes telling me that I'd lied as I poured a full bottle of antiseptic on his wound and then gave him a supersized penicillin shot in the shoulder. I remember ripping and wrapping my T-shirt, crisscrossing it under a leg, around a shoulder and neck. I don't remember stripping off my bloody clothes, but I do remember sinking into the tub, and how even with my eyes closed I could still picture the stiff bundle of bandaged-up doggie that lay on the bathroom floor. And I remember how I wondered if anything I'd done had helped, or if I'd done just the opposite of what one was supposed to do when your dog got bit by a wolf.

What I don't remember is why I decided to take Stew Pot upstairs after I'd finished my bath. I do remember lugging him up, and then the words I said.

"I'll keep you safe," I promised. "I'll sleep here beside you tonight."

It was one more promise I wouldn't keep.

Chapter Twenty-six

I'd hardly settled Pot into his beanbag and covered him with my blanket when I heard Ol' Yeller chug up the road to the house. Truck doors slammed. The front door banged. I held my breath for the sounds of the next two doors banging, but then I figured I'd left them open. I heard Mam's gloves slapping down on the kitchen counter. Thanks to the hole in the floor I could hear everything. Thanks or no thanks . . .

"I'm not asking you to stay." Mam's voice had a knife-sharp edge to it.

"You're still my wife," came my dad's quick reply, "and I was not saying I wanted to stay. It was a suggestion. An idea only. I could live here between jobs. Until I get the money to do that film I'm thinking of making. But you seem to think this is your own private territory."

There was a long pause. I crept to the hole and lay with my ear to the floor.

"What I think is that it's high time we got divorced. Legally. Desertion should be reason enough."

I heard the *bam* of the fridge door. Above its hum I could hear my dad snort. *We should put up a sign,* I thought.

PLEASE, NO SLAMMING DOORS— FRIDGE WITH DELICATE NERVES!

My dad had probably driven up not long after I'd left for the hill—had they been doing nothing but arguing the whole time? It was a good thing I was already flat on the floor because all of a sudden my tummy felt really icky. *They have no idea I'm home,* I thought, *and that I can hear every word. . . .*

"As if you hadn't kept moving on," my dad snorted again. "It was not my fault that I couldn't find you. And my daughter. My only child. And I know that you got my letters because they never were returned to me."

Mam stalked out of the kitchen and my dad followed, his cowboy boots making angry hard sounds on the floor. If they'd looked up they'd have seen my face peeking down from behind the grate in the ceiling. I could've almost reached down and plucked my dad's black cowboy hat off his head as he stomped by beneath me. Their lights turned the air jittery, like the way it is just before an electrical storm. My dad was like flashing lightning, while my mom held her lights close as if she were shielding herself from his strikes.

Mam turned, fists on her hips, and leaned toward him. "How many letters?" she demanded. "One a year? No, I didn't tell Blue when I got the last ones. You want to know why? Because each time you said you were planning to come back, and you didn't. I didn't tell her because I didn't want to break her heart any more than it'd already been broken."

Up in my attic, I wondered how many times a heart could be broken, and if it would always show cracks, or if it was maybe self-mending. Somehow I had the gut feeling that soon I was going to find out.

My dad whipped off his hat. I could see a grin on his face, the kind you get when you yell "Gotcha!" "So!" he said. "You *admit* you were running and hiding from me."

I wanted to pound on the floor and yell *STOP! It's me you're playing your games with and I HATE hide-and-seek!*

"Well, this time you found out where we were. But then you waited a whole week to come out here. And then you turned around and left without letting Blue or me know if you had any intention of returning. You let her worry and wonder—"

My dad broke in. "It is my business what I do. And I am back now. That should be enough."

Mam lifted her chin defiantly. "Well, it's not," she said.

Upstairs, I rooted silently, *Way to go, Mam!* But what I heard next sucked the breath right out of me.

"Well, what I really came back for is my guitar," my dad said. His hand shot out and he squeezed my mom's arm. "I was afraid you might slip away again, given your record. You still have it, no?"

"No." Mam pulled away and brushed at her shirt.

The fridge quit its humming. The air inside the house turned heavy and still, as if the house itself was hunkering down before a big storm.

"No?" my dad asked. Around him the air churned and turned dark as a thundercloud. "*No? My guitar*—you have any idea what it was worth?"

"We needed the money," Mam said, her voice deadly calm. "So I hocked it. And then there's the matter of my saddle, the one with the silver trim. . . ."

I pressed my cheek to the floor and closed my eyes as I waited for the big clap of thunder I sensed was coming. I heard books and things clattering to the floor, glass shattering, and the fridge suddenly rumbling. Out of the slits of my eyes I stared at the dust bunnies under the bed, and at my just-in-case box and my dusty old suitcase. No wonder I'd hidden under the bed when I was little. No wonder I'd blanked out the fights. . . .

Downstairs, my dad muttered something I couldn't make out, while my mom said something sharp back at him. I looked back down the peek hole. I could see my mom's back as she crouched to pick up a book. She straightened and held the book to her chest, patting it as if it were alive, as if she were comforting it. She put the book on the pile she'd made on the couch. Around her I could see her lights spreading out as if she was now trying to shield and protect everything in the whole room.

"This is a very big house for two people," my dad said as he turned in a circle, looking about as if he'd just now noticed its size. "A very big house for someone who is just a hired hand."

My mom flipped her hair out of her face. I could see her chest puffing up. "I *manage* this ranch," she said, putting a whole ton of weight on the word.

Upstairs in my attic I sat up. My shoulders lifted. That's what she was. My mom, the ranch manager. Really, that was quite a step up from just being a "hand."

I bent over the grate again.

"And this room," my dad went on as if he hadn't heard what she'd said. "Why is there a 'No Trespassing' sign on the door?"

Don't you dare! I thought as he lifted the latch and pushed the door open. *That's my room!* I wanted to yell down. *How can you just come in and act like you can take over? And now you're going to spoil everything—Mam'll see my creations before everything's ready, before the candles are lit, before Mr. Mac gets here tonight. . . .*

I was about to jump up when the next thing Mam said stopped me cold.

"Blue's doing this as a surprise. She wanted Mac to come out. . . ."

Cripes! That had to be the very worst thing she could've possibly said!

"So, *Mac,* is it?" My dad's voice snaked up through the hole in the floor.

Watch out, I wanted to yell down to my mom. *He's getting ready to strike. . . .*

"She must think he's quite a guy. You must think so too. Is that why you haven't left before now?"

Mam flashed him a cold, steely look.

"That's it, isn't it?"

"I've stayed for my own reasons." Mam lifted her chin and stared straight into his eyes. "And because I knew it was what Blue wanted. . . ."

My dad broke in. "And so she made this man some fancy-looking—what would you call this?—*furniture.*"

I heard a loud cracking sound and my mom's voice shouting, "NO!"

I shot up, anger snatching my breath away. So what if we—both of us—liked Mr. Mac! So what if I'd made Mr. Mac some, *what would you call this?—furniture!*

Stew Pot groaned, twisting about in the beanbag as he struggled to get to his feet. Gently, I pushed him back. "Sweet hero dog, don't move a hair," I said. "Don't you dare try to go down those stairs, you understand? Stay!" I fluffed up the beanbag, settled it under his head, straightened the blanket, kissed my hand to his forehead, and tore down the stairs. At the bottom I stopped and gripped the wall as the thought sank into me.

The reason my dad was being so horrid was because he was drunk.

I stormed through the kitchen. Mam's back was to

me as she stood in the doorway to my room. She swirled in surprise and held out a hand as if to warn or to stop me. I brushed it away. Without a word, she moved aside.

My dad stood in the middle of my room in a round of bright sunlight with a red willow branch in his hand. He squinted at me as if wondering how I'd suddenly appeared in the doorway. He looked down at the branch in his hand and then dropped it as if he'd been scorched.

Sometimes it made me dizzy to see lights change so quickly, flashing out, then taming down in the blink of an eye. I held on to the doorway as my dad's lights settled around him.

Part of me stared at the tall stranger standing in the shaft of sunlight with his lights shifting around him, and another part looked beyond him at the toppled table and the chair that'd been on the receiving end of a really good kick. Some part of me noticed the broken bits of branches, tufts of birds' nests and feathers and the two turquoise pillows that lay scattered across the wood floor, along with the books and the now-shattered vase I'd so carefully placed on my table—when was it, just a few hours ago?

"I see you're back," I said. To my own ears my voice sounded hollow.

I'd stormed down all set to scream out my anger. Now all I could feel was a huge emptiness growing inside me, in the place where my heart used to be. *This is not who you are,* I wanted to say to my dad. *And we are not who we were just an hour ago. None of us will ever, ever be the same. . . .*

Somewhere a ringing sound started up. *Brinnnng!*

Brinnnng! It sounded far, far away. Mam squeezed my shoulder. "I left a message for Mac," she whispered. "He must be calling back." She disappeared into the kitchen.

I concentrated hard on the circle of sunlight where my dad stood. I tried to block out the rest of the room.

"Did you find the Nutella?" I asked. My tone was so polite it surprised even me. I could've been asking him to please come have a glass of ice tea. The effect might've been spoiled by the hiccups that suddenly came out of nowhere.

"It must not exist in Wyoming," my dad said. His face turned red, and I wondered if he only now remembered that he'd gone off to look for that chocolaty stuff.

Somewhere far, far away, someone was calling, "Blue . . . Blue . . ."

That's my name, I thought, but I didn't move. I was inside a bubble where nothing and no one could reach me, where nothing could ever hurt anymore. I could see my dad's mouth moving, but the words didn't make any sense. Inside my bubble the outside world didn't exist.

Mam's hand shook my shoulder. "Blue. Blue. The phone call's for you. Are you okay?"

"No," I said flatly.

"It's Clyde, down at the store." My mom's eyes poured into mine. "It's about your friend. . . ."

I hiccupped my way through the kitchen and lifted the phone to my ear. I could hear a rumble of voices and what sounded like cups clattering on counters.

"Hello?" I squeaked.

"Blue, you there? You seen Shawn lately? He's gone

missing. Thought we'd better call up to Far Canyon, since it's the nearest place to his grandma's."

"No," I said, and I hiccupped. "It's been a while. . . ."

Above the background noise I could hear a gruff man's voice counting up the days since he'd last seen Shawn, saying it'd been four days, no, maybe five, darn kid. He was hard to keep track of, what with the way he was always off helping some relative or the other or foolin' around out there on those tribal lands. . . .

"Blue says she hasn't seen hide nor hair of him, either," Clyde said to the crowd in the store.

"Clyde." I gulped. "What happened?"

"His horse came back without him. Showed up this afternoon at his grandma's place. Minus his rider."

I held the phone out and frowned at it. Clyde's voice came through. "Seems he told his grandma he was riding over to go help his uncle with the haying. Seems his uncle wasn't aware he was coming, so no one worried when he didn't show up. Well, thanks anyway, Blue. Don't worry. We're getting a search party together," he said, and hung up.

I just stood there opening and closing my mouth like a fish.

Chapter Twenty-seven

I stared down at the strange object I held in my hand. Mam reached over and hung up the phone. She looked worriedly into my eyes. "Do you have any idea where he is?" she asked.

I shook my head. But I did know. In the back of my mind I could see a black hole. *The entrance to the underworld . . .*

I could just imagine calling Clyde back, saying, *Wait a minute. Listen, I saw some fuzzy lines stretched out along the ground not too long ago, and I told Shawn about them, how they seemed to meet up in a star at a certain place in the mountains. He got all excited and I bet he's gone off . . .*

Yeah, right.

From somewhere outside my bubble I could hear my mom's voice explaining what'd happened, and then my dad's saying, "What is the big deal? Probably the kid did not tie up his horse. Why, I myself have had a horse run off. What you do then is you put one foot in front of the other. You *walk* home."

I tried hard to think through the fog that had taken the place of my brain. Shawn and I had talked about the ley lines on my birthday—when was that, a week ago? He could've taken off the next day, or soon afterward.

And then, in spite of all the bad stuff that had happened that day, I felt a guilty little tingle of joy. Maybe that explained why he hadn't been back to our tree. . . . And when exactly, I wondered, had I started thinking of it as *our* tree?

Still, I couldn't imagine Tivo just walking away, though I'd never seen Shawn tie him up. No. Something had to be terribly wrong. Maybe he was hurt. Maybe he couldn't put one foot in front of the other. Maybe he *couldn't* walk home. . . .

I tottered out of the kitchen as if I were sleepwalking and stumbled up to my attic.

Numbly, I reached for the backpack that lay in its usual place by my bed. I dumped my colored pencils and journal onto the bed and checked to be sure I had water, matches, and my sack of trail mix. Then I stuck a hand under the pillow and grabbed Grub's black button eye and stuffed it into my pocket. I pulled a long-sleeved shirt out of the closet and tucked it into my backpack. Stew Pot's eyes followed my every move.

I sank down by the beanbag. How could I possibly leave him? Honestly, all I wanted was to crawl in with him, close my eyes, and forget about wolves and wounded doggies and fathers who wrecked things. Forget about kids who'd gone missing. But how could I? It was *my* fault that Shawn had gotten himself into this fix, whatever it was. It was up to me to get him out of it.

Through the hole in the floor I could hear my parents' low, bickering voices. My dad said something about packing up. I sat up and leaned toward the hole.

"The best thing would be for you to leave this desolate place," he said. "Just pack things up—"

"Don't tell me what I should do," my mom's angry voice broke in.

"You prefer to stay *here* when I am asking you to come with me? I still have very strong feelings for you."

"I think you've already shown me exactly how much you care," Mam said, and I could imagine her lifting her chin and giving my dad one of her looks.

Pot struggled to lift his head. "Don't listen," I whispered. He soaked up moods like a sponge, same as I did. How could I possibly work on Stew Pot with everything all stirred up like this? I took a breath.

I'd have to hurry if I was going to find Shawn before dark.

I felt as if I'd fallen apart and now had to gather up all the scattered pieces of myself. I closed my eyes and imagined I was outside soaking up the bright sunlight. I held my hands over Pot's wound and opened my eyes and watched as the light slowly grew. I could see Pot's lights growing brighter. I sat there with my hands over Pot's wound until finally he relaxed. When he started to snore I took my hands away.

Pot's lights fluttered and grew dim.

I sat still and tried not to cry. It all felt so hopeless. How could I possibly leave him? What I'd been doing just wasn't enough. What had I been thinking? What if I'd been fooling myself all along? I stared at my hands. What a strange thing it was to even *think* they could heal. Maybe my dad was right. Maybe the best thing really would be to leave this desolate place. Maybe I'd gotten—what was the word?—"delusional." I'd read about someone being that way and I'd looked the word up. It meant they'd had a false or mistaken belief or idea about something. That seemed to fit me to a tee.

The attic suddenly grew dark as a cloud covered the sun. I sighed. It was getting late. I pushed myself out of the beanbag and looked down at my sweet hero dog. In his rip-wrapped bandages he looked like a furry black caterpillar shedding its skin. I imagined a chrysalis of light forming around him. "Heal inside your silvery cocoon, little butterfly," I whispered. "Only please. Please. Don't fly away while I'm gone. . . ."

I grabbed my cap, slung my pack over my shoulder, and tiptoed down the stairs.

They were both in the kitchen. Mam stood with her hands on her hips, looking to me as if she'd grown ten inches taller. My dad had his head down as if he were studying his boots. He looked up when I opened the door. "You going somewhere?" he asked.

"Yes," I said. I lifted a shoulder and shifted the pack on my back.

"But I am here! I am back!" my dad said. "You are angry about the chair, the little table, I know. That's a strange thing for a child to do. Building furniture? But I will fix the silly little things you made and make them good as new." My dad beamed a smile at me. It was such a charming smile. . . .

I shook my head.

"We will do it together," he said. "Like a father-and-daughter team. I will show you how to make a much better chair. I will show you what I can do."

"I think you've already shown me," I said.

The words hung in the air. I imagined them lining up like beads on a string next to Mam's words. Mam and I looked at each other. My dad looked from me to my mom, but none of us spoke. In the silence I could hear my dad swallow.

My heart pounded as I stared at my dad, maybe really seeing him for the first time, and maybe even seeing him for the last.

Through the window behind him I could see the sun glinting off the roof of his new-model truck, see the dull rusty top of Ol' Yeller beside it. Our truck was so beat-up it was a wonder it even made it to the barn. But it had carried us here, and it could take us somewhere else, if

Mam and I decided to go. I had the feeling that we'd be making those decisions together from now on.

I looked at my mom, standing there holding her head tall. She had that look in her eyes. The one she got when she was zeroing in on a calf, about to twirl her rope and lasso it. If I'd been my dad, I'd have been careful.

"I've got to go," I said before she could say anything.

Mam held up her hands as if to say "Wait!" but I kept on.

"Stew Pot's upstairs. He's in bad shape. He had a war with a wolf. Please check on him and take him to the veterinarian. I gave him a big shot of penicillin and doused him with antiseptic. But he's hurt bad and you'll have to take care of him."

I walked to my dad and reached a hand up to his neck. He bent down and I kissed him on the cheek. I touched his scar with one finger. He reached out for me, but I stepped away. "Bye, Papa," I said. I turned to Mam. "Don't worry," I said. "I think I know where Shawn is, but I can't explain it."

I was out the door before she could question me.

"Oh. I forgot," I called over my shoulder. "Don't have a heart attack when you go into the bathroom."

I got hung up before I even got started. How had I forgotten about my backpack when I tried to go through the fence? And then, what with my hands not working quite right, it took ages to get all untangled. Down by the house a truck revved up, backfired, and roared down the road. I stood without moving, counting the seconds it took for the sounds to fade. Three minutes exactly was all it took for my dad to roar out of my life.

"Put one foot in front of the other," he'd said. That's what I did. Walked away, slowly, not looking back, taking forever to hike up my hill.

Maybe it was just the late-afternoon sun striking my tree, but its lights seemed brighter than ever. It seemed to glow as if it'd become some sort of holy place.

I pulled Grub's eye out of my pocket and found it a little nook in the shaggy bark of the juniper's trunk. I thought of a zillion wishes. Finally I boiled them all down into one.

"Just let everything be for the better." I sighed. "Thanks."

I shielded my eyes and looked out from my hill. Far, far away, over the Owl Creeks, the stacked clouds had reared up into scary dark thunderheads. Far below, along the stretch of road that led to the highway, red dust ghosts trailed behind a small speck, playing peekaboo as they passed behind hills. I watched the dust billow up as the speck on the road suddenly stopped.

I couldn't breathe. In my head I could see him. My dad, sparks flying as he pounded the steering wheel with his fists while the dust settled around his pickup. He was thinking about turning around and racing back up the road to the ranch and running after me and grabbing me up in his arms and begging me to forgive him. I could see him turning all pretty rainbow colors as he told me how happy he was to have found us again, and how it didn't matter one bit that my mom sold his guitar because it was really me he'd come back for, and not that stupid guitar.

He almost did this, I know.

For a long time the truck sat there. But then the ghost dusts rose once again, and when they reached the highway I lost him.

I bit my lip, trying to hold back a sob. Then I turned away. I'd wasted too much time. Already the thunderheads pawed at the sky. I fanned my face with my cap. At least it wouldn't be quite so hot with all those clouds coming in. I scanned the mountains to pinpoint the spot marked by the shale landslide where I thought Shawn might be. If I hurried, I could get there in, what? I calculated the distance. Two miles, maybe, going slantways over the hills to the edge of the deep forest. Then I'd have to go up into the trees to get to the point across from the landslide landmark. From there I'd climb down into the gorge. Shawn had said something about the cave being hard to spot if you didn't come upon it from above. But I'd find it. If I jogged all the way, it shouldn't take long. . . .

I launched myself over the ledge and slipped and slid down the hill, almost crashing into the tree where Shawn always left Tivo.

I should've saddled a horse!

No one would've objected. I could run back. Catch a horse . . .

I almost did. I even took a few steps. But no. Mam

would certainly see me, and she'd be so full of questions and doubts that it'd make my own worries worse, and I'd want to run up and check on Stew Pot, and then I'd never, ever tear myself away. . . .

Eyes on the ground, one foot in front of the other, I started off. I climbed the hill Shawn and I had ridden up with me on the back of Tivo. At least I didn't have to cross the creek—I was headed in the opposite direction this time. Once I was on the high ground that stretched up toward the mountains I could jog along at a good pace. Dodging prairie dog holes, prickly cactus, and gnarly sagebrush, ignoring the grasshoppers that flit up and out of my path, I ran.

I hadn't gone far when I tripped. Gasping and trying hard not to cry, I blinked up at the mountains looming ahead, and at the dark clouds sneaking down over their tops. Suddenly the whole day caved in around me. I slumped over my knees. I had to be totally bonkers. What had I been *thinking*? I'd have as much luck finding Shawn as I would a tick on a bear.

I'll go back, I thought as I sat nursing my knees. *I'll call Clyde and tell him my weird little story and get help with this search.* It was only because of everything going on at the house that I'd run off like I had—who could blame me?

I rubbed my knees, picked the burrs out of my socks, and was about to scramble up when I felt rather than heard something behind me. I twisted around.

They could've dropped out of the sky, Lone One and Light of the Dawn. They'd come up so quietly, Lone One with that mischievous look in her eyes. Sure enough, she tucked her head down. I jumped up, holding my hands out in front of me as she charged. The small horny black bumps on her head dug into my hands as she pushed hard against me. I skidded backward. But—it wasn't a bad butt. More like a nudge, really, as if she just wanted to have fun, the way I'd seen antelopes playing butting games with one another.

Something inside me soared as a thought struck me. *If I start running, they'd be so curious they'd run after me.*

I spun around and took off.

In about two seconds they'd sprinted right past me. I followed behind. Even a lame antelope could run faster than I could, but having them ahead of me spurred me on. I ran as fast as I could—faster than ever I'd run before. After a while the fawn dropped down, panting, behind a sagebush. Far ahead, Lone One stopped, looked back, and waited for me before she took off once again. "You're too fast," I yelled when all I could see was the white flag of her rump. It didn't matter that sometimes I couldn't even see her because of all the gullies and hills; she'd taken off in the right direction. It was almost as if she were following along those strange lines of energy that led toward the cave.

I ran past my tiredness and worries, ran past my heaviness, ran till my hurts didn't hurt anymore. Ran till I felt like I'd burst through a barrier and was floating along on pure air.

I barely noticed the cows lifting their heads as I darted by. I didn't pay attention to the winds picking up, or to the gloomy clouds bubbling and boiling around me. And

I didn't even see the flash of white light but I heard its furious *crack!* and I hit the ground hard.

"Cripes almighty," I said into the dirt as I plastered my hands to my ears. I couldn't tell where the lightning had struck, but it hadn't been far away. I peeked through my fingers at the tan blur streaking back down toward her fawn. *Please stay safe,* I thought. *I couldn't have made it without you. . . .*

I ducked as another silvery flash ripped through the sky and slashed into the forest behind me. I squeezed my eyes shut as thunder boomed over the hills and rumbled and roared down the canyons. When the echoing grumbles faded away I lifted my head.

It was only a skip and a jump to the shelter of the forest. I scrambled up and ran for it. Brushing aside branches as I dashed into the trees, I stumbled over a dead limb and sprawled on the ground. Looking up, I saw that the tree nearest me was a huge fir with branches hanging down to the ground. Crawling on hands and knees, I wiggled under its droopy branches. A thick carpet of brown needles covered the ground. Shrugging the pack off my back, I yanked out my long-sleeved shirt, crammed my arms into it, and then pulled out my bottle of water. While I guzzled it I pulled out my sack of trail mix. I shifted it from one hand to the other. Then I held up the bottle and frowned at how much I'd drunk. I took one more swig and jammed the bottle back into my pack, along with the trail mix.

I'd better save it for Shawn. He'll be even thirstier than I am, and a lot hungrier too.

I thought about how everything that had happened today had gone as wrong as it possibly could. The day had for sure hit rock bottom.

I covered my ears as a deafening boom shattered the air and shook the ground around me. My hands trembled as I cleared away twigs and branches and burrowed down into the soft carpet of needles. I curled up with my pack for a pillow and lay listening to the deep, low rumblings.

Chapter Twenty-eight

My first thought when I opened my eyes was that it was early dawn of a brand-new day. In a split second it hit me that it wasn't. I bolted up with a start, my mind racing now. I rubbed my eyes and uncurled myself, squinting out through the scraggly branches.

The sun was going down, not coming up. I must've slept for at least several hours. Cripes. I waited for what seemed like hours until the storm finally drifted away. I'd really have to get a move on if I was going to find Shawn before dark.

I grabbed my pack and crawled out of my green cave and stumbled to the edge of the forest. *At least the worst is over,* I thought as I stood brushing off dirt and needles. The wind had picked up, but the storm had drifted away and now the sky to the east had turned dark and scary looking. Still, with all that blustery show, not one drop of rain had fallen. That didn't seem fair. This whole forest was so dry and thirsty-looking it was practically begging for rain.

I started off, walking as fast as I could along the edge of the forest. I hadn't gone far when a blister popped up on one heel. A bit farther on I doubled over with a stitch in my side. I plopped down and tugged off my boot. Shook it. Picked the burrs out of my socks. Took a deep breath.

I sniffed the air. Was that smoke I smelled?

I wrenched my boot back on and scrambled to my feet.

If there's a fire, it has to be far away. Scent travels, I said to myself. Then I said it out loud because that's what I wanted to believe.

I sniffed the air again. Slowly I turned in a circle, peering out over the landscape. It must've been my imagination, I decided. There wasn't a ghost of smoke, not a wisp or a whisper anywhere that I could see.

The wind gusted behind me, shoving me forward and whirling dust into my eyes. I pulled my shirt tight around me and walked faster. It wasn't far now to the ridge across from the landslide. I'd have to head back into the trees and then hike along the ridge until I found someplace where I could climb down. In the bottom, Shawn had said, there'd be a creek. It might be just a trickle, he'd said, but if you followed it down you'd find the hidden mouth of the cave.

"One foot in front of the other," I found myself saying as the wind pushed me along. I grabbed on to my side as the stitch in it nearly doubled me over again. Now I was chanting over and over the words to that Indian prayer. "Where I walk is sacred, sacred is the ground. Forest, mountain, river, listen to the sound. Great Spirit circle, circle all around. . . ."

Under my boots, the dry hill grass crackled like paper. The wind rattled and drummed through the trees. Above me, hundreds of rosy finches swarmed out of the cliffs.

Holding my side, ignoring the blister, I sped up. I was almost to the ridge. From there I'd head into the trees. *"Whew,"* I said out loud, and I breathed a huge sigh of relief.

That's when I smelled it for sure. I looked up, dreading what I might see.

On a pale rosy cliff high above me rose a swirl of white smoke. A patch of red glowed against the dark green of the forest. I watched, stunned, as the red patch flared up and turned bright orange and black. Watched as the flames suddenly leaped from one tree to the next.

A feeling of horror ballooned up inside me. I froze, my mind a big blank as I stared at flames snaking their way toward a scraggly dead pine out on the highest point of a cliff. I stood petrified as the flames snatched at the tree and then leaped up its trunk and turned it into a flaming red torch. Then, with an earsplitting *crack*, the tree exploded. Blazing limbs and fiery red bark whirled through the air and came tumbling and crashing down into the forest below.

There was a sound as if the jittery trees were clapping. As I stood there the applause turned into a roar.

Within seconds, before my wide eyes, it seemed as if the whole forest had burst into flames.

I couldn't think. My feet, though, didn't need brains to know what to do–*run!* Run away, run as fast as they could, run, run, back to the ranch! That's what I started to do. Then suddenly a freezing cold terror spread through me. I couldn't. *I couldn't.*

Shawn. He was out here somewhere. . . .

"*Shawnnnnnnnnnn!*" I shrieked as I started to run where only a fool would go. Shoving aside branches, leaping over fallen tree trunks, I tore through the trees toward the ridge. Behind me I could feel the fire's heat and hear a terrible roaring as if a huge monster train was crashing its way through the forest. If I didn't move fast, it'd be only minutes before it reached me.

Through the trees, to my left, I could see the gray landslide. I cut toward it and stopped short at the ledge and gaped down. My stomach lurched into my throat. The cliff dropped about forty feet almost straight to the ground.

How was I supposed to climb down? I'd never make it, at least not here. . . . Quickly I scanned the ridge. Way back where I'd come from, only much farther down, there was a place where I could easily get down. Farther up, toward the mountains, it only got steeper. I looked over my shoulder. A gust of wind whipped a shower of sparks in my direction. Behind me, the fire gobbled up one tree after the other. It was too late to turn back. I was trapped.

Even if I fell, nothing could be worse than staying up here.

I crouched and reached for the exposed root of a gnarly old pine that stuck out of the side of the cliff. *Don't look down,* I told myself, *and don't look back toward the fire.* I stretched a foot over the ledge and swung my foot back and forth, feeling for a foothold. My toe touched a slab. It felt as if it might crumble with my full weight, but what choice did I have? I clutched the root with both hands and swung my other foot over the cliff.

Only the gnarly root and the toehold kept me from sliding straight down. Then my other foot touched a shelf. Slowly I let go of the root. For a moment it seemed almost as if I hovered in midair, and then I snapped back close to the wall and clutched wildly at it while my toes explored the narrow shelf. Then, clawing at the wall, I inched my hands down till I crouched hunched on the outcrop. I dangled one leg over and felt for another foothold. I climbed down to it. From one narrow ledge to the next, I let my feet feel their way down. The footholds felt as soft as hands, but they didn't crumble. And then, when I'd almost reached bottom, I let go and slid down the rest of the way.

I leaned in to the cliff. If only I could've stayed there forever, arms spread out and my cheek pressed against the cool face of the cliff. If only I didn't have to *think.*

Slowly I pushed myself away from the wall and looked around. Down here, the light was gray-gold and fuzzy, but up there, on the rim, white smoke puffed up like Halloween ghosts tweaking their sheets in the wind.

But even down here, I didn't feel safe. What if those

trees on the rim caught on fire and fell into the canyon? I had to find the cave. Find it fast.

Wheezing from the smoke, I plunged through a tangle of berry bushes and shrub toward the center of the narrow valley, toward what had looked from above like a gray river of rocks. Huge boulders and chunky shale slabs clogged the creek bed. I scrambled up onto a boulder and turned in a circle, looking around. A trickle of water thin as a garden snake twisted down through the rocky creek bed.

"Just follow the water," Shawn had said. "It disappears into the cave."

Chapter Twenty-nine

I scrambled down off the boulder. I hadn't gone far when the trickle seeped under a boulder as big as a truck and disappeared out of sight. Even climbing up on the highest rocks and looking around, I couldn't for the life of me figure out where the water came out.

The creek bed twisted between steep canyon walls that jutted out and then drew back into deep shadows. I was directly across from the gray shale landslide. My eyes darted to every gash, scar, and dark shadow on both sides of the canyon walls. A feeling of hopelessness sank through me. There was no sign of a cave.

And even worse, no sign of Shawn.

It wasn't until I looked up at the rim and saw black smoke boiling up that I realized I'd been praying. *Please,* I prayed, as if my very life depended on this one word. *Please, please, please,* I repeated over and over as flames leaped at the trees overlooking the canyon. "Please," I said when a sound rose as if the trees were now moaning in pain. "Please," I said as they exploded and came crashing down into the canyon.

In spite of the heat I felt myself turn icy cold.

"Please," I whispered. "I'm here to find Shawn. Please."

As I said that last "please," a quick, sudden knowing washed over me like a wave breaking over my head.

I was in a place where I shouldn't be, looking for a cave I was supposed to know nothing about. It was such an ancient, secret, forbidden cave—the entrance to the underworld—that the water ghosts and little people had made it invisible.

And suddenly something, I don't know what, but *something* felt different. All the panic I'd felt seemed to lift out of me, the way you might feel if you'd just aced the most challenging, most tricky test ever. Or maybe how you might feel if you'd gone through some kind of initiation. And it was right at that moment when I heard the loud gurgle.

I looked down.

A clog of twigs and leaves gushed out from beneath the boulder I stood on. The litter bunched up and then swirled and slowly started floating down through the alleyway of gray boulders. They snaked around a jagged outcrop and then disappeared out of sight. I was about to jump down and follow along when I spotted a pile of debris heaping up along the edge of the outcrop. It suddenly bulged up, and then with a gurgle it disappeared into a narrow slit at the foot of the cliff.

The entrance to the cave was just a mere crack in the earth.

"Hang on, Shawn," I cried and I slid off the boulder and stumbled over the rocks toward the place where the pile of leaves and twigs had vanished. I'd been searching for an O- or a U-shaped mouth—no wonder I hadn't seen it! Then, pushing my backpack ahead of me, I wriggled through the narrow opening.

Talk about a mouth. The cave entrance was clammy and dark and it drooled and smelled like sour breath. I had a sense of teeth grazing my head, and the strange, eerie feeling that I could be swallowed whole in one gulp.

A shaft of smoky light streamed through the crack and then evaporated into the total black night of the cave. In the dim light all I could see was the narrow, slimy ledge I'd wiggled onto and a few rocky stairlike shelves that dropped down from it and then dissolved into darkness. The trickle of water dribbled over the ledge and then vanished into the cracks between rocks.

"Shawn?" I shouted into the blackness.

In a clear crystalline voice the cave called out, "Shawn! Shawn! Shawn!"

I held my breath. Silence.

My shoulders slumped. I could feel all my hopes come crashing down, one on top of the other. It had been too much to expect. After everything that had gone as wrong as it possibly could, I'd hoped that something good would happen. Maybe even something *miraculous*. Like for Shawn actually to be there. In the cave. Safe. Alive. Of course he'd probably be injured. Something had for sure kept him from getting back to his grandma's ranch—but he'd be waiting for me and totally thrilled out of his boots that I'd found him.

But . . . maybe I was too late. What if he was . . .

I couldn't even *think* the word. I took a deep breath and shouldered back into my pack and slowly, carefully wormed my way off the slippery ledge.

Blinking to get used to the dark, I inched down the steplike ledges. They seemed to go on forever. I was about to give up and just curl up where I was when my feet touched dirt and what had to be the bottom of the very deep hole.

Total silence. Total darkness. Total stillness and *nothing.*

Good thing I wasn't afraid of the dark. Except maybe *this* dark . . .

I got the heebie-jeebies staring into it. It was a black so black that I couldn't even see my own lights. There was no up, no down, no left, no right. It was like the confusion I'd felt once when I'd gotten caught in a blinding blizzard, only this time it was a total blackout instead of a whiteout. Holding my arms out in front of me, I slid a foot forward on the dirt floor. My legs wobbled like a horse that'd been ridden too fast, too far.

I was safe, but just try to tell that to my body.

Inch by inch I felt my way forward, the jet-black darkness so thick it was as if I waded through ink. Twigs, leaves, hard stones, and soft things crunched under my boots—oh thank goodness, thank heaven that nothing squirmed or wiggled beneath them! I bent over and groped around on the ground for sticks, leaves, twigs, anything that I could use for a fire. Blindly, wildly, I pulled my stash to me and heaped it up into a pile. I felt in my pack for my matches. Stopped breathing. I'd lost them. No. There they were. My hands shook so badly that it took half my box of matches before I got one that sparked. I tucked it into my pile, hunched over it, and blew. As a blue flame blazed up and grew I put more twigs in it and then I squinted around at the darkness.

I was definitely in a deep hole. Huge, by the little bit of it that I could see by the feeble light from my fire. For a quick second, as my fire flared up, I glimpsed dark red and ocher-colored slabs heaped along one side of the cave. Against the wall ahead of me was a jumble of sticks and brush that had probably been washed there by water. I shuddered as the thought hit me that if a sudden downpour flooded the cave, that'd be the way I'd end up, too. Smashed into the wall with a bunch of sticks.

I dragged myself over to the jumble of sticks and hauled back an armful. I dropped them and made one more trip and then plunked myself down by my fire. I pulled my trail mix and bottle of water out of my pack.

I drank all the water, but I couldn't swallow one bit of the trail mix.

This is what it must feel like to be at the bottom of a bottomless pit, I thought. Somehow it was easier to think about being deep underground in a black hole than it was to think about the fire raging outside. Or about how I'd come within a pinch of getting caught in it. Or about who might be caught in it now. Because one thing was for sure. Shawn wasn't here in this cave.

And of course it wasn't Shawn's fault that I'd risked my life to come find him. It wasn't even his fault that I'd abandoned my poor sweet doggie when he'd needed me most. And then run out on my mom who, come to think of it, was probably crazy with fear because by now she'd surely spotted the fire. It wasn't anyone's fault that I'd run from my dad. Run from throwing all the horrible words I could've or should've hurled at him before I left.

Or was it the other way around? Hadn't *he* thrown out those horrible words—hadn't *my dad* been the one who'd run out on *me*?

I was *so* tired. . . .

I tossed the last of the sticks into the fire. Not bothering about the bumps and lumps in the dirt under me, I lay down, stuffed my pack under my head, and stared up into the darkness. The fire suddenly blazed up and I flinched.

There were *teeth* over my head. No, not teeth—they were stars shining above me, a whole Milky Way of shimmering pale greenish crystals twinkling down from the roof of the cave. I seemed to be smack in the middle of a gigantic geode.

Beside me, all around me, fallen stars lay scattered about in the dirt. I picked up one and wiped off the dirt. It looked like pale greenish light frozen in stone. I held it to my cheek and it felt like tingling ice on a sore spot.

I lay back with the fire flickering off the thousands of pale greenish crystals and called out Shawn's name once again. "Shawn! Shawn! Shawn!" the crystals sang back.

Chapter Thirty

"Blue?"

Is it morning already? No, it can't be. It has to be the middle of night because it's so dark, but didn't I just hear my mom calling my name?

"Coming," I moaned. Then, "Lemme sleep," I muttered, snuggling back into my pillow. *Geez, but it's lumpy. And this bed is so hard. . . .*

My eyes popped wide open. It was pitch-black. Except for—except for the fire, which had burned low. My fire. I was on the cold, hard floor of the cave. I must have fallen asleep. My skin started crawling up inch by inch from my toes to my skull. I grew as still as a rock. Ages went by. I tried not to think of how my shoulders were cramping and my elbow was itching and how I really, really did have to sneeze.

"Ahhhhchoo!" I muffled the sneeze with my hands.

From far, far away, as if coming up out of a deep hole, I heard it again. "Blue?"

I sucked in my breath. "Sha—Shawn?"

"Friend?" The voice floated up from somewhere deep down under the ground.

"Shawn, is that you?" My heart about leaped out of my chest. "You're here in the cave! But where are you?"

"I dreamed you. I'm a ghost. I'm dead" rose a flat, deadly calm voice.

Ohmygod! Did that mean I was dead too? Goose bumps rose on top of goose bumps as I clutched at my shirt—it seemed real enough—and then felt behind me for my pack. It felt solid. . . . And for sure the crystal I still gripped in one hand was rock hard and solid. I tucked it into my pocket.

"Are you dead too?" rose the voice.

"Shawn, you stop that right this minute," I shrieked. "I mean it. You're creeping me out!" I pinched the back of my hand. It hurt. There was no way I could be dead.

"Is this a dream?" the voice floated up dreamily.

"Wait a minute. Make a noise. Say something. I'm coming to find you," I said, my voice calmer but still trembling.

"What are you doing here?" the dazed-sounding voice wondered.

"Looking for you, Shawn, that's what I'm doing. Been all over the mountain, almost. It's on fire, Shawn, you know that? No, of course you don't. Keep talking. I'm trying to figure out where you are." With the way those crystals seemed to pick up sounds and then fling them back, I couldn't tell where the voice came from.

"I'm down in the underworld," growled the very low, grave, serious voice. "Don't come near me."

"Okay, Shawn, I get that you're in this direction," I called back almost as gravely. I staggered dizzily to my feet. "Cripes, it's pitch-black in here. Just a second while I get this fire going. . . . Keep talking."

I fumbled about for the sticks I'd gathered—when? I had no idea what time it was, or even what day it was or how long I'd slept. I couldn't tell up from down or front from back. And I guessed it would stay that way because I'd already used up my stash of kindling. I blew on my almost-dead fire and stirred it with a stick, and then placed the stick on it. It flared up but didn't make a dent in the enormous black night of the cave.

"You sound awful real . . . ," rose the doubtful-sounding voice. "But watch out. Don't come near me, you'll fall."

"I'm coming, Shawn, like it or not," I said, muffling a big *ouch!* as I tripped, stubbing my toe. Holding my hands out, I blindly shuffled along the rough floor toward the place where the voice seemed to be coming from.

"Listen, I've got a flashlight." The voice for the first time sounded hopeful. "It's really weak, the batteries are almost out, but I'll shine it up."

A pale shaft of yellow light glimmered up.

"I see it. I see it," I called back excitedly. I groped my way toward it, my eyes stretching for things beyond what they could see, and bumping smack into what felt like a big slab of rock. I walked my hands up the smooth vertical wall of the slab. Now, with my heart actually pumping again and my energy suddenly pepped up to the max, I could see the faint glow of my hands and the blue-white light streaming out of my fingers. "I'm alive," I whispered, and for some strange reason I almost burst into tears.

And then there it was right in front of me. The yellow light. It shone up from the depths of the earth.

"Geez, Shawn," I managed to say. "How'd you get down there?"

"There's a rope. It's hanging down from the other side of this hole. At least I think it is. . . . I'm a bit . . . dizzy. . . ." The beam of light swayed back and forth as it searched across the walls for the rope and finally found it. The light suddenly went out. "Don't try to come down here," Shawn said. "Please."

"This may sound stupid, but if you got down the rope, why can't you climb back up it?"

"Right. I fell. I think I broke my arm. I can't climb back out. I tried, but one-armed . . ." Even from high above I could hear him let out his breath. "It was real dumb to come to this cave and not tell anyone where I was going. . . ."

"You're not kidding. Double dumb, because I just did the same thing."

The light flicked back on. "You're kidding," Shawn said.

"I wish I were. But listen, Shawn. Don't move. Just

keep the light on while I go around to the side of the hole where the rope is. I'm coming down." The light wavered, found me, and then slowly moved toward the rope. I followed, crawling carefully forward on hands and knees. I was on a shelf of sorts. A shelf that dropped down—I stared at the point of light—maybe twenty feet. I couldn't see Shawn at all, just the bright spot of his flashlight.

"I heard the spirits singing my name," Shawn said, back in his dreamy voice. "I thought I'd gone to the spirit world."

"Always sneaking up when I don't know you're around, Shawn. Just like you," I said as I reached the place where the rope was attached. "You climbed down *that*?" I said, then quickly, "Not that I can't do it too. . . ."

It wasn't a ladder, but just a rope with big knots tied into it for footholds. I knew I could do it. I mean, after all, hadn't I just climbed down a cliff with a raging fire at my back? This would be a piece of cake. Nothing to it.

"Don't come down. If you fall, we'll both be stuck in this hole. . . ."

He had a point. Who would come find us? Thanks to our combined brilliance, no one even knew where we were. But what choice did I have?

"I can't leave you, Shawn," I called down. "It would take me forever to get back to the ranch and then back up here. And besides, I don't know that I could even get there right now. There's a huge wildfire burning outside. It's maybe even worse now—the whole range is probably blazing."

I slid over the ledge. Clung for dear life to the rope . . .

"I'll sit here below you and try to soften your fall, if you do fall, that is. But try not to," Shawn called up, and below me I could hear him moving around.

At least he could move. And actually, with the big knots tied in the rope, it really was a piece of cake climbing down. *"Oops,"* I said. "Did I kick you?"

"*Ni hinch*. My friend," Shawn whispered. "It's really you."

Now that my feet had touched bottom again (how many levels did the underworld have?), I felt like falling to pieces and crying my heart out and even telling him what a dumb klutz he was and that I was thrilled to the bones to have found him and that even if he didn't like me, well, I loved him, I really did love him, so there. And I almost did that. But what I did instead was lean dizzily over him, feel down his arm, swallow, and say, "Wow, Shawn. You really got yourself into a pickle."

"Arm doesn't hurt much anymore," Shawn said, and he put his good hand on top of mine and held it against his hurt arm. "Did at first, and it felt a lot worse after I tried to climb back out. But I made this sling out of my T-shirt, and it's much better now."

Which made me close my eyes and say a quick prayer for my hero dog Stew Pot.

The light suddenly sputtered and dimmed.

"Better turn off the flashlight," I said, although really

I just wanted to look him over real good and make sure there was nothing worse wrong with him.

"Yeah, I've been trying to make it last," Shawn said, switching it off. "I turned it on every once in a while just to see light. Just thinkin' about how it would be when it went totally out . . . Oh man. Keep touching my hand," he said, and his hand clamped down harder on mine. "I can't tell up from down in this black hole."

"How long have you been down here? Have you had anything to eat? Drink? Geez, Shawn," I sputtered, rearing my head back and studying his lights. I shuddered at the thought that he might've died in this hole if I hadn't found him.

"Came here two days after you told me about those lines. I told my grandma I was going to go help my uncle with the haying. It was a lie. I couldn't tell her I was going to this cave—it's not a place where she'd allow me to go. I thought if I was lucky I'd have myself a vision. But I should've done it the right way, with an elder to guide me." Shawn stopped, out of breath.

With my hand, the one that wasn't still gripped tightly in his, I brushed back the hair on his forehead. Somehow I could tell that he smiled.

"I wasn't going to be gone long," he continued. "Day or so, maybe. Now I've lost track of time. I had an apple and two baloney sandwiches in my pack. But there's plenty of water. It trickles down over the wall and then disappears into a hole. Don't go near it. It's slippery over there. . . ."

"The entrance to the underworld," I breathed.

"Shhhh!" Shawn said, his hand suddenly holding mine like a fist. "It's a spirit thing. Our lower world is a place of dreaming and visions. I can't talk about this, Friend. You shouldn't be here." A long pause. "And neither should I."

"I understand, Shawn. Don't worry, you don't have to say any more. I've got some trail mix in my pack, but I left it up in the cave. Saved it for you, though. Just in case . . ."

"I'm not very hungry. My stomach must've shrunk." Shawn grunted. "Funny way to lose weight, no?"

"Well, we've got to get you out of here. This may be a sacred hole, but it's clammy as all get-out. It's a wonder you haven't turned into a mushroom." I reached down and felt the ground. "Here, stretch out on the dirt," I said, kneeling and holding my hand behind him and gently pushing him backward. "Let's see what's going on."

"How can you see? All I see is black, black, and more black."

"I see your lights, which are pretty darn bright considering what you've been through. And I see my own lights shining out. I could hardly see them at all when I first got to the cave, I was so totally pooped." I waved my fingers and watched my own blue-white lights flash into the darkness. I'd have to pump up my lights, bring into myself all the light I possibly could if I was going to be able to help him.

"This dark's like a sponge absorbing the light," I added. "I've never seen anything like it. It must've been awful. . . ."

"I did a whole lot of praying," Shawn said, sucking his breath in as he tried moving his arm. "But you know what? I knew you'd come."

"You did?" I reared back in surprise.

"Yeah. I had this strong feeling that things were going to turn out the way they were meant to."

"If I told you how close I came to not making it . . . ," I said, my stomach clenching into a knot just thinking about the fire and my mad dash toward the invisible cave. I swallowed, trying to gather myself together again. Now wasn't the time to fall apart.

"Okay, listen," I said, bending over him. "I'm gonna run my hands over you, above your body, to check things out. I'm feeling something like an electric spike coming out of your arm and I see a spear of light where the bone's probably fractured. Not a bad break. At least it didn't cut through your skin, thank goodness. You know, Shawn, I might be able to help it a little. . . . Want me to try?"

"Wrap it again, you mean?" Shawn asked, surprised.

"Well, you already did that and it seems to have helped. But no. I'd like to use light."

"Do it. Please. Friend? You know what? When I heard my name being called out of the darkness the sound seemed to be everywhere. I could've sworn I even saw stars shining above me. I was sure I'd died and flown up to the Milky Way."

This cave. The world was so full of mystery. Here I was, in a place that I'd spotted because of some glowing lines I'd noticed one morning. And then there'd been that strange feeling I'd gotten right when I'd almost totally given up hope—the feeling that I'd been put through some sort of test and that I'd passed it with flying colors.

So really, why should I be surprised that the cave might actually, *really* be special? And that the crystals might have their own energy? I pulled the crystal out of my pocket. Maybe there was some way I could use it. In the darkness I swept the crystal over Shawn's body as he lay stretched out on the ground.

"Feel's like I'm being feathered," Shawn said dreamily. "My uncle uses eagle feathers, and this feels the same way. What are you doing?"

"I'm trying to brighten your lights," I said. "There are different places up and down your body where light seems stronger. Just holding my hands over these places makes them brighter. That's good, that means they're getting healthier, and all their bright rainbow colors are coming back really strong too. You're fantastic at healing yourself, Shawn."

"Wait!" Shawn grabbed my hand. "You said there was a fire? What happened to Tivo?"

"Tivo went back to your grandma's. That's how she knew something was wrong. The fire didn't start till late yesterday afternoon." I smiled to myself as I felt his grip on my hand relax. Now he could put all his attention to healing himself. "Now *shhh*," I whispered. "Let's see what the two of us can do to make this bone heal more quickly."

I took a deep breath. What had I gotten myself into? Like yeah, just stick your arm out and let me wave my magic wand over it, and pretty quick it'll stitch itself back together again, no hitches, no glitches, no witches required. Just little ol' batty me.

What *had* I been thinking?

But weren't we in a special place? I had the feeling that anything could happen here.

We'd do it. The two of us together. We'd heal his arm.

I grew still as still. I put all my intention on my *intention*. If I'd learned anything since we'd arrived at the ranch, it was that you had to be clear about what it was that you wanted. And then to not be surprised when magical things actually happened.

And then I just kind of got out of the way. I let go and let it happen. As I kneeled beside Shawn I could see my own lights growing brighter and brighter until I could no longer tell where I ended and where he began.

Chapter Thirty-one

The smell of smoke was not the first thing that I noticed when I woke—this morning the world smells of wet sage. We've had two days of showers and last night it *poured*, so the wildfires must finally be almost out. It seems more like a month than just a week since they started.

Mam about rattled my brains out when they hauled Shawn and me back to the ranch. Then she cried. It took several days for her to get back to her usual self. She even brought me breakfast in bed that first morning. I seriously doubt I can expect that today, though (yawn!) it still might be worth a try. But I reckon I've already milked my sprained ankle for all it was worth.

Honestly, you'd think that after whatever it was that happened in the cave to make Shawn's arm strong enough to climb out of the hole, healing a sprain would be a breeze, right? But no way. I can barely put any weight on my foot. Maybe I need to get Shawn to come heal it. Or maybe I just needed some time to myself up here in my attic room. I've got lots to put down in my journal.

Not that Shawn's arm was totally healed, but it's so much better that hardly anyone believes it was really broken. You should've seen all the winks and sideways glances we got when we came up with *that* story. You better bet he's getting ribbed something awful about hiding out in that black hole until a white girl had to come find him.

So things are getting back to normal, if such a state exists. Rumors, though, are running wild as mustangs across the reservation. The only way to round them up and get them all corralled is to tell what really happened.

First, my apologies to the tribes for trespassing, though Shawn says not to worry; they're so thankful that he was found. And my sincere thanks to the search parties and the firefighters who risked their lives looking for us. And to Mr. Mac and his crew.

I'm sorry for the years Mam says I swiped from her life. Really, how was I to know that a wildfire would start up and then grow till it covered thousands of acres? Or that she and the whole rez would come to believe we were goners?

I mean, there we were, Shawn and I, down in that black timeless hole. He was lying stretched out on the floor while I kneeled beside him. Time seemed to float by. And then suddenly Shawn grabbed my arm.

"You're on fire!!!" he called out, his voice sounding shaken and scared, as if he'd just noticed—well, me, on fire.

But I knew it wasn't fire he was seeing.

"Tell me," I whispered.

"It's dark, but I *see* you. You're glowing as if you're on fire! You're like the most *beautiful* rainbow."

I reached down and touched him. He was shaking like leaves in the wind.

"The black isn't black anymore," Shawn whispered, his voice sounding dazed. "For a moment this hole lit up—it actually glowed. Then I think you were holding that crystal and saying my name when one of those sounds struck me and rang me like a bell." He stopped. "And my arm. Feel it."

I ran one hand down his arm. Then I felt it with both hands. It certainly felt more—what was the word? Hitched together?

"Toto," I whispered, rolling my eyes at the roof of the cave, "I have a feeling we're not in Kansas anymore. We must be over the rainbow. . . ."

Shawn sucked in his breath. "I feel like a candle's burning inside my head," he whispered. "The light's so intense I don't think my body can hold it."

And he burst out crying. He cried so hard I thought the hole would fill up and we'd float to the top on his tears. They were happy tears, though, the kind you might cry when your most incredible prayer has been answered.

"I see them," Shawn kept saying, and then he'd cry some more. "You did something. I don't know what, but now I can see them. I see your lights. I see *auras*!" And suddenly he burst out laughing.

I laughed too. It felt so good, as if our laughter was dissolving all the horrors of yesterday, as if the bad memories were swelling up to the top of the hole and floating right out of the cave. Finally Shawn reached over and took both my hands in his. "Thank you," he gasped, "for whatever it was that you did."

"Well, it wasn't me," I said when I could talk. "It took the two of us to make this happen. Really, I just let the light do all the work." I thought about that for a minute. I bit my lip. I couldn't say that I'd chanted his name with such a huge feeling of love that maybe that had had something to do with it too. "But you know what?" I went on. "No one's going to believe that your arm was actually broken."

"No one except the old ones." Shawn sniffed, wiping his nose on his sleeve. His lights glowed so brightly he lit up the hole. I felt awed at the sight of him.

"The elders," Shawn went on, "they know the power of song and they know about healing. They'll believe us. And you and me. *We* know what happened down here."

We hung a high five. Our hands clapped and held, and the bluish white light from our fingers reached up through the dark like a prayer.

Shawn took a deep breath and got unsteadily to his feet. He rubbed his arm. I reached out at the same time and his fingers gripped mine. I could feel my face getting red, feel something pulse up my arm and down into my heart. A glowing pink light swelled out around us. We stayed like that for the longest time, both of us grinning and not saying a word.

Shawn's stomach suddenly rumbled. He patted it. "I think I got skinny down here," he boasted. "And this is sure one tough bone. I'm ready to climb out of this hole. I'm strong as a bear." And he growled.

I flicked on the flashlight. Its weak golden moon found the rope and trailed up the knots to the top. Shadows swung back and forth like giant spiders as Shawn grabbed the rope. It made me think of those tales where a rope falls out of the sky or a bean stalk grows up to the clouds. They always ended with the hero climbing up it and finding himself in a whole different world.

A world twenty feet up.

There was no way he could make it. He'd break his arm again. Or worse, his neck or his leg.

"Better move back or I'll squash you like a bug if I fall," Shawn warned as he reached up. He tested his arm and pulled himself up to the first knot. Then he reached up again and climbed to the next knot.

I closed my eyes and crossed all my fingers. I twisted my legs like a pretzel, crossed my eyes, and inside my boots I even tried crossing my toes.

"Hey, little bug," he called down. "I was just kiddin'. What, don't you *believe*?"

I unpretzeled myself. Maybe for good and forever, now that he'd put it like that.

Slowly, taking his time, resting at each knot he came to, Shawn climbed up the rope and with a yell of triumph he pulled himself over the top. I clapped so hard I about broke the flashlight. Then, scuffing a hole in the dirt with my heel, I stuck the light into it and aimed its pale yellow moon halfway up the rope. Then I grabbed hold of the rope and hitched myself up the knots, past the moon, and out of the underworld.

We scrambled over the rocks that guarded the hole, and then to the barely glowing embers of my fire. I hurried to the jumbled-up sticks by the wall and lugged back all I could carry, and in no time we had us a fire.

High above, up by the entrance, a shaft of smoky light sifted through the narrow mouth of cave. "Wait here while I check on what's going on outside," I ordered, though Shawn had already plopped down and was pulling his boots off, flexing his toes and warming his feet by the fire. I left him and climbed up the rocky steps to the ledge and poked my head out of the crack.

In the smoky dawn light I could see that the fire had swept through the canyon. The black stumps of trees still smoldered and smoked. The willows and shrubs were burned toast. I coughed and ducked back into the cave like a turtle tucking its head into its shell.

"The fire's still smoldering," I said when I got back to where Shawn sat warming his feet. "We'll have to wait till it's safe to go out. But now, food," I said, and I smiled at myself for not having eaten up all of the trail mix. We sat munching and stirring the fire while Shawn asked me a zillion questions. I tried as best as I could to answer them.

What does blue light mean when it flows out of your throat? Green just sparked out of your chest. Why? The yellow that for a second hovered over your head—what was that? That pink cloud around you—around both of us! What does that mean? And when you were saying my name, why did lights bubble up like huge colored mountains?

"You'll have to figure that out for yourself," I said. "It's trial and error and looking as hard as you can until it begins to make some sort of sense. When you get used to seeing the lights you'll pay more attention to the ones that look different, like dark holes or spikes or tentacles. There'll be lopsided lights and lights that look scary. You'll be able to tell when someone's happy or sad or angry or jealous, or when there's something seriously wrong, like maybe illness. It's like being a snoop, so you'll have to be careful and, most of the time, hold what you see to yourself. But your great-grandmother said you'd use this to see into people's souls for healing, right? She was saying you'd be a medicine man."

He stirred the fire, frowning. "That's one thing I don't understand," he said. "The thing about the rainbow petroglyph. About finding it and then being able to see rainbows. I'm seeing rainbows, but I didn't find the petroglyph. How can that be?"

We had no answers.

For the longest time we sat and stared at the fire. I thought about Pot and my poor, probably worried-plumb-out-of-her-mind mom. When I thought of my dad it was as if somehow, in this short bit of time in the cave, I'd let go, and let *him* go. Maybe Shawn hadn't been the only one to get healed.

Beside me, Shawn had burrowed down into his own

thoughts. The fire burned low. We threw on more sticks and let it burn low again. Above us the pale greenish crystals twinkled and glowed.

Finally Shawn stood up and stretched. He reached his hands out to the four corners of the earth, down to the earth, and up to heaven. The firelight flickered off the crystals and for an instant the whole cave seemed to glow almost as brightly as Shawn. Against the smoky light he was almost transparent; against the dark he was light.

It seemed like we'd been down in the cave for a very long time, so we both figured we should take our chances with the smoldering fires. We shouldered our packs and said our good-byes to the cave. I held my crystal to my heart and thanked it. I so badly wanted to slip it back into my pocket. But no. There was something else I'd learned on this journey to the underworld. And that was that the little people and water ghosts that the Indians believed in might really, actually be real. Or at least real *spirits,* if that was the same thing. They might really be protecting certain places. So I carefully placed the crystal back on the ground where I'd found it, and then, with Shawn following slowly behind me, we climbed up to the mouth of the cave.

I poked my head out. The red sun of late afternoon shone through the smoky haze. "It looks safe enough," I said, and I squeezed myself out through the crack. Shawn squirmed out behind me, joking that coming in he'd fit tighter than a cork, but now . . .

He stopped.

Black skeletons of trees lifted leafless arms up to a

hazy sky. Charred stumps of trees smoldered and smoked. Ashes covered the ground and the boulders and rocks. It was an almost-lifeless, smoky-gray moonscape.

"Did you ever see anything like this?" Shawn asked, his voice plumb full of wonder.

I shook my head. "Pretty sad, isn't it?" I muttered.

But Shawn was so wide-eyed it looked like he'd been blinded by a spotlight. He reached down and picked up a small sooty rock. "It's like I've been blindfolded all my life," he said as he looked at the rock as if it were a diamond in disguise.

As we hiked, Shawn kept reaching out to touch the scorched bark of a burned tree or the withered, curled leaves on a willow or a charred root sticking out of the cliff side.

Climbing up a steep rocky slope was so easy, compared with the way I'd come into it. When we reached the top we stood panting and catching our breath. The charred hill grass stretched like a black sooty carpet across the hillsides. To the east, along the mountains and down in the gullies and canyons, the fire still raged. In the distance an airplane passed in and out of the clouds of white smoke. A helicopter dangling a big bucket on a long rope whirred toward the fire. We waved and jumped up and down, but it didn't see us. It disappeared into the billowing smoke.

"Think they saw us?" I asked hopefully, though it was obvious they hadn't.

Shawn shrugged. "It will be as it's meant to be," he said.

Geez, he was sounding like an old medicine man already. "Goofball," I said.

At the rate we were going it'd be dark long before we got to the ranch. Every two steps or so Shawn stopped and looked around as if he were walking about in a dream. "I'm in a whole new world," he exclaimed. "I've never really seen color before. It's like I've lived in the dark and have just walked out into sunlight."

He bent to stare at a gopher that poked its startled head out of a hole. "Creature of light," I heard him whisper. "We're *all* creatures of light."

He dropped far behind. I'd have been running full speed down the slopes to the ranch and my Stew Pot and my worried-sick mom if Shawn hadn't been so weak and so dazed by—well, by the light. It was already late afternoon, and we still had a long way to hike.

Now, looking back, I can see there were signs. Nothing you'd normally think twice about. Like for instance the rocky outcrop ahead of us. We wouldn't have even seen it if the trees all around it hadn't been burned to a crisp. Even then I wouldn't have paid any attention to that particular bunch of big rocks if the top of it hadn't suddenly been spotlighted by the rosy rays of the sinking sun. I wouldn't have gotten the brilliant idea to climb to the top and signal for help.

Already I could hear the *chop-chop-chop* of another helicopter as it whirled up from the lowlands to the fire.

A thick band of burned trees and shrubs surrounded the outcrop. Shelflike ridges made it look like it wouldn't be too hard a climb. I charged through the trees and tore up the outcrop in a mad race with the sun, and then I stripped off my shirt and waved, whooped, and hollered my head off.

The helicopter ignored me. The ray of bright light faded as the sun went behind a big cloud of smoke. "What a bummer," I said. My shoulders drooped. My legs felt limp as noodles.

Down below, Shawn slowly threaded his way through the burned grove. I stared at his face streaked with soot, at his matted hair, at his jeans and shirt caked with dried mud. *He sure looks scary,* I thought. And then I glanced down at myself. *"Boo!"* I said.

"I'm headed down!" I called when I saw that Shawn was starting to climb up the outcrop to join me. Just then an airplane buzzed out of the clouds of white smoke. I waved my shirt and thought that the plane tipped its wing.

"Don't come any farther," I called down to Shawn, and I jumped to the ledge just below. He'd already climbed halfway up, but he stopped and waited and when I got to the ledge above him he reached up to give me a hand. As I took it he gasped.

"Oh, I'm so sorry! Did that hurt?" I asked, scowling at my hand as if it had bitten my friend.

"Behind you. *Look!*"

I turned stiff as a stick. A rattlesnake? That's all we needed. . . .

There, on the flat face of the rock behind me, a petro-glyph. Three etched lines arched high above three lumpy

rows of what could only be the symbol for mountains. A lone stick tree stood on top of the highest mountain. It stretched out two limbs to the rainbow.

Or it could've been a person. It could've been Shawn himself, raising his arms up in praise of the rainbow and lifting the sky with his song.

The pickup struggled up the blackened hillsides, traveling now where no road existed, making its way around boulders and sagebrush. I'd climbed back up to the top of the rocks when we first heard it, and had stood there wildly waving my shirt. When I was certain they'd seen me and were headed our way, I shot down to meet them.

And that's how my ankle got sprained.

I didn't cry. I really didn't. Even when I fell in a lump on the ground. Because there they were, hopping out of the truck, running toward us, Mr. Mac yelling back to Dingo in the cab, "They're okay, it's Blue and Shawn, and they're safe!" And then he was carefully feeling my leg while over his shoulder Slim John beamed and kept wiping his eyes. Meanwhile Jakey was guiding Shawn to the truck, careful as if he were glass because I guess Shawn's eyes were so wide and starry they figured he must be in shock.

Which, in a way, he was.

And then Mr. Mac was lifting me in his strong arms and brushing my hair with his lips and saying, "Miss Blue, you sure know how to scare the heck out of a fellow." And Slim John kept looking at my hands and then at my leg, expecting, I suppose, that I'd reach down and magically fix it.

And before I knew it we were bumping down toward the ranch, somewhere along the way finding a road that wound through the hills toward Shawn's grandma's ranch, which must've been closer than ours. And Shawn was tugging an oily, crumpled paper sack out of his pack and plopping it on my lap saying, "It's yours. I saw you put it down before we left the cave. But it belongs to you. And thank you. . . ."

And Slim John was patting my knee and wiping his eyes with his shirtsleeve as I held up the pale greenish crystal.

Mam met up with us just before we got back to the ranch, gunning Ol' Yeller, roaring over boulders and brush as if she were driving a tank. Seems that she'd finally figured out where I'd been headed. She'd read through my journals and found the parts about the ley lines and where they met up, and a bit about Shawn and his rainbow.

Honestly, I'm hardly even mad about it. Even the really personal, secret parts that she read, stuff about how much I'd fallen for Shawn, and then all the things I'd written about my dad, and the way I felt about packing up Ol' Yeller every two months. It was all there. She must've read every bit of it.

It stopped her in her tracks. She says she's ready to make some big changes. Some of which, by the way, would've been made anyway because of what happened after our clash with my dad and after I ran out the door.

My dad had decided I needed counseling. Mam had

told him she probably needed some too, for not having put a proper end to their marriage. My dad had slammed out the door saying she could have her divorce papers any old day she wanted.

I expect anytime now I'll get a letter saying he's ever so sorry for breaking my chairs and, along with them, my heart, and that he loves me, and to heck with that old guitar. And if I don't get a letter, well, I know I'll survive.

But I love happy endings, and just the fact that my hero dog, Pot, survived makes a perfect one. He's here in his beanbag, beside me, a little worse for wear and tear, but able now to limp down the stairs. We took him to the vet's clinic the day after I got back. Most dogs wouldn't have survived a wolf attack, the vet told us. It was a good thing I'd been there to scare it off, and what I'd done afterward had been just right. Stew Pot was one lucky dog, she said. But we already knew that.

Of course Mam had practically dropped to the floor when she ran up to my attic and saw him all wrapped like a mummy in his beanbag—especially after the shock of those bloody bandages I'd left strewn across the bathroom floor.

It had been about then that she'd heard the pickup drive into the yard.

But it hadn't been my dad coming back. It had been Mr. Mac. By then she'd plumb forgotten that she'd called him to come up for the grand opening of my room. Which of course was by then in a total state of disaster. But I gather he'd been really touched. Maybe even more so than he would've been if it hadn't been for the ruined—well, whatever you want to call them. "Furniture" is a word that maybe really is a bit too grand.

Mostly, Mam told me, Mr. Mac just ran his fingers through his hair and said that I was the darnedest kid he'd ever known. Which I'm taking as a great compliment.

He'd come zooming up to the ranch, though, because he'd gotten the word about Shawn when he'd stopped at the trading post. He'd called Slim John and Jakey and Dingo to come help with the search. They'd decided that Mam should stay home just in case. At that point the fire hadn't yet started up and she'd been more worried about Stew Pot than me.

But it wasn't long afterward that she spotted the smoke. That's when she about tore out her hair. And that's when she read through my journals.

Honestly, I forgive her. Given the way things have turned out.

I gather that Mr. Mac has been thinking about taking the cows off this place, at least for the winters. And I gather that he'd like Mam to come help out at his other ranch, the one that's closer to town and to schools.

I'd miss this place so much, even though Mam has said that if we do this, well, we'll be back here next summer. I think that will happen, especially after all the rosy-pink lights that had floated around the two of them when Mr. Mac brought me home. For once I spied to my heart's content. Just watching their lights made me happy.

My bums would come with us, but I'd miss Lone

One and Light of the Dawn. I'd watched Lone One run back down the hills toward her fawn, so I was pretty sure they'd been safe. Antelopes don't like forests and places where they can't see every little thing that's going on. I knew they'd head for the wide-open spaces and safety. Right now, this morning, they're below my window next to the log cabin, happily stripping petals off the sunflowers that have sprung up all over the place, both inside and outside our garden.

Mr. Mac is coming over this evening. So is Shawn, and he's bringing his grandma. I've gotten my room back in shape, in spite of having to hobble around on one leg. This time we're having a real ceremony. Shawn's grandma will be doing the blessing.

Shawn asked me to be his helper at the Sun Dance that's coming up next week. His uncle is the medicine man for it. They'll hold the ceremony up in the hills in between Crowheart and Ft. Washakie. It's a big deal, I gather, though I haven't been to one yet. The men stay in a circular lodge made of branches and pray as they blow through eagle-bone whistles. And they don't eat or drink for four days. You can't even chew gum if you go there to watch, Shawn says. Just watching you chew it might make the dancers thirsty. Shawn says his cousins will show me what to do, but not to worry because I'd be supporting him just by being there for him. He explained that the Sun Dancers do this as prayers for their family and friends and for all of us, and they also pray for a vision.

But Shawn's doing the Sun Dance to say thanks. Lots

of big thanks, he says. He can't get over the way his great-grandma's story came true.

So things are getting back to normal. Through normal, as Mam always says, is a state not on our map. Still, it feels like a regular, ordinary day here at Far Canyon Ranch.

The only thing at all unusual is a double rainbow in the morning sky.

Acknowledgments

The Wind River Reservation does exist. What takes place on it is a work of fiction, separate from the real-life community of the Shoshones and Arapahos. To the people of this land of high mountains, big winds, and blue sky go my love and respect.

I wish to express my heartfelt thanks to Vernon Lajeunesse and to Carrie and Darwin Griebel for their encouragement in reading through my manuscript. To all my friends here, my life has been enriched by having crossed your paths.

I owe a huge debt of gratitude to my literary agent, Charlotte Sheedy, who believed in and encouraged me and sent care packages of delicious goodies through the mail. She is truly an earth-mother agent. My thanks to Melanie Cecka for guiding me through the maze of writing my first book. For cheering me on and for the hot-from-the-oven oatmeal cookies brought to my desk, I thank my love, Rod Johnson.